the wrong Place

THE WRONG PLACE

ASPEN RIDGE

SASHA PIERCE

SNOWBOARDING TERMS

In The Wrong Place, there's a fair amount of snowboard-related jargon that the average non-boarder may not understand, or even just skiing in general. I decided to provide you with a short list to help.

Black Diamond - hardest terrain/highest skill level rating for ski runs, based on the mountain's difficulty. Easiest runs are green, intermediate are blue. There are also 'double black diamonds' which are considered extreme difficulty

Moguls - small bumps on the terrain with narrow paths between that have to be navigated accurately

Terrain Park - a special section of a ski resort

that features a variety of equipment especially designed for tricks - boxes, pipes, ramps

Groomer - runs on ski hills that are 'groomed' by machines to tamp down the loose powdery snow and create a more stable surface

Bowl - refers to the shape of the mountains and how the snow lay in the valley. Typically not groomed and 'ski at your own risk' runs.

Snowboard Cross - a style of race that involves multiple participants traversing a course of obstacles on snowboard, with the first to finish the winner

Slalom - a short downhill race with two participants where individuals have to successfully navigate around poles and come in with the shortest time to win

Half-pipe - a short downhill course with tall curved sides, resembling a pipe cut in half, where the goal is to score as many points as possible through the performance of complicated tricks as the boarder criss-crosses the pipe for momentum

Slope Style - a race where participates traverse down a longer run filled with objects and jumps, and the goal is to score as many points as possible through the performance of tricks

Tail grab - grabbing the board mid air on the back edge with the trailing hand

Indy - Grabbing the board mid-air on the toe edge between the bindings with the trailing hand

Wildcat Weddle - a combo of two distinct movements: Wildcat is a backflip that keeps the board parallel to the riding line, so the rider does a sort of 'side' flip without losing momentum. A Weddle is grabbing the toe edge between the bindings with the lead hand

Backside Rodeo 360 - a Backside Rodeo involves initiating a backside turn off the jump, popping off the heel edge, and then performing a backflip with a 180 turn to land switch. More rotation can be added to make it a Backside Rodeo 360 or more

Switch - Snowboarders ride sideways on their boards and typically have the same foot forward. Landing or taking off 'switch' means they have the other leg in front, which is a different skill

Heel edge, toe edge - refers to the part of the board in front or behind the feet. Boarders intentionally ride one edge to maintain control

Catching an edge - inadvertently losing control of the board because the wrong edge is in the snow. This results is a pretty hard fall, particularly if the boarder is going fast

CHAPTER ONE

STELLA

Tiny crystals of ice beat at my face relentlessly as I raced down the powdery slope, but I hardly felt them. Strapped into my board, music in my ears, and all of my focus on the obstacles in my path—there was nowhere else I felt this alive. And much to my parents' chagrin, there was nothing that held my focus in this way. I did alright in school, but I wasn't the straight-A student my brother was. My parents always complained that I just didn't apply myself, and they were right. I didn't *care* about grades... they had no bearing on the future I chose.

The only thing I'd experienced in my life that felt right, that felt like I was *exactly* where I was meant to be, was on a snowboard. Raised in a family that owned a ski resort, I was literally born to be on the slopes. Out here, no one could stop me; it was like I had wings. I *flew*.

Even with the frosty air, I was sweating under all of my layers. Snowboarding was deceptively physical—even though it looks smooth and effortless to the casual observer, it requires constant control of the muscles and awareness of your surroundings. I was an athlete, and I trained like one. Blood sang through my veins as I prepared for the approaching jump, crouching down only to spring up at the right moment to catch air. I had just enough time to execute a perfect tail grab before I straightened my legs, taking the impact with my right leg before easing down on my leading edge. Perfect.

As I merged with the traffic on the lower black diamond, I eased off the speed and stretched my complaining quads, switching to my heel edge and coasting through the flat spot where other winter sports enthusiasts were dismounting the chair lift. And even though my legs were already aching, I turned my board to the trail on the right instead of the easier route to the left. I'd promised to meet my dad for lunch in town, so this was my last run for a couple of hours. Might as well make it count.

When I tipped over the edge, I picked up speed, heading straight for the patch of moguls, where a few skiers were carefully picking their way through the mini hills of snow. Moguls aren't for the faint of heart, but they're especially challenging for a snowboarder—you have to make a series of sharp turns to navigate in the valleys between them, and it's easy to catch an edge and fly asshole over elbows the rest of the way down.

My eyes remained trained on the path in front of me, my body twisting as I navigated heel-toe-heel-toe-heel-toe. I carved through the moguls like a hot knife through butter. When I was nearly through, a body that was tumbling instead of carving flew down the hill to my right, forcing me to turn and break my speed. My music was so loud I didn't hear him coming, but that was kind of the point. Hearing people coming up behind me was distracting, so music helped me block them all out and focus.

I finished the moguls and drew a deep breath, then steered myself toward the person who had such a bumpy ride down the hill that he still hadn't moved. His board was strapped to his feet, and fortunately, he wore a helmet. However, he was also spread eagle on his back and I couldn't tell if he was conscious or not.

Dropping to my knees next to him, I yanked my ear buds out and shoved them in a pocket. This close, I could tell he was young, maybe twelve or thirteen.

"Hey bud, you okay?" His head turned slightly my way and his jaw worked even though no sound came out, so he was at least conscious.

The boy drew in a slow, creaky breath, stretching his jaw wide like he was struggling to get more air in his lungs. The metallic flash of braces shone on his teeth, but I didn't spot any blood.

"That's good. Just focus on breathing. Looks like you hit hard enough to knock the air from your lungs... it hurts like hell, I know. Just keep working on in-out slowly, okay? I'm going to check to see if you did any major damage." I felt carefully along his arms and legs, paying close attention to his reaction. His breath was coming more regularly, and he didn't jerk away in pain when I touched him, so he appeared to be intact.

"Can you lift an arm for me?" The boy did as requested. "Great, now the other one." Once he obliged again, I instructed, "Okay, now I want you to move your board a bit so we know your legs are working. Just bend and flex to wiggle your toe edge." His board moved accordingly. "Excellent. Now I want to get a look at your eyes. Can you lift your goggles for me?" I demonstrated, sliding mine onto my helmet above my eyes. The boy reached up slowly and did the same, and when his gaze landed on my face, his brown eyes grew as big as saucers.

"Oh shit, you're Stella Blackwell!" His voice cracked when he spoke, but it was still deafeningly loud. Clearly, he was breathing fine now.

"Busted," I grinned. "What's your name?"

"Dylan. Man, my friends are NOT going to believe this! Can I get a picture with you?" His cheeks had been pale a moment ago, but now they were fiery red.

"Well, let's focus on sitting up first, Dylan. Sound good?"

He nodded and pushed himself into a sitting position.

"How do you feel?"

"Super embarrassed I wiped out in front of Stella-freaking-Blackwell," he admitted, his blush deepening.

"Well, don't worry about it. I used to wipe out all the time. Still do occasionally," I added with a wink. "But what I meant was, how does your head feel?"

"Oh, I'm fine," he answered quickly. "But seriously, there's no way my friends will *believe* I met you. I told them all I was going to Aspen Ridge for our family ski trip and I was going to see you—everyone knows you're getting ready for the trials here—and they all told me that was stupid and there was no *way* you'd be on the regular slopes with everyone else. But you are!" Dylan whipped off his gloves and dug into his jacket pocket. "Please, one photo? They won't believe it otherwise. I promise I'm your biggest fan! See?" He showed me the background on his phone, which was a glamorous shot from a campaign I did for Branton Snowboards last year.

Now it was my turn to blush. How could I say no? "I'm very flattered. Come on, let's get you up. You don't want to take a photo on the ground, do you?"

"Yes!" He crowed before a horrified look crossed his face. "I mean, no, I don't want the photo on the ground. Hold on." He popped up on his board and brushed the snow from his clothes, grinning maniacally.

Fortunately for Dylan, I'm so short that I barely had a few inches on him, despite being a fully grown adult. I positioned my board just behind his and asked, "May I?" Holding my hand out for the phone.

Dylan was so flustered by this point that he had a hard time unlocking it, but eventually we figured it out and I leaned in close to snap a few photos. The kid was grinning ear to ear, and it was impossible for me to ignore the tiny flame of gratification I felt. Sometimes, I needed to be reminded that there were people in the world who thought I was something special; who traveled here just hoping to get a *glimpse* of me. That I was good enough, and something I was passionate about mattered to other people. That even if my own family didn't, there were lots of other people out there who supported my dreams.

When I had taken a fair number of photos for Dylan to choose from, I straightened and tried to hand back his phone. But before I had the chance to move away, he whipped his face toward me and planted a fat, sloppy kiss on my cheek.

I froze in absolute shock, staring at Dylan, who gave me an impish grin. Quick as lightning, he tucked away his phone and snatched up his gloves.

"I'm never washing my lips again!" He declared with gleaming eyes before taking off down the mountain at top speed. He waited until he was a few hundred feet away to yell, "I LOVE YOU STELLA!"

That broke me out of my shock with a giggle, but then he added, "I KISSED STELLA BLACK-WELL!!" in a shout that echoed across the wide expanse of trail as he sped along toward the bottom.

I should have seen that one coming.

Sighing, I put my earbuds back in and adjusted my goggles. As embarrassing as it was to have a boy in the midst of puberty shouting across the mountain that he'd kissed me—not to mention potential repercussions from the implication that I was some kind of pedophile—his adoration was flattering all the same. Making a mental note to have Andrea, my social media manger, check later to see if Dylan posted anything about it. I caught speed and carved my way down the mountain, trying to hold on to that warm glow as I prepared to meet my dad for a lunch that was sure to be a lot less amusing than an encounter with a hormonal teenage boy.

SEBASTIAN

I CRUISED SLOWLY down Glacier Run, my eyes darting across the swarm of bodies to scan for anyone who might need help. It was the largest green at Aspen Ridge and was always full to bursting with people who could barely remain on their feet. It had taken me a couple of weeks to calm down and stop assuming everyone on the ground was in imminent danger. I was learning to recognize when it was a simple case of 'fell over their own crossed skis' versus 'probably broke something.' A lot of time, as ski patrol, we didn't witness the accident. But usually other people did, and when a large crowd gathered around an individual, it was typically a clue they had a nasty fall.

I paused at the intersection between Glacier and Black Bear to observe for a moment.

It felt odd to be back here. Right, but also wrong somehow. Aspen Ridge was the scene of my popularity as a teen, with a bunch of things like being best friends with Reece Blackwell buoying me up to legendary status; not to mention being homecoming king and having a squad of admirers before I graduated. It wasn't something I'd ever sought out, but I certainly enjoyed the attention at the time.

Now I was back and it felt like a failure, somehow, returning here six years later with very little to show.

While my mind was wandering, Gary, my team lead, pulled up beside me and drew in a deep, satisfied breath.

"Another day in paradise," he observed mildly.

"Yeah," I agreed, shifting gears. It was a bluebird day, not a cloud in the sky, and the air temperature was almost too warm for so many layers of clothing.

"Are you getting settled in?"

"Yeah, I am. Reece hooked me up with an employee rental, so it's furnished and everything. I can't complain."

Gary scratched at his silver beard with a mitten and turned his knowing ice-blue eyes on me. "I meant adjusting to civilian life, the change of pace compared to the military."

"Oh. Yeah, it's okay. You might be surprised, but the Army wasn't all go-go-go all the time. There was actually a lot of sitting around doing nothing."

He chuckled. "Yeah, I remember that part; it was the same for the Marines. But it's still different in the civilian world. And given every-thing you went through in six years, I can imagine it's still a change, even if it's a welcome one."

Sweat beaded on the back of my neck, my throat constricting. My mind short-circuited with flashes of explosions, overturned humvees disap-pearing into clouds of dust, deafening silence, pools of dark red everywhere... the smell of death filled my senses.

Blinking rapidly, I swallowed and clenched my fists, drawing in a deep breath of fresh moun-tain air and bringing myself back to the present. "Yeah, it's a change. But at least I can put my medic skills to use here. And it's nice to be home."

Gary's inscrutable eyes didn't miss a thing; he asked me that question on purpose to observe my reaction. While the ski patrol had been happy to welcome me to the team, Gary was the most cautious. It took a while, but I found out he'd retired from the Marines as a Gunny Sergeant. He didn't talk about it, but when he met my eyes, I knew he saw through my composed smile.

It's impossible to hide the truth from someone who's been there.

So I understood his caution now. He was watching for signs I wasn't as well as I claimed to be. Making innocent references to things I tried very hard not to think about. Testing me.

The silence stretched between us as I held his gaze, almost too long, before Gary replied. "Yeah, it's nice to call a place like this home."

"Definitely. I grew up here. It was the first place I thought of when my contract was over."

"Did you work for the resort back then?"

"Nah, I was far more intent on riding the snow than shoveling it back then. I mean, I worked here during the summer, of course, just so I could afford a season pass and some new gear."

"Of course. Are these your old skis?"

"Nah, I gave all of that stuff away before I left. I didn't think I'd be back here for a long time. It was strange to get back on these things, and I wouldn't know what to buy at this point. But Reece has more than he even knows what to do with, so he's letting me borrow some so I can figure out what I want for next season."

I flashed him my widest grin, but Gary still hadn't cracked a smile. He continued observing me with his shrewd 'ancient warrior' expression.

When he still didn't speak, I felt obliged to continue the conversation. "It seems like a good season so far."

Gary nodded slowly. "The snow has been

good. Not too many major emergencies, and only a couple of snowstorms bad enough to shut us down for a day. Which reminds me, it looks like we have another coming in tomorrow afternoon. If it's as bad as they're saying, we'll have to shut down early and likely remain closed for a day or two. Are you feeling confident enough to hit the bowls tomorrow?"

I nodded. "Yeah, I'm pretty solid. I hit a few of the double blacks today and it was smooth. I haven't gotten into much deep powder though."

Gary sniffed. "Alright. I want you to run the bowls tomorrow morning, get a feel for them. I'll probably send you to do a sweep if we have to shut down early, make sure the mountain is clear before we close the lifts."

"I can do that, but why me?"

That drew a twitch of a smile from Gary's lips. "I dunno if you've noticed, kid, but you're at least two decades younger than most of the patrollers this year. Some of us aren't as springy or bendy as we used to be. Besides, anyone you find back there will probably be closer to your age than mine, and I don't feel like taking lip from snowboarding punks when I'm trying to look out for their safety. You can handle it, right?"

"Sure thing, not a problem."

"Good. We'll talk more about it in the morning meeting. For now, why don't you go over to Peak 8 and check in with Jeremy, see where he needs some help."

"Yes, sir."

"Bah, don't call me sir, kid. I work for a living."

"You got it, Gary." I pushed off and meandered slowly toward the lift before he could say anything else. Everyone in the military knew better than to call an enlisted Marine 'sir', and I'd done it just to annoy him. I was growing tired of feeling like a bomb he was waiting to go off.

Sure, I went through some shit I didn't want to talk about with anyone, let alone an all-too-knowing retired Marine with wary eyes.

But I was fine. Some things just weren't worth dredging up repeatedly.

It was far better to let sleeping dogs lie.

CHAPTER
TWO

STELLA

I shoved another fry into my mouth to stop myself from snapping back at Dad. Even though I was expecting this lecture, it didn't make it any easier to stomach. We were seated at the bar in Aspen Ridge Brewery and I was seriously considering making a run for it, despite the pile of excellent fries that remained on my plate.

"...your mom and I are worried about you, Estelle. We don't want you to get hurt again." His dark eyes were serious, and nearly the same shade of brown as his thick eyebrows. "I know you're an excellent boarder, and I'd never discourage my daughter from having a snow hobby—snow is our family business, I *want* you to love it!—But snowboarding isn't a *career*. At some point, you're going to have to join the rest of us in the business, and I just don't see why you're so resistant to putting in a few hours with your brother to learn the ropes this season."

As if we hadn't had this conversation about a thousand times already. "Dad, the regionals start in a few weeks. I'm spending every hour I have preparing for them. My focus is 100% on qualifying for nationals, and from there World Cup, and then-"

"Estelle, I know how the system works. We did this with you last time. Trust me, I haven't forgotten." His voice took on the clipped tone reserved for 'definitely don't continue down this line of conversation.' "I know you feel cheated you didn't make it to the Olympics last time. But that's the thing about these events, Bug. They're dangerous, and you can perform each one perfectly a thousand times and then one time you're a half second off..."

"Yeah, I *know*," I snapped. I sure as hell didn't need him to remind me. It was *my* shoulder that got broken. *My* body that had multiple fractures and ended up set in plaster for weeks. It was me who had to watch the Olympics from my bed instead of standing on a podium with a medal hanging around my neck. I was *quite* aware of what could happen. "That's why I'm doing more events; if I do well enough on snowboard cross and slalom, I may drop out of half-pipe altogether. Maybe even slope style. But those were my two strongest last time and these new ones are untested for me. Which means I have to practice even *more,* so I'm ready to compete. I don't have time to dink around in the kitchen with Reece."

Dad gave me the head tilt and lowered eyebrows that were his version of rolling his eyes. "That's not fair, Estelle. You know your brother does a hell of a lot more than 'dink around in the kitchen.' He's managing all of food service plus the event hall by himself. He could certainly use some help-"

"Then *hire* someone to help him!" My voice turned shrill, but I was too pissed to care at this point. "God, you guys are unbelievable. Any other family would be stoked to see their daughter on the Olympic stage, and you guys act like I'm just some lazy wash-out waste of space. I train all day, *every* day. I start out in the gym, lifting weights before the sun comes up. Then I'm on the slopes until sunset, working on my skills for four different qualifying events. Then I hit the lap pool and finally the sauna before I come home and barely have dinner before I collapse into bed. I'm probably the most dedicated person in this family and you guys all shame me for it. I don't have a lot of time left, Dad. If I don't make it this season, I'm done. There's no way I can keep this up for another four years hoping to place again. I sat out and lost my injury re-invite at your insistence because you promised-" he opened his mouth to speak but I cut him off, "you *promised* I could try for the next Olympics. This has been my dream since I still had baby teeth. It's the only thing I've ever wanted. I've done everything you asked me, and now I'm primed and ready to start my Olympic run and you're on my case to go waste my time shadowing Reece in the kitchen."

"Estelle, it's not like-"

"How's everything going over here?" Tessa stepped up with an unnaturally bright smile and cut Dad off completely. "Are you guys thinking about some dessert? Stella, do you need a box? You should probably try to get a few more fries in before you get back out on the slopes. We're all rooting for you to make nationals this year," she added with a wink.

I shot her a grateful smile. "Thanks, Tessa. I

really appreciate your support. But I'm pretty full and I should head out, anyway. Only a couple hours left of daylight." I hopped off my barstool and gave Tessa a hug. "Thank you," I whispered into her chestnut locks.

"No prob, Stella. I got you." She whispered back, then released me with another wide grin.

I grabbed my coat from the back of my chair and planted a kiss on Dad's cheek. "Thanks for lunch, Dad. I'll see you at home for dinner!" And I darted for the doorway before he could say another word.

I could have waited for him to drive me back, but I sure as hell didn't want to sit in the car with him and expose myself to yet another lecture about the futility of continuing to try for the Olympic team at the feeble old age of twenty-two. Jesus, they acted like I was ready for pasture.

Instead, I marched to the bus stop and hopped on the yellow line, which was a 5-minute ride from ARB to the condos where we kept a ski locker for our gear. Well, some of it, anyway. My parents hit the snow so infrequently they didn't even keep gear at the house anymore. My boards and helmets had taken up most of the space at home, and I even had spillage into here thanks to my generous sponsors.

While I waited to reach my stop, my temper simmered. I knew they were just worried about me. Reece said they nearly lost it when I landed that trick wrong and didn't get up. I couldn't recall a single time my parents had fussed over me more than the week following the accident that had cut my Olympic dreams short.

And it wasn't entirely on them I skipped the next year, when I could have landed an invitation to nationals without qualifying because of my injury. To be honest, that fall really rattled me. I'd had plenty of falls—there's no way to avoid them when you're flipping and spinning in the air, learning new tricks and trying to remember when to kick your feet out. But that one had knocked me out cold. I woke up in an ambulance, strapped to a stretcher, with no memory of how I got there. All I knew was pain like I'd *never* felt before.

In the end I'd dislocated my shoulder, broken my clavicle and two ribs, and given myself a concussion and severe whiplash. I got through all the physical therapy and recovery and put on a brave face... but the first time I stared down the hill at the half-pipe, a freezing sweat drenched my body and I nearly hurled.

That was the first time I ever walked away

from a run, and it took me weeks to work up the courage to go back.

But I'd put in the work, built my strength and control, and worked my way up from just sliding from one side to the other on the half-pipe to low jumps, then simple tricks, and finally back up to the kinds of stunts that win gold.

It still terrified me every time. I clenched my teeth so hard I was certain they'd shatter, and followed my coach's advice on spotting the ground so I didn't lose track. But it wasn't fun anymore, and I could never admit that to my family no matter how much I needed outside encouragement. They would just use it as fuel to keep pushing me to quit.

Speed wasn't a problem for me—I loved it. Racing down the hill at a break-neck pace forced me to just react to upcoming obstacles, no time to over think. If I was confident that I'd hit high scores on snowboard cross and slalom, I'd drop out of the trick series altogether. It was leaving the solid ground and losing track of which way was up that made me sick to my stomach. I'd never been afraid of a trick before the one that could have left me paralyzed for life, and now three years later I still hadn't gotten over that fear.

The only problem was that being petite and

strong made me an excellent competitor for jumps. I could get air far more easily than girls who were bigger than me, and I'd trained as a pre-teen to build up my upper body and core strength. My dedication to the sport had me in Aspen Ridge's state-of-the-art gym so much that my parents finally built my weight room just to keep me home more.

The bus pulled up to my stop, and I thanked the driver before hopping off and heading to retrieve my board. There were still a couple of good hours of sunlight to ride. I briefly considered heading to the back bowls, but I'd have to cross two peaks and by the time I got there, I'd only get one run in. Better to stick to the black diamonds here at Peak 6 and just work on my technique. I could hit the bowls tomorrow.

If we had lights like Snowshoe Ridge, I'd be able to keep going for hours, but no one liked that idea. I used to head over there to enjoy the extra snow time, but my coach insisted I get the swimming in to keep me limber and mobile.

Plus, it was weird patronizing another mountain when we literally *owned* this one.

I gathered my gear and boarded the chair lift alone; with music in my ears and the warm afternoon sun on my cheeks, the ride was pretty good despite the icy breeze that sought every path to my skin through my multiple layers. This was my happy place. Even so, I was already dreading going home tonight; I was sure to receive a guilt trip from my mom about how rude I'd been to Dad. They always had each other's backs.

Guilt slithered in my belly. I complained loudly and often that they didn't support my dreams, but truthfully, they had supported me a lot. I'd had snowboard coaches and swim coaches and strength coaches before I even got my first cell phone. They funded trips to Argentina in the summer so I could keep practicing when Colorado was green. They built me that gym and paid for all of my gear—until I got sponsored by Branton Snowboards, who now paid me and provided anything I wanted for free. I still lived at home and had my own car, which I rarely drove in the winter since I spent most days on the hill. I'd never had a 'real job' in any sense of the imagination.

So it wasn't that they weren't supportive, but maybe not supportive when I needed them the most. I knew my pre-ordained destiny was to eventually step in and help run Aspen Ridge, perhaps even help it grow. Dad and JJ had actually been resistant to putting in the terrain park at first; now it was one of our most popular attractions. Pros came and practiced their tricks early season until they set the competition courses up. I'd been begging my dad for years to have Aspen Ridge host the X Games, or even a Red Bull event, but I always got a flat no. He insisted JJ wouldn't go for it, but I suspected he didn't even ask.

Which pissed me off, but there was nothing I could do about it. Now that Ellie was taking over for JJ and James ran mountain ops, it felt like I had a good chance to convince the new generation of Aspen Ridge to modernize. Competitions were a huge draw for pros and spectators alike, and everyone needed food, places to stay, and entertainment. It would be great for Aspen Ridge.

I actually thought about Aspen Ridge a lot and had plenty of ideas to improve, but my parents didn't want to hear what I had to say. If I so much as mentioned 'snowboard', it was like they tuned out completely, assuming the next words out of my mouth were only about me. I represented a demographic they rarely thought about or planned for, but if Aspen Ridge wanted to have customers thirty years from now, we had to project into the future instead of trying to hold on to the past.

When I reached the top and dismounted the chairlift, I stepped into my binding and continued to Snowcat Trail without slowing down. If I pushed it, I could get at least five runs in before dark.

If I *really* pushed it, I might get in six.

Crouching, I lowered my center of gravity and picked up speed with a smile curling my lips.

CHAPTER
THREE

SEBASTIAN

"Hey, thanks for having me over. I haven't exactly stocked my fridge yet." I followed Reece through the door to his condo and started kicking snow off my boots and unloading my gear into the ski closet.

"Not a problem. It's nice to have you back. To be honest, I spend so much time alone lately I'm really looking forward to the company." Reece grinned as he pulled off his beanie and hung up his coat.

Just then, the telltale meow of a demanding feline carried down the hallway. I was removing my boots when the brownish-grey striped cat slunk around the corner and rubbed itself against Reece's leg. It had a bright red bowtie wrapped around its furry neck.

"But I have no reason to be lonely," Reece cooed at the cat in a baby voice, and I stifled a laugh. "Baxter's always here for me, aren't you Bax?" The animal purred loudly and rubbed against Reece's auburn beard. "Sebastian, this is Baxter. Baxter, this is Sebastian."

He held the cat out to me like he expected me to shake its paw, and I stood there on one foot holding my boot and completely at a loss about what I should do.

"Um... hi Baxter. That's a very nice bowtie you have on?" I felt ridiculous talking to a cat, but Reece seemed pleased, so I continued. "I didn't realize this dinner was black tie. Am I under-dressed?" I questioned the cat.

"Baxter just likes to look his best, don't you Bax?" He continued in his special 'talking to the cat' voice. "We pick out a bowtie every morning so he doesn't get bored." Finally, he gave the cat a kiss on the head and set him down, where Baxter began meowing non-stop and weaving in and out of his legs.

I stared in mild disgust at this display, wondering what had happened to my 'guy's guy' friend in the last six years. Reece just chuckled fondly, and when he caught my expression, his grin turned sheepish.

"I told you I spend a lot of time alone. Anyway, he's good company, doesn't bother me too much except at dinner time. You ready?"

My snow gear was all stacked neatly away, and I nodded. "No offense, man, but I think you need a girlfriend."

He released a booming laugh and spun on his heel, leading the way from the foyer into the condo.

The place was clearly recently remodeled, but even with all the modern upgrades, it kept the charm of a classic ski chalet. Lots of wood accents, a stone fireplace, and plush leather furniture. But the most startling feature was the solid wall of windows looking out over the ski hill. The condo was situated along the outermost run on Peak 5, and I could see all the way from the top of the mountain, highlighted by the setting sun, to the base of the run where the cross-peak gondola was loading passengers. It was the kind of million-dollar view people saved for years to experience for one week. One perk of being an heir to Aspen Ridge: sweet slope-side lodging at zero cost.

At first thoroughly distracted by the view, I remembered I was actually here to catch up with my friend. I turned back around and headed for the kitchen where Reece was already up to his elbows in produce at the kitchen island.

"Can I help with anything?" I offered. It had been far too long since I'd had a home-cooked meal, and the thick steaks on the counter already had me salivating.

"Nah, I'm good. Help yourself to a drink if you want," he gestured to a backlit bar built into the wall beside the fireplace.

"Don't mind if I do," I agreed with a grin. "Can I fix you something?"

"Yeah, that'd be great. There's a bottle of whiskey from the Cedar Creek Distillery. Can you pour me two measures over ice?"

"You got it." I plucked two glasses from the bar shelves, scooped some ice from the mini icemaker, and poured. I carried both glasses back to the island and slid one over to Reece before I took a sip of my own.

"Wow," I commented. "I can't say I'm an expert, but this is pretty good."

Reece nodded, switching from cutting carrot sticks to slicing an onion like a pie. "Right? They're a tiny distillery, but they have a really high-quality product. They've already got it in most of the liquor stores in Denver."

"That's great. Are they actually in Cedar Creek?"

"Yeah, they are. Local couple that just had a passion for whiskey and wanted to make their own."

"That's really cool. I admire people that just *know* what they want to do with their lives."

"Well, what about you? Now that you're out of the Army, what's your next step?" Reece barely paused in his chopping to take a sip before he was right back at it.

"I still have no idea, man. When I joined, I thought *that* was going to be my career. I was so sure, and then... well, you know." I'd told Reece all about my struggles during my enlistment, and when I decided not to reenlist, he was the first to suggest I come back to Aspen Ridge.

He nodded soberly. "Yeah, I get it, man. Most people don't grow up with a family business like this to inherit. Guess that makes me pretty lucky."

Even though he said it, it didn't really sound like he felt that lucky.

I chose my next words carefully. "Are you... not happy with working at Aspen Ridge?"

"No, I am! I mean, I don't want to sound ungrateful. My dad and JJ basically created this position for me because they knew how passionate I was about food. They paid for my culinary school, the whole nine yards. And I love it. There's nothing I'd rather wake up to in the morning than that view." He gestured behind me toward the windows.

Despite his insistence, there was still something to his tone that left me questioning. "Okay, you're grateful... but...?" I prompted, taking another sip and gazing at him patiently.

Reece drew a deep breath and let it out in one gust. "But... this isn't *all* I want to do," he admitted finally, moving on to the pile of small red potatoes.

"So, what else do you want to do?" This was news to me, but it intrigued me all the same.

"This," he lifted his glass and took a sip.

"Drink?" I asked.

"No, jerk, I want to make whiskey. And bourbon. I want to open a distillery."

"That's a great idea," I nodded. "Distilleries are popping up everywhere now. They're really popular. Aspen Ridge has the brewery, and that's awesome, but a distillery would be really cool."

"Right?" Reece's eyes were bright, his voice excited now that I'd validated the idea. "We'd call it Aspen Ridge Distillery, of course, and we'd make and bottle everything in-house. We could serve it in all the bars and restaurants in the resort, sell it in the gift shops and local stores, and people could take a bottle home from their trip to enjoy. If we planned well and built a big enough footprint, we could look at expanded distribution in the future, and making special small batches for the festivals... there's so much we could do. Of course, we'd donate a percentage of every sale to the local charities, and we'd have a tasting room with a mixologist and we could do tours..." as he reached the end of his speech, the excitement in his voice dissipated.

"Well, that all sounds like a great idea to me. When are you going to get started?"

"Never," he snorted.

"What? Why? It's a great idea and definitely will be a profitable business."

"Dad and JJ said no way. Even though Ellie Tremont—you remember Ellie, right? She was a few years older than us, JJ's daughter?—even though she's taken over for JJ, he's still on the board. I'd have to get the board to agree to the investment, and they won't even let me do a proposal. So it's dead in the water for now." Reece tossed the vegetables with olive oil and seasoning, then arranged them on a baking tray and slid it into the oven.

"That can't be it, man. It's an outstanding idea, and if you guys don't do it, someone else will soon."

He washed his hands and dried them on a towel, then took the seat beside me. "I told them that, too. But I don't have the votes to overrule the board. I'd need Ellie, her older brother James, their cousin the Dubois kid, and Stella all to claim their stake and agree to it before I could try to persuade the board. So chances of that are slim to none." He tipped back the rest of his drink and stood, gesturing to my glass. "Refill?"

I held it out to him wordlessly, and he moved over to the bar.

"So, is Stella still being a punk kid with no responsibilities?"

Reece gave me a dark look over his shoulder. "Hey, be nice. She had that accident just weeks before she would have gone to the Olympics. That was everything she had worked for her entire childhood, and like that," he snapped his fingers, "it was gone. It took her a long time to recover and since then she's been training like crazy, preparing for regionals to see if she can get one more shot at the Olympics. I'm really proud of her for sticking with it."

"Yeah, I mean that's cool. She was always super driven about it. I'm just wondering where she goes after that?"

"Dad and I have discussed it. When he retires, he'll need someone to take over building and expansion, and James was interested in it. So maybe Stella could take over mountain ops. She's more passionate about the runs and the snow than the rest of us combined, and she's got all these ideas-" he stopped, interrupted by a loud bang from the front door opening and closing.

A husky feminine voice called out, "It's just me, Reece. I decided I can't face Mom and Dad for dinner. I hope it's okay if I hide out with you for a few hours."

Reece brought me back a full glass and grinned. "Speak of the devil..."

"And she shall appear," I finished, the words a croak that I tried to cover with a sip of my drink. Muffled thuds and thumps sounded from the foyer and I waited with a smug smile, my heart suddenly pounding. The last time I'd seen Stella, she had glared at me with absolute hatred—it had nearly broken my heart, but it was my fault and I knew I'd deserved it. In fact, I'd gone out of my way to make her hate me. At school she'd been a skinny, kind of awkward girl with long blonde braids who dressed like a skater punk and wore braces. That mental image was burned into my mind, along with the girl I knew outside of school —the one who enjoyed hikes and swimming and was impossibly sarcastic and sweet. Either way, in my head, she was still a teenage girl.

But when Stella walked around the corner, I had to blink my eyes several times to register what I was seeing.

The woman who stood before me scarcely resembled the teenager I remembered. Freed from her snow gear and wearing nothing but leggings and a tight-fitting shirt, this woman had clearly grown into her curves. She was in the process of releasing long, ice-blonde locks from a loose braid, and her lips were full and glossy.

I was partially hidden behind Reece, but she didn't even glance our way. Heat built in my chest, my pulse continuing to rise. I knew this would happen eventually, but I hadn't been prepared for it today. Nothing like facing the consequences of your youth when you least expect it.

Stella walked straight to the fridge and started digging without acknowledging either of us.

"What are you making for dinner? It smells amazing! I hope you made enough to share, but if you didn't, that's fine. I'll just heat up some leftovers."

Reece cleared his throat. "Uh, Stella, I don't think you noticed I have a guest."

"Oh!" She straightened immediately, sorting through glass containers. "Is it a girl? *Please* tell me it's a girl. I'll just nuke this pasta a la vodka and be out of your hair," she promised, turning around.

I knew the exact moment she recognized me. Her crystal blue eyes were bright with excitement when she turned, a wide smile on her lips revealing perfectly straight, pearly white teeth with zero trace of braces. As soon as her gaze landed on me, her entire face fell into an expression of horror. She froze, her arms wrapped around several containers of leftovers, and stared at me without saying a word.

"Stella, you remember Sebastian?"

───────

───────

My body locked up, my eyes wide in terror. I imagined I looked just like the deer-in-the-headlights scenario people loved to use.

He was even hotter than I remembered. As a teenage girl, I thought he was so grown up when he left, but this Sebastian had definitely become a man. He still had the close-cropped, inky black hair that was tousled from his hat; those bright chocolate-brown eyes I'd drawn endlessly in art class, framed by thick lashes that any girl would kill for; and the full lips that girls whispered about in school.

And the dimples...

But now he had wide, muscular shoulders to go with his warm brown skin, and hands that looked strong and adept. My heart stuttered and raced, heat rising to my cheeks. After all this time and what he did, I thought my crush was dead and buried. But it resurfaced with a vengeance in a matter of moments.

In the brief seconds we sized each other up, a thought flitted through my brain that this was my second chance. He'd crushed and humiliated me in the cruel way only teenage boys can, but we'd been *kids* then. I wasn't a dorky freshman chasing him around with heart eyes—even though I was still pretty short, nobody could mistake me for a teenage boy now. My body finally filled out, I ditched the braces, and rid myself of the acne. Now men of all ages watched me walk by, so I'd clearly grown out of my ugly duckling phase. He'd been away for six years. Maybe we could finally put our past behind us...

"Hey there, *Estrellita*." Sebastian drew out the syllables of the nickname I'd loathed pretty much my entire life, as if not a single day had passed since he left. His expression slipped into that same sarcastic smile, and I suddenly felt like it transported me right back to six years ago.

Hope crashed and burned in my stomach. Nope, he was definitely still the dick who broke my heart in school.

My brows dropped, and I gave him my best superior glare, hauling my leftovers toward the microwave. "Hey Sebastian. I'd ask how you've been, but I don't really care."

Reece, always the peace-maker, intervened. "Hey now, you two. Stella, I have another steak and there's plenty of vegetables in the oven. You can put those back and save them for another day you want to raid my fridge. Want a drink?"

I paused, weighing the pros and cons of having a perfectly cooked steak that required sharing a table with Sebastian, against the idea of eating the suddenly much less appealing leftovers but being able to scarf them down in peace, alone in front of the TV.

SASHA PIERCE

Reece knew exactly where my head was at. "Come on, Stella, you haven't seen each other in six years, isn't it time to let bygones be bygones? And I know you never turn down a steak. Besides, that pasta hardly has any protein in it... what would your coach say?"

He had me there. My head fell back, and I released a frustrated groan. "Fine, I'll have steak, but pass on the booze. I've got to hit the weights early tomorrow, and I always feel like shit when I drink."

My big brother beamed and scooped me up for a hug in his burly arms. "I knew you'd make the right choice."

His squeeze was too tight; I drew in a pained gasp and he set me down immediately.

Reece's cheeks flushed behind his auburn beard. "Sorry, Stella. I keep forgetting... you'd think I'd remember by now."

"It's fine. I know you don't do it on purpose. You're just a big oaf," I flashed him a teasing grin while I massaged my ribs.

Sebastian's aggravatingly smooth voice interrupted our familial banter. "Did you get hurt *again*?"

I shot him an annoyed glance. "Again? What do you mean again?"

"Reece told me how you got hurt a few years back, but that's got to be healed by now. So I assumed it was a newer injury."

His know-it-all tone set my teeth on edge. "Well, sorry to disappoint you Dr. Delacruz, but it's still the same one. Something about how my ribs set and healed was slightly off, so when I work hard, the area swells up and gets sensitive."

His suddenly sympathetic voice took me by surprise. "I'm sorry. Chronic pain can be really debilitating." Despite his gentle tone, I would not fall for it. He liked to set me up just to crush me harder. It was his signature move in high school.

"Yeah, like you know anything about it." I tossed my hair and turned back to Reece, who'd already seasoned a third steak and was preparing his tray for the grill.

Reece paused and turned to me with a solemn expression. "Stella, Sebastian actually-"

"It's fine," Sebastian cut him off quickly. "No worries."

With a sigh and a shake of his head, Reece picked up his tray and exited onto the deck.

Sebastian watched him go with a confused expression. "Is he... going *outside* to cook?"

"Yeah. He insists the only proper way to cook a steak is over an open flame, so even in the dead of winter, he uses his grill. Even got a special roof extension added on out there to keep the snow off of his baby."

I dug a slice of bread from the pantry and started pulling off pieces to eat, leaning against the counter and doing my best to look casual. Maybe I could make him believe I'd forgotten what he did all those years ago.

Sebastian focused on his drink for a few minutes, then glanced up. "So, you're doing another run for the Olympics?"

"Yup." If he wanted to talk about my favorite subject, I wouldn't stop him. But I wasn't going to fall into the trap of gushing.

"That's cool. You were so geeked out over it in school you used to practice waving from that step stool in your living room like it was a podium. Do you remember that? Good to see that some things never change." He smirked at me over his glass and waited for my reaction.

Even though my jaw clenched with annoyance, I refused to give him the satisfaction. Instead, I affected a bored tone and replied, "Yeah, I actually got lots of practice when I placed at *regionals*, then *nationals*, then the *World Cup* a few years ago. I have so many medals now, I just started tossing them in a drawer."

"Good for you, *Estrellita*." His grin widened, revealing those damned dimples.

Folding my arms over my chest, I leveled him with my best glare. "Could you not? You know I've always hated that nickname, and that hasn't changed in the last six years. My name is Estelle. Most people call me Stella. I *prefer* Stella."

"Aww, but *Estrellita* is so much cuter! And it suits you. You were always a little star."

Fury boiled in my stomach, and my blood ran hot through my veins. "You know what?" I snapped. "You're right that some things never change, because you're still a fucking dick."

He laughed, which only pissed me off more. "Come on, I'm just teasing you. I would have thought you'd grow out of this teenage angst over a silly nickname."

As if it was just about the nickname. "Yeah, well surprise, I still don't like people picking on me," I shot back pointedly. "How about you get a clue and stop treating me like a dumb kid? If you hadn't noticed I'm grown, and I don't like stupid nicknames."

"Well, that's the thing about nicknames; no one gets to choose their own."

"Alright, then your new nickname is Dickface McBallsack."

He shrugged, his face ambivalent. "If that's what you want, but it's really a mouthful to say. Could we shorten it to Dickface? What about just Ballsack? It has a nice ring to it, doesn't it?"

"Why don't we just go with Twatwaffle then?"

"Oh I like that one."

"Well, we can't have that. Now it's Buttboy McTool."

He shrugged nonchalantly. "Whatever you want, *Estrellita*."

The rage boiled over. "I want you to *stop fucking calling me that!*"

"Woah, woah, simmer down," Reece interjected. "Man, I can't leave you two alone for five minutes before you're at it like cats and dogs." He set the tray of perfectly grilled beef on the stove, the scent making my stomach rumble despite the ball of fury within it.

"Yeah, well, I know which one of us is the *dog*." I glared at Sebastian.

A slow smile spread across his face. "Whatever you say, *pussycat*."

"I knew you'd come out with some sexist shit eventually. I heard the Army is full of perverts. I guess *that* rumor was true. Is that why they kicked you out?"

Sebastian's smug expression dropped, and I

felt a flicker of satisfaction that I finally pierced that infuriating armor.

Reece glanced up from the oven and hit me with a warning tone. "Stella, that's enough."

I turned my fury on him. "What the *fuck*, Reece? Why are you *always* on his side? Even after what he did to me in high school, you believed him over me. So now he can sit here and say *whatever* he wants and I have to take it, but the *second* I stand up for myself and say something back-"

"You don't know what you're talking about. Just let it be." My brother's face was deadly serious, the same flat look I get from Dad when he's about to lose his shit.

I glanced at Sebastian and was shocked to see that all of his smug self-assuredness was gone, replaced by an expression of immeasurable grief. My throat grew thick, and I swallowed, unsure of what exactly was going on. Clearly, there was more here than I knew.

"Fine. Whatever. I'll set the table." Ignoring the both of them, I retrieved placemats, napkins, and silverware from the cabinet and crossed to the dining room, my blood still boiling. It wasn't an enormous room, just big enough for a round table that sat four. Reece and Sebastian spoke in voices too low for me to hear, and I didn't give a shit that they were probably talking about me. By the time I finished and returned to the kitchen, Reece had already dished up three plates and they were heading to the table.

I grabbed a glass of water and returned, only to discover they'd chosen the outer seats, leaving me sandwiched in the middle.

Fan-fucking-tastic. Nothing like an awkward family dinner to allow me to relive all the humiliation I'd tried to put behind me for six years.

Gritting my teeth, I claimed my chair. It was a minor consolation, but Reece had given me the largest steak of the three. I was determined to focus on the good and ignore the bad, aka Sebastian Delacruz.

Apparently, I wasn't the only one determined not to break the peaceful silence, because I was almost through with my dinner before Reece cleared his throat.

"So, Sebastian, how are you liking ski patrol?"

My silverware dropped to my plate with a clatter, and I stared at him in disbelief. "You put this jerk on ski patrol? Jesus. That mountain was my *one* refuge and now it's not even safe on the slopes any more."

Sebastian's tone was infuriatingly condescending when he replied, "Actually, that's the purpose of ski patrol, *Estrellita*. To ensure the safety of everyone out there enjoying the mountain. And yes, Reece, it's going well. It took a couple days for me to get used to skis again, but turns out it's like riding a bicycle after all. So far, it's been pretty calm."

My eyes narrowed, and I glared at him, returning to cutting my steak aggressively. "Oh, I know your type; the guys who love the power trip and chase people down just to kick them off the hill for riding faster than the tourists who can barely stay on their feet. Made any teenage girls cry today?"

"Ooh, someone's bitter." Sebastian's smirk returned along with that enraging, sarcastic tone. "Listen, princess, everyone has to follow the rules, even you."

I snorted, matching his energy head on. "I avoid the greens and the slow areas for exactly that reason. That's not a problem *I* have, but I've seen a lot of snowboarders just minding their own business and getting crapped on. For some reason, ski patrol always has it in for us."

"Not as far as I can tell." His smirk widened, and he raised an eyebrow. "I guess you must still be rolling with a group of deviants."

I pushed back from the table in disgust. "Ugh,

just because we're not all homecoming king or freaking quarterback for the football team, that doesn't mean we're deviants. My friends may not fit the mold, but they're good people."

Reece, maddeningly, sat in complete silence with his eyes trained on his plate as he ate extremely slowly.

Sebastian tilted his head. "Wasn't that you and your friends who got busted for spray painting the homecoming float?"

A bubble of laughter tumbled out of me at the unexpected memory. "Yeah, that was us," I answered with my own smirk. "That prank was *hilarious*. You sat up there all smug on your throne and had no idea about what we wrote on the back. God, people were *crying* from laughing so hard."

Reece snorted, then quickly cleared his throat, trying to cover up his laugh. But I caught the glint of amusement in his eye before he refocused on his potatoes.

"Well, if you think the sort of humor that centers on farts is hilarious, I suppose it might have been funny. Regardless, I'm not the one who had to do a hundred hours of community service along with an in-school suspension, so I rather think I came out ahead in the long run."

"Worth it." I shoved the last bite of beef into

my mouth and grinned at him smugly. He hadn't gotten into a lick of trouble for what he did to me, so it had been my only recourse.

And quite satisfying.

Abruptly, Sebastian changed tracks. "So what have you been doing while I've been gone? I mean, I know you were injured and then you've been training, but surely you must have gotten a job, a place of your own to live?"

The feeling of smugness withered away. "I devote all of my time to training. I have the sponsorship with Branton, so that and snowboarding are my only jobs right now."

"Ah yes, your 'modeling career.'" He said it in such a disdainful way my hands flexed with my sudden desire to punch his smug face. "So I take it you still live with your parents? No desire to fly the nest, huh? I imagine it's easier, not having to pay for your own food or anything." He eyed my empty plate meaningfully, implying that I was some kind of loser freeloading on my family.

Reece finally stepped in. "We're *all* proud of her dedication to her goals. Stella will find her place with Aspen Ridge once she gets through this Olympic run and ends up on a podium with a big shiny medal around her neck." He cast me a warm smile, and I returned it gratefully.

"Oh, I'm sure everyone is *very* proud. But like, what are you going to *do*? Surely you'll need some kind of education to help run a business as big as Aspen Ridge. Do you feel behind that you don't have a degree? Have you taken any community college courses?"

This constant needling was bringing my temper to a boiling point. "No," I answered. "Right now I'm training for four separate events and I barely have time to sleep, let alone study."

Reece looked up at me with alarm. "Stella, I thought you were going to drop half-pipe?"

"I haven't decided yet," I sniffed. "My highest scores have always been half-pipe and slope style, and I'm not as confident with snowboard cross and slalom. So I'm gonna start out with all four and see what happens."

Color crept up Reece's face, visible even beneath his auburn beard. "What could happen is that you crash on half-pipe again and are too injured to do ANY of the events. Is that what you want?"

"Of course not! But it's difficult for anyone, and it's dangerous for every person who rides down that pipe. I'm no different from the rest of them."

"You're different to *me*, Stella. You're my little

sister. God, we all lost it when you got hurt. Is that what Mom and Dad are pissed about? That you haven't dropped out of half-pipe?"

I drew in a deep breath and let it out with a slow sigh. "Part of it."

Sebastian chose this moment to insert himself into a conversation that clearly had nothing to do with him.

"Yes, don't let your family, your friends, or even reason stop you from doing what you want, *Estrellita*. Perhaps if you end up a paraplegic, you'll still think it was *worth it*." His entire demeanor had changed, a disgusted expression on his face that was nowhere near playful.

My eyes drifted to Reece, who had a similarly unpleasant expression.

Standing abruptly, I picked up my plate. "Well, this was fun. Thanks for the support, guys." I swept back to the kitchen with my dishes before he could say anything else.

By the time I had them rinsed and in the dishwasher, Reece and Sebastian were just standing up. I hustled to the foyer and started pulling on my snow pants.

Reece popped his head around the corner. "Stella, are you leaving? I thought you'd want to stay for dessert."

"Yeah, I've had enough of this treat, thanks. I still have to go get my laps in. I came straight here from the hill." I stepped into my snowboard boots, then started tightening the boa fastener, just enough that my feet wouldn't slide around inside. It wasn't a long walk to the bus station.

"I made the brownies you like..." he offered in a regretful tone. He was clearly remorseful for getting on my case about the events.

He *almost* convinced me to stay. Reece's peanut butter scotch brownies were my absolute favorite dessert on earth.

Then Sebastian's taunting voice carried from the kitchen, and I was immediately over it.

"Oh, she probably can't have dessert. What would her *coach* say? It's surely harder to do all those death-defying tricks with a belly full of brownie."

My chin dropped, and I glared at Reece. "Nah, I'm good. I'll have one tomorrow at lunch when I come back for that pasta, and your place is a little less *crowded*." After zipping up my jacket, I pulled my gloves from my pockets and gave him a hug that he returned gently, conscious of my ribs. "Love you. Thanks for dinner. It would have been a lot more pleasant with a little less company," I added pointedly, backing away.

"Eh, give him a break. He's been through a lot in the last six years, Stella."

"Yeah, well, so have we all. That doesn't give everyone an excuse to act like a dick."

Reece sighed heavily. "Well, everyone is worried about you, even though we're excited for you, too. But I know he gets under your skin. I'll talk to him, okay?"

"Thank you. Best big brother ever." I grinned and pulled on my hat.

"I know. I'll leave a couple brownies for you in the fridge, on top of the pasta. And I'll fix you a salad. Can't have too many vegetables." He smiled fondly at me, then shoved his hands in his pockets. "Now get out of here, and text me when you get home, okay?"

I rolled my eyes. "You're almost as bad as Dad. It's like a ten-minute bus ride to the pool, and a five-minute walk to our house. This is Aspen Ridge, Reece. What do you think is going to happen?"

"All the same, text me, please."

"Okay, okay, I'll text you."

CHAPTER
FOUR

STELLA

E ven though I evaded the argument last night, Mom and Dad were up especially early to hit me with it in the morning. I thought I'd get my workout done and slip out before they made it down for coffee, but apparently, they were determined to have this talk.

"Estelle," Mom sighed, her thin fingers wrapped around her mug. She was leaning back slightly against my dad's chest, who had braced himself against the counter. They always did the united front thing. It'd be sweet if they weren't united against *me*. "It's not that your dad and I don't want you to pursue your passions, but we'd just like you to show even the *slightest* interest in the business side of things."

I kept to the other side of the gleaming kitchen island, arms folded over my chest. "If you recall, I *have* shown interest in the business. I've come to you with a lot of ideas, and they all get shot down."

"Now that's not fair, Bug," Dad piped up. This was the other thing they did, alternating who speaks, so it's always two against one. "We built the terrain park from your suggestion. Some of the other things just weren't as feasible."

"Not *feasible*?" I choked. "You're kidding, right? Hosting a huge televised competition would require some planning, but I'd hardly say it's not feasible. Snowshoe Ridge did the X-Games last year, and I told you guys we should bid for that *three years* ago. If they found it feasible, surely we could have."

"Estelle, please lower your voice. There's no need for a shouting match," Mom chided.

My eyes rolled, but I attempted to control my volume. "Regardless, it's not true to say I've shown no interest in the business, and you know it. But this is the most important season of my life, and I'm training for four events. Surely you can understand that I can't slack off of training to shadow Reece around or sit in an office."

Dad cleared his throat and shifted with obvious discomfort. "That's something we wanted to talk to you about, too. We're still not convinced that you need to do all four. Wouldn't it be better if you dropped the half-pipe and slope style, so you can focus on the other two?"

My eyes narrowed. "Safer, you mean. It would be *safer* if I avoided the events that included tricks."

Mom glanced backward briefly at Dad, then returned her gaze to me. "Yes, Estelle, that would be safer. And I think we'd all feel a lot better knowing that those events were off the table."

"But they're my *best* events. I don't know yet how I'll do in slalom and snowboard cross. It'd be stupid to restrict myself to those when I know I win medals in the other two."

"Bug, you know the reported times of your competition; About ninety percent of the time you're actually home—which isn't much, I admit —you spend researching how everyone else is doing. And your coach said you're already outperforming the known front-runners. He's confident you'll sweep the regionals in all categories, so you should be, too."

"I'm glad David is confident, but until I actually do some comps and see how I stack up, I'm not planning on being too cocky. The race isn't won until it's over, right?" It was shitty of me to throw that back in his face, knowing it was something he said to encourage me for years, but I was definitely over it.

Mom tried again. "We just think—and David agrees—that you're training a little too hard, baby. I know you like to stay busy, so we thought if you had a couple hours doing something else—whatever you want to do—at the resort, it would give your body and mind a break from the training and also get you more involved with Aspen Ridge, that's all."

Grabbing the jacket I'd thrown it over the bar stool, I slid my arms into the sleeves. "Thanks for the advice, but I'm actually on my way to do a normal 20-something activity and have coffee with a friend. I'd better not be late—I so rarely have time away from training, after all." I zipped up and headed for the door. "Bye, great talk."

"Estelle, wait-" Dad called after me, but I was already gone.

Heading for the bus stop, I realized I was still plenty early to meet Madison. And, in my haste to get out of the house, I completely skipped grab-bing my prepared snacks and overnight oats.

I hoofed it into town since the indignation was still running hot through my veins. David wouldn't approve, but I'd find something to eat at Bear Paw, and I could rustle up some snacks at Reece's when I stopped in for lunch.

A fresh snow had fallen overnight, just an inch, but it sparkled in the morning sunlight and made everything look clean and crisp. I drew in a deep breath of cold air, held it for a moment, then released it in a white cloud of vapor.

I loved winter. Of course summer was nice, and fall, and even spring, but winter in Aspen Ridge had always been my favorite. Mom wasn't wrong; I always needed to stay busy, and there was just nothing better than spending the short winter days on the slopes, followed by an après-ski cock-tail or meal with friends, cocoa or cider next to a roaring fireplace while snow drifted outside, hot tub sessions with snow crusting my hair...

Of course, this season was all work, no time for play. No room in the diet for fondu or rum and cokes when I'm trying to be an Olympic athlete. It did sort of feel isolating to have every spare minute spent on training and none for friends or fun. It wasn't easy by any stretch of the imagination.

Which was why I'd begged Madison to meet me at Bear Paw this morning, just to catch up. I was planning for a hard ride this afternoon, so I granted myself a couple of hours to be a normal person for once.

I reached the corner of Birch, the secondary thoroughfare that branches off but runs parallel to Main, and watched the blue line bus rumble past on its way toward my house. Walking had been a good choice; I was already only three blocks from Bear Paw and the bus took a rambling route to get there.

It was barely twenty minutes after dawn and the morning light was cool and pale. Even so, Aspen Ridge was already bustling. Tourists dashed into local breakfast joints for fuel before they hit the slopes, locals delivered their wares to shops, shuttles arrived from the Denver airport to drop off even more tourists keen to strap on their skis. And likely, no thought given to the fact they were now over eleven-thousand feet above sea level. I grew up here, so I had no problem with the thin air. But there was a reason all of those oxygen bars remained afloat in town and were already open.

I finally crossed Main and slipped into Bear

Paw, where warm coffee-and-pastry-scented air blasted me in the face. Immediately overheated, I unzipped my jacket and searched for Madison's long chestnut hair.

It didn't take long to find her in our favorite cozy chairs by the fire, and she wasn't alone. Another girl, who looked similar in the face but taller, leaner, with very light brown hair, sat engaged in conversation with my friend.

"Hey Mads," I threw my jacket on an empty chair and grinned. "Who's your friend?"

Madison hopped out of her own chair and hugged me. "Stella, I'm so glad you texted last night! It's been ages since we hung out. This is my cousin, Genevieve. Vieve, this is Stella Blackwell."

The new girl stood up with sparkling eyes and a bashful expression. I barely reached her chin. "Stella, it's so great to meet you! I don't really follow sports, but of course I've heard of you. And Madison has talked about you a ton over the last couple of years."

"All good things, I hope?" I turned to give Madison a dubious expression with one eyebrow raised, and she grinned.

"Mostly... aw, who am I kidding? You know all I do is sing your praises. You're like snowboarding goals, and we're all so jealous but super proud of you, Stella."

My cheeks warmed at the compliment. "You're the sweetest! I'm dying of starvation so I'm going to go order. Have you already got something coming?"

"Not yet. We barely sat down before you arrived. We thought we'd be waiting longer, but apparently everyone's early today!"

"Perfect, because now I can treat. Let's go."

Despite their protests, I got the entire order on my card. I knew Madison didn't expect me to treat, but I also knew that the cost of living in Aspen Ridge was high, and even though we paid our instructors well, a lot of them took on second jobs. So I enjoyed helping when I could.

Once we had happily settled in our seats with steaming mugs, and I had an enormous egg and bacon croissant sandwich to tame my growling stomach, we got to the business of catching up.

"So Vieve, are you here on vacation?" I prompted her, then took a satisfying bite of my breakfast.

"Sort of," she glanced down at her lap as if she was embarrassed.

I was expecting more of an answer than that.

"Sort of?" I said around my mouthful.

"Vieve's visiting to see if she likes the place," Madison replied. "She'll finish her degree next semester and she doesn't really have anywhere else to go. She was supposed to move in with her boyfriend, but he dumped her out of nowhere right before Christmas and now she's got to rethink her plans."

The tall girl's cheeks grew rosy, and her eyes didn't lift from her cup.

I choked down my bite. "Oh man, that sucks. God, guys are the worst, aren't they?" It wasn't exactly an asshole boyfriend, but I could certainly relate in a general sense.

"Yeah, pretty much," Vieve agreed. "We were together for three and a half years, and then we were about to go on a winter vacation with his family and he just broke it off an hour before we left for the airport."

"What?!"

"Yeah, it was super shitty," Madison agreed, blowing on the steam billowing from her mocha.

Genevieve expanded. "He'd been hinting that he was going to propose on that trip—they were going to his family cabin in Tahoe where his dad had proposed to his mom. And then—boom—he changed his mind and told me to pack and be out of his apartment when he got back."

"What an asshole!" I exclaimed, rather too loudly because it drew the attention of almost everyone in the coffee shop. Dropping my voice, I added, "I'm so sorry. That's freaking awful. Did you find another place to stay?"

Genevieve had finally lifted her eyes, apparently less embarrassed now that the story was out. "Technically, I've always had a dorm room, but I had stayed at his place since the school year started. So most of my stuff was there. I got a couple of friends to help me move it, and then Madison was kind enough to invite me here for the rest of my winter break. I head back next week, which sucks if I'm honest."

"Yeah, she's already in love with the place," Madison added smugly. "Aspen Ridge gets them every time."

"I'm not really a winter person, but it has been nice hanging out with you at least," Vieve said to her cousin with a smile. "So I'm looking forward to more of that."

I had to interrupt. "Uh, excuse me, did you say you weren't a winter person?" I leveled an insulted gaze at her. "We'll certainly have to change that!"

Genevieve laughed and Madison nodded in agreement. "Oh yeah, absolutely. She's just not a winter person because she's never gotten to see how good it can be. We'll change her mind."

The taller girl just shook her head. "I like winter, just from the inside, like this," she gestured to the crackling fire. "I'll take a cozy seat and a good book any day."

"Do you ski, or snowboard like me and Mads?" I asked, curious.

"Nope, never tried it. I'm not the athletic adventurer type. I prefer a pleasant walk, or perhaps a leisurely bike ride. That's about my limit."

I exchanged a glance with Madison, who shrugged her shoulders.

"So, what are you interested in?" I probed. "What's your degree?"

"Biology," she answered. "I want to be a veterinarian. I love animals."

"That's cool," I replied. "How long does it take to become a pet doctor?"

"Eight years," Genevieve answered. "I'm finishing up my undergrad this spring, and then I have four years of veterinary school."

"Wow, that's really cool. And how old are you, if you don't mind me asking?"

"I'll be twenty-two in the fall."

"That's awesome," I replied, a cold sliver of

embarrassment settling in my chest. She was younger than me and already half-way to being a veterinarian. I barely coasted through high school with a B-minus average and that was the extent of my education.

As if she sensed the change in my mood, Madison interjected, "What about you, Stella? You're a *world class* snowboarder on her way to the Olympics!"

"Seriously," agreed Genevieve, "that's so incredibly cool. I can't imagine what that must be like. Madison said you train all the time."

Gratification spread through my chest, warming away the previous feelings. "It's not that big of a deal," I deflected humbly. "I'm no different from any other athlete dedicated to their sport. We're all passionate about something."

"Nah, I'm not falling for that," Madison snorted. "Vieve have you ever seen videos of her? Stella does tricks I can't even *dream* of attempting. She catches so much air, honestly I don't know how she does it. I'd be so freaked out I'd completely forget what I was supposed to do and just hope that I made it back to earth safely."

"It's not all that complicated. I work out a lot, practice the moves again and again in the gym and then in this giant outdoor inflatable air bag. So by the time I try for the first time to land it on the snow, I've already landed it hundreds of times on a safer surface."

"It's still awesome," Genevieve replied, and Madison nodded in agreement. "Few people can do it. I have seen some clips of you, and you're incredible. I *know* you're going to win this year."

At this point, my heart was full to bursting with pride. There's nothing like girl friends to boost you up when you're feeling low.

———

AFTER MY LUXURIOUS gab session with Mads and a promise from Vieve that she'd let me know when she was back in town, I hoofed it back to my family ski locker to gear up.

The sun had come out fully and brightened the sky to a brilliant cloudless blue, the snow already disappearing from the rooftops under the warm rays. When I had equipped myself to do battle with the mountain, I grabbed my pack and set out for the lift. I had water and a couple of snacks, and despite my best intention to leave it behind, my flask was tucked in there as well. I probably wouldn't need the liquid courage today, but it had become a sort of crutch and I hated to leave it at home... just in case.

On my way up, I checked my watch, calculating how many runs I could get in before I needed to break for lunch and head to Reece's condo.

It was a perfect morning, hardly any tracks on the black runs and a fresh layer of powder over the groomed tracks. Music in my ears, my body rested and charged up from my meal, and nothing in front of me but miles of pristine mountain slope.

After a few runs to get my body warmed up and my blood pumping, I angled my board toward the terrain park. I was vibing, conscious of other skiers as I crossed the trails but minding my own business, when a skier in a bright red ski patrol jacket zipped in front of me then hit the brakes, blasting me with a snowy rooster tail and forcing me to stop or crash into him.

I wiped the snow from my face and glared at Sebastian with fiery hate. "Dude, what the actual fuck??"

"Hey, *Estrellita*," he smirked, and he was lucky I wasn't quite close enough to hit him in the face because he was definitely due for a knuckle sandwich. "I wondered if I'd see you today."

"Yeah, well, I hoped that *wouldn't* happen, but here we are. Isn't that little move you just pulled the sort of shit that people get in trouble for with the ski patrol?"

"Nah, that's kind of a grey area. I can argue that you were going to cross my path, and I had to stop before we crashed. They tend to favor one of their own over a random snowboarder, you know."

"So glad you're settling into your roll as slope-side douchebag, Sebastian. Now, if you'll excuse me, there's a terrain park calling my name." I shifted my weight and swung my body around, planning to pass around him by carving downhill and continuing my trek.

However, the jerk wasn't satisfied with just blasting me with snow and cutting me off the one time. Apparently, he was determined to do it again.

"Are you sure that's a good idea? It doesn't sound like your family wants you doing those tricks. Reece told me what happened-"

"Yeah, well Reece can think what he wants, but it's my career. Besides, I stopped caring what you thought sophomore year," I added pointedly.

His tone abruptly turned colder. "Your choices affect other people, Estrellita. It's pretty selfish of you to pretend like you're the only one who gets hurt when you fall."

"That's rich, coming from you. Oh, I forgot, you don't hurt people by accident. You do it deliberately," I snapped. "What I do is none of your business, Sebastian. This is my life, and I don't recall giving you a say about how I live it."

"I care about your brother, and he's worried about you, so it's my business by proxy."

My fury reached the boiling point. "No, it's really fucking not. Ski patrol doesn't give you a free license for harassing me about my life choices. Keep it up and I'll report you. I may be a snowboarder, but I'm not 'random' and believe me, if I have a complaint about you, they'll deal with it."

His eyes narrowed with obvious anger, jaw flexing as he clenched his teeth. "Fine, do what you want and damn the consequences, right? Far be it for those of us who care about you to voice our concern. Good luck, Estrellita. I'd say I hope you don't break your neck, but I guess it's none of my business."

With that, he pushed off, carving a neat run down the hill.

Racing blood echoed in my ears, but I was flush with the victory of making him leave first. I pushed off toward the terrain park with a grin, but in the back of my mind, I had to wonder...

What the hell did he mean by 'those of us' who care about me?

CHAPTER
FIVE

STELLA

I did a few tricks, but the adrenaline from my fight with Sebastian made me shaky and I didn't trust myself on the big jumps with less than perfect concentration. Instead of hanging out longer, I headed toward Reece's condo for lunch and to stock up on supplies for the rest of the day.

When both my belly and my pack were filled— my brother, bless him, had prepared several power snacks for me and left them in a neat stack in his fridge—I swapped out for one of the warmer jackets I kept at Reece's and headed out once again, with the plan to head for the back bowls.

Since they're steep and have fewer obstacles, they make for a great place to practice carving with speed. Especially since the snow piles up there, it's perfect to work on keeping speed through the thicker drifts.

Once I got on the other side of the mountain, the blue sky day abruptly became more threatening. Huge grey clouds that were nearly black on the bottom were heading our way. The sky below them appeared dark and misty, a sure sign that they were dropping snow, and a lot of it.

Still, I had time for a few runs and spent a good forty-five minutes just to get here, so I was certainly going to take advantage while I had the time. The storm looked to be a few hours out, at least. The slope below me was still sparkling in sunlight, with hardly any skiers in my path.

It was a good move; the snow was great, and because there was so much fresh powder I felt confident pushing myself harder on speed. Wiping out on light fluffy snow differed completely from eating it on a groomed trail. That could get rather painful since the snow was packed. Here it was like a deep feather pillow, as long as you landed right.

I enjoyed a few runs, racing against time as those threatening clouds moved ever closer. The long lift ride back to the peak gave me time to have my snacks and stay fueled up for the next run, and as long as the sun was warm, it was a fantastic time.

When I reached the peak again, the clouds were blocking the sun from the entire slope aside from the very top, and not far off, the world disappeared in a veil of grey.

With no time to lose, I maneuvered down to my favorite run and absolutely flew down the mountain. Snow was already hitting when I reached the bottom, and visibility was swiftly degrading.

I *had* to get one more run in. I hopped on the chairlift and rode back to the peak, glancing over my shoulder at the heavy clouds every few seconds.

When I reached the top, Todd, the lift operator, almost refused to let me go back down.

"I dunno, Stella, this one is pretty bad. Did you look at the radar? It's going to be sitting on us for a couple of days, from the looks of it."

"All the more reason for me to get in one more run, Todd," I pleaded. "I need all the practice I can get for regionals and this is going to kill *days* from my training. I swear I'll be careful and I promise I'll go straight down and get on the chair. No more arguing."

He scratched his beard thoughtfully. "I know you're a killer boarder, Stella, but if something happened to you, your dad would kill me. Not to mention Josh can't come back up until you do."

"I swear I'll be fast. *Lightning* fast. I'll be back up so fast it'll be like I never left. Pleeeease?"

He sighed heavily. "Okay, but straight down and straight to the lift, Stella. I mean it. And if you get in trouble with ski patrol, it's on you."

"Deal! Thank you, Todd. I'm gone!" I turned and zipped down the trail that traveled along the peaks. If this was going to be my last ride for a few days, I was going to make it a good one.

I went straight to the steepest part of the mountain and stared down at my route. The storm was hitting even faster than I expected. Visibility was already low just a few hundred feet below me, and the mountain actually disappeared less than halfway down.

I swapped out the polarized lens on my goggles for a yellow low-vis, then drew a deep breath, and hopped over the edge.

SEBASTIAN

THE CHAIRLIFT from the bowls was still running when I arrived at the peak from the other direction. Sharp icy wind, peppered with snowflakes, assaulted my face as soon as I crested the top. Sure enough, the approaching storm had arrived, and was close to crossing over the mountain. I peeked over the edge and my heart immediately sank... there was practically zero visibility. I had only skied back here once this season, and for all my bravado, I was still getting used to being on skis again. It was one thing to carve down a black groomer in this weather; it was a completely different thing to take on the wild snowdrifts in the back bowls.

On this side of the mountain, they didn't maintain things the same way. There was even a warning at the top of the chairlift from the resort side that people crossing over were doing so at their own risk, knowing that if they end up in trouble, there could be a significant expense attached to helping them. Ski patrol couldn't sled someone out back here—it required a rescue chopper.

Just the thought made my stomach queasy. Flashes of another time I'd been in a different rescue chopper filled my brain and flooded my veins with adrenaline.

But if the lift was still going, that meant someone was still down there. Otherwise, they'd have closed down to prepare for the storm.

I didn't have time to travel along a few hundred yards of peak to the bowl-side lift to find out how many I was looking for—I needed to get down the mountain and get the hell out of there.

Drawing in a deep breath, I turned on my skis and shot down the drop-in ramp.

The snow was deep on the mountain, but actually pleasant to carve on. I took a wide route to make sure I had eyes on the entire face and didn't miss anyone. Traveling as fast as I dared while still maintaining my situational awareness.

By the time I estimated I was halfway, visibility was so poor I wasn't sure it was worth me even being out here. Like as not, I could pass someone without even realizing it. Most likely, whoever it was had already safely mounted the chairlift, and I was back here for nothing. Even so, I was not someone who left a person behind, no matter who they were, so I continued my long slow trek back and forth with as much speed as I could comfortably go. My heart raced, the clock ticking in my head a warning that I was swiftly running out of time.

When it reached the point that the lift operator had to close down or risk getting stuck, he would go no matter who was still out here. That was protocol. I knew that somewhere back here was an emergency warming house, although I didn't know exactly where. It existed precisely for this reason, but it didn't get used often. Fuck, it would be so embarrassing if I got myself stuck back here and had to wait it out. *Everyone* would know. It would hardly show that I'm a capable ski patroller.

Anxiety getting the better of me, I picked up my pace, traveling a shorter distance across the mountain as I drew closer to the bottom. The only way I knew I was close was that the slope started leveling out. I knew the layout of the hill, and I'd studied the schematic as part of orientation, so I was reasonably confident I could make my way to the lift despite the nearly complete lack of visibility.

I turned again, curving back toward what I approximated would be the path to the chairlift, and pushed myself to go a little faster.

I was practically on top of it before I realized there was something ahead of me in the snow.

Shit, is that a person? Or a rock? It was a flash of black in a white world, but my adrenaline immediately kicked into overdrive.

Somehow, I knew it wasn't a rock. A sick feeling dropped in my stomach, and I pulled up to the black thing in the snow, popping out of my skis quickly so I could get to the ground.

This close, I could definitely see it was a person. The black I'd spotted was the back of a helmet and a backpack, half-buried in the snow and quickly being covered with more.

Fuck, they're upside down in the snow. Not moving. I had no idea how long they'd been here, but it wasn't good. They were small, likely a teenage boy judging by the all-black baggy clothes and edge of the snowboard peeking out from the accumulating snow. A swift feeling of gratitude that Stella was at the terrain park flashed in my mind, but I had to focus on the here and now.

I risked disturbing any injury to his neck or spine, but there was no way around it. The most important thing was to make sure he was breathing.

The sick feeling grew, and the tremors started, my blood so loud in my ears it drowned out the howling wind. I dug around the body and confirmed the pack was strapped around his waist.

Bracing myself, I grabbed onto the pack and tugged, using my strength to flip the person over. I lifted him to one side, then performed the flip, preparing to perform CPR and check for injury.

Then I saw the long blonde braid, crusted with snow, that hung out of the helmet. I tugged down the face mask, exposing plush lips and a narrow chin. Definitely not a teenage boy.

No, no nono nonononono. My body froze completely, and an icy feeling doused me like a bucket of water. *Not again.*

It couldn't be...

I stripped off my thick gloves, ignoring the freezing air on my hands, to lift her snow-covered goggles.

Fucking hell.

It was definitely Stella, and she was completely unconscious.

CHAPTER
SIX

SEBASTIAN

"Stella? Stella?" I tapped her cheek to see if I could rouse her, but she didn't respond. Holding my hand over her nose I could feel warm air that proved she was breathing shallowly, but her lips were already turning blue and I had no idea how long she'd been out here.

Suddenly remembering protocol, I radioed to command. "This is Delacruz, I've found an unconscious snowboarder in the back bowls. I repeat: This is Delacruz, I have an unconscious snowboarder with unknown injuries on the back of Peak Nine. Requesting immediate rescue."

I waited, but the only reply I received was static. Despite how good our radios were, weather like this was bound to interfere. With a sinking heart, I pulled out my phone, but there was zero reception. I didn't know how injured she was, how long she'd been out here, or how to get help. Visibility was so poor at this point I was just guessing where I needed to go, at any rate.

Fuck it, there was no time to waste.

I replaced her goggles and mask, then tugged her hood on, zipping it up to help protect her face. Then I pulled off my pack and dragged out a small coil of cord. After unbuckling Stella's feet from her board, I folded the bindings down and lay it in the snow next to her.

She was lucky she's so small. It wouldn't be comfortable, but it was the best I could do in a pinch.

With one hand, I turned her body to face away from me, and with the other I slid the board under her back. The top binding landed right at her mid back, but hopefully the pack and her layers would prevent it from being too painful. After looping the rope under her arms, I hooked it around the binding, then pulled the ends toward the top of my makeshift sled.

I got my skis back on and retrieved my poles,

then maneuvered around her so I could tie the ends of the rope around my waist.

Then I started moving.

Fortunately, there was still a small amount of slope to get us some momentum, but the snow was so heavy and thick it was like slogging through quicksand.

I didn't know how long it actually took me; I was singularly focused on finding my way to the emergency warming house where there would be heat and medical supplies, not to mention a stronger radio that had its own mini tower. My body had shut down all emotion ages ago, with pure adrenaline being the only thing pushing me forward. They say that in the military we train and train and train, so that when things happen, we can react on instinct; our bodies will innately know what to do. And sometimes it was a gift to shut down my feelings and just follow those heavily ingrained instincts. Right now, my first mission was to get Stella out of the snow so I could assess her injuries and call for help.

I followed what appeared to be the trail, since it seemed reasonably flat with trees at an equal distance to either side. I knew that the warming house was less than a hundred yards from the chairlift. Of course, the lift was shut down now, no attendant in sight; he'd have been insane to wait. If he was still here, he'd be stuck with us, since the winds were too dangerous to ride the lift at this point. That meant they'd already radioed in that a rider was stuck here, and Gary knew I'd come over here, too. Not necessarily a comforting thought, but it was the only good news I had to hold on to.

Pressing on, I dragged Stella behind me with robotic movements. It was only a few more minutes before I could see the tiny shack that was our destination, blanketed by snow. Already there was a foot of fresh powder piled up in front of the door.

After untying myself from Stella, I clicked out of my skis and propped them against the wall, then tried the door. It wasn't locked, but it seemed to be stuck. It took a few solid hits with my shoulder to dislodge it, and then I turned and dragged her inside.

It was not, by any sense of the word, spacious. The tiny room held a single bed, a cupboard, a wood stove, and a closet with a toilet and a minuscule sink. Since it was a space for a stranded lift operator, they clearly didn't design it with two in mind.

And it was not warm. They kept the heat at a minimal setting to ensure the pipes didn't freeze, so it was at least warmer than outside, but we wouldn't be taking our jackets off soon.

First thing, I lit the oil hurricane lamp, then located the thermostat and cranked it up as high as it would go. The furnace groaned in protest but started pushing out more warm air from the register on the wall. I knew the cabin's heat ran off of a tiny fuel tank, and they stored a small ten gallon water tank under the sink. The toilet was little more than a seat over a hole in the frozen ground... I tried not to think too hard on that one.

After I got my gloves off, I untied Stella from my makeshift sled and freed her head from her mask and goggles. Her cheeks were still deathly pale and her lips hardly better, but I could see the faint white curl of warmth in the air when she breathed. I didn't want to get her snow gear off to assess her injuries before I got the room warm enough, so I left her fully clothed but removed her backpack, then scooped her up from the ground, placing her on the single bed and covering her with a nearby blanket.

My eyes darted between the small iron stove and the radio in the corner as I struggled to decide which was most important. Getting the fire going would be crucial; the fuel tank wasn't meant to support heat at full blast for multiple days.

However, I needed to let everyone know we were here and that Stella could be injured, but she was safe.

Finally making the call, I flipped the switch on the tiny battery-powered generator and crouched down before powering on the radio. It was already tuned to the patrol channel, and someone taped a helpful list of others next to the dial. There was static on the line, but that was to be expected in this storm. I keyed the button on the handset and brought it to my mouth.

"Patrol command, this is Delacruz. Do you copy?"

After a slight delay, they responded. "Hey Sebastian, it's good to hear from you. We were getting worried." Despite the static, Gary's voice was soothing, and it sent a warm wave of relief through my tense muscles.

"Unfortunately, I don't have good news. I'm not alone. I've got Stella Blackwell here with me in the back bowl warming house. She was passed out in the snow, and I'm not sure how extensive her injuries might be. I haven't assessed her other than verifying that she's breathing. The snow is pretty bad back here."

"Copy that," Gary responded, his voice crackling over the static. "We'll let her family know, but you're going to have to make do for a while. This storm is going to hang around for a couple of days, absolute blizzard conditions. There's no way anyone is getting to you until it passes."

"Roger, understood." Panic rose in my throat again. What if she had broken something? What if she had internal injuries?

Gary continued. "You should have some emergency supplies in the cupboard to your left: bandages, braces, gauze and tape. There's also a box of power bars and some drink mix, along with a kettle to use on the stove. The backside of the cabin has a pile of chopped wood. I recommend bringing in as much as you can now before you get snowed in completely."

"Roger," I repeated. "Anything else?"

"There should be two sleeping bags under the bed, along with a few extra blankets. Do whatever you have to stay warm, and just hunker down. We-" a sharp crackle, coordinating with an eerie howl of wind outside, cut him off.

"Gary, are you there?"

Static was my only reply for nearly a minute before he returned. "We may lose contact for a while until it clears up. Do your best, Sebastian. We'll try to keep checking in-"

Static consumed his voice once more, and a

dark sense of foreboding told me that was the last I'd hear from him for a while. I shut off the generator, then stood and crossed the small space to check on Stella again. Her cheeks had regained some color, her lips more rosy, but she was still out cold. Trusting Gary's advice, I ignored the small pile of wood next to the stove and pulled my gloves back on to go get more.

In the corner behind the door hung a snow shovel and a large rope bag for wood. Hallelujah for small favors! I snatched the shovel and braced myself for the cold, then opened the door.

We'd been inside for such a short time, but the blizzard outside was still a shock to my senses. I quickly scooped the snow away from the doorway, tossing it to the right and clearing a small landing, before depositing the shovel inside and grabbing the bag.

It didn't take me long to walk around the cabin, but the snow was growing deeper by the minute. I could see the edges of the path where the lift attendants cleared a trench to the wood, but it was filled nearly to my knees with fresh snow already.

Fortunately, the snow was blowing from the other side, so when I turned the corner it wasn't as bad. A pair of bright blue tarps crusted with snow covered the wood stack, which rose far over my head. Without hesitation, I got to work, shoving as much as I could into my bag, then hauling it back to the door.

Even though the logs made an incredible racket when I dumped them on the floor, Stella didn't stir. I managed several more loads—until there was no empty floor space—then repeated the process, dumping my loads of chopped wood just outside the door. Once I had a sizable pile, I pulled one of the tarps around and used it to cover the new pile I made, tucking the ends into the snow. I'd have to dig it out, but at least it was more accessible if we needed it.

When I was blessedly back inside, the cabin was noticeably warmer, and I stripped off my jacket before checking on Stella again. Still no change.

I got a healthy fire burning in the tiny stove, then set about stacking the wood in every nook and crevice I could find until the space was reasonably clear again.

By now I was sweating from the exertion and the stove was putting out an incredible amount of heat, so I turned down the thermostat to save on the fuel oil, then turned my attention to Stella.

Her cheeks were rosy now, flushed with

warmth, and her breath was no longer visible in the air. Carefully, I lifted her head and pulled back the hood on her jacket, then unbuckled her helmet and gently removed it with one hand while I cradled her head with the other.

Fortunately, there was no blood, and a gentle exploration of her skull showed no obvious damage. The helmet clearly did its job.

The rest of her body was still a question. It felt odd undressing my best friend's little sister while she was unconscious—nearly impossible to consider her just another patient—so I tried to rouse her one more time.

"Stella? Stella, can you hear me?" I pulled off her gloves and checked her fingertips, but they looked normal—cream and peach, no dark pooling of blood or redness from swelling. I gave her hand a squeeze and tried again. "Stella?"

Her eyes scrunched, an expression of pain crossing her face before she gasped loudly and her lids fluttered open.

"What? Where... *Sebastian?* Why are you holding my hand?" She sat up quickly and her eyes immediately began to roll back into her head.

"For fuck's sake Stella, lay down before you pass out again." I braced her back against my arm and tried to lower her gently, but she fought me.

"Why the hell am I here with *you*? Where is here?" Her tone was impossibly snotty for someone who'd just been rescued from a snow pile on a mountain. She blinked rapidly as if trying to clear her eyes, turning stiffly to look around.

Annoyance replaced concern, and I couldn't help growling back at her. "We're here because I found your stubborn, reckless ass facedown in the snow in a fucking blizzard, Stella. I dragged you to the warming house and you've been out cold for over half an hour. I'm fairly certain you have a concussion and I'm *trying* to assess your injuries, so would you please just fucking lay down and cooperate?"

She finally complied and allowed me to lower her onto the bed. "Jesus, even while saving someone, you still manage to be an asshole."

"Yeah, well, only you could be a fucking brat while being rescued," I retorted. "Now I'm going to ask you some questions. Do you want to take off your jacket?"

"Yeah, I'm hot," she replied in a slightly less snotty tone.

"Okay, before we do that, does anything in your body feel painful, swollen, injured or unusual in any way?"

Stella thought about it, clearly used to doing

this sort of assessment exercise before. "My ribs ache, but that's nothing new. Mainly I'm just boiling."

"Good. Okay, I'm going to help you get this jacket off." I unzipped it, then tugged on the sleeve so she could ease first one, then the other arm out. "Better?"

"Yes." She drew in a deep breath, then winced. "Yep, ribs definitely hurt."

"Okay, but not anything unusual?"

"As far as I can tell."

"Alright. Now I want you to wiggle your feet and tell me if you feel something."

Both of her heavy boots wiggled back and forth, and she gasped. "Knee," she ground out between clenched teeth. "Left knee."

"Okay. I need to get your boots and snow pants off so I can take a look. Is that alright?"

With her lower lip pinched between her teeth, she nodded. "Yeah."

As gently as I was able, I popped the release on her right boot, tugging the wires loose and easing the tongue out until I could slide the tight-fitting boot off with minimal jostling. Stella helped without complaint, pointing her foot to make the removal smoother.

I repeated the loosening process on the left

boot, glancing up at her face before I tried to pull. "Are you ready? If you can point your foot without too much pain, it'll go faster."

"Just get it over with," she growled, her fists clenched at her sides and her entire body tense.

I raised her leg by the calf and gently started working the boot off. Stella drew in a deep breath then breathed out slowly while pointing her toe, enabling me to slide the boot completely free. Once I set her leg back on the bed, she relaxed and drew in another deep breath.

Already dreading the next part, I sighed. "Alright, now it's time to take off your pants."

STELLA

I'VE HAD INJURIES BEFORE. I had epic wipeouts on national tv. Millions of people had watched me land that trick wrong and get hauled off the half-pipe, unconscious, on a stretcher.

None of that came close to the humiliation of having Sebastian-fucking-Delacruz apparently finding me facedown in the snow and turning into my personal nurse. Aside from a nasty headache, difficulty seeing clearly and an apparently injured knee, I felt pretty normal, but something told me he would not take my word for it.

Now, if I didn't *know* him, it might have been romantic. Hot ski patrol hero rescues injured snowboarder, tends gently to her injuries, and they fall in love in the middle of a snowstorm.

However, this was Sebastian we were talking about, and the chance of romance between the two of us was in the negative numbers. While there was nothing but concern in his chocolate eyes now, as soon as he decided I was okay, it would turn into a never-ending diatribe about my lack of concern for my safety with a refreshing dose of humiliation for good measure. Guaranteed.

His hands were steady as they unsnapped my snow pants, tugging the zipper down and releasing the velcro on the sides that kept the thick material snug to my waist. Propped on a pair of pillows, I had a decent view, and that traitorous teenage girl in my head crowed with delight at the sight of her crush undressing me.

Sadly, she didn't really grasp context.

"You're going to need to lift your butt for me to slide these off," Sebastian stated mechanically, completely unaware of my inner hormonal angst. "Use your right leg to push up and try not to use your left at all."

"Got it," I replied. "Let me know when." I did one-leg bridges all the time, no sweat.

He positioned himself at the foot of the bed between my legs, then reached up to grasp the material at my hips. "Okay, go ahead."

The flush on my face had nothing to do with the heat from the stove—my brain was absolutely running wild with this image. Somehow I followed instructions and pressed my hips into the air on my right leg alone, while Sebastian pulled my outerwear down to my knees and left me in only my long underwear.

"Okay, good. Lower down, I'll do your right leg first, then the left."

My lips clamped shut, and I allowed him to undress me without a single word. The slight jostle as he tugged on my left leg definitely hurt my knee, but I'd had worse. My sweat-soaked underclothes cooled immediately, releasing the heat that was trapped against my body from the waterproof outwear.

Once he had the pants off, he gently worked down my thick wool sock, then tugged up the pant leg and pushed it up my calf. If he was grossed out because my body was drenched in sweat, he didn't say a word.

With the way his hands were running slowly up my leg, I said a silent prayer of thanks that I'd bothered to shave this morning.

Free of fabric, my knee now received a thorough examination. Sebastian's deft fingers probed gently along both sides, up my quad and behind my knee. He didn't say a word until he'd finished.

"I don't think you have any major injuries. It seems slightly swollen here," he pressed more firmly above my knee, and I hissed in response, "but nothing serious. I think you somehow strained your lower quad, or perhaps the tendon. Some ice and rest should take care of it."

"Thank you, Doctor Delacruz," I replied flippantly. "Do I get a sticker for being a good girl?"

Sebastian rolled his eyes, but I didn't miss the half smile that brought out one of those dimples. "I'm not done with you yet, Stella. I still need to see how bad this concussion is." He came around and helped me sit up. "How do you feel? Dizzy, headache, nausea?"

"It's not that bad. I've had worse."

Sebastian pinched the bridge of his nose. "You were passed out for over a half hour. I'm doing this *for you*. It'd be great if you could help me out here."

I heaved a sigh. "Okay, fine, yes, I have a headache. My vision is a little blurry and I feel kinda off."

"Do you remember falling?"

"I..." I thought about it a minute, but I couldn't pull the memory up. "The last thing I remember was cruising down the hill, trying to get to the lift, but visibility was low. Then I woke up in here with you undressing me."

"So headache, blurry vision, disorientation, memory loss, and loss of consciousness for an extended period. Yeah, I'd say you have a pretty serious concussion. If we had access, we'd be taking you to an ER, but it's not an option right now." His gentle fingers probed around my head, and I allowed myself a brief inner cringe at him touching my dank, sweaty hair before he found a tender spot at the back of my head.

"Ouch!" I yelped. His fingers withdrew immediately.

"My best guess is that you somehow caught an edge and tumbled downhill, hitting yourself in the back of the head with your own board. Let me see if I can fashion a couple of icepacks for you."

"Okay, Sherlock, how did you come to that conclusion?"

"It's elementary, my dear Watson," he

smirked, affecting a terrible British accent. "Based on your injury, and the mark on the back of your helmet," he added in his normal voice with a wink. He placed it in my lap, and even with my blurred vision, I could see the distinct horizontal divot marring the back.

Sebastian rummaged around somewhere behind me; I was too stiff to turn around and fatigue had already brought my head back to the pillows. Closing my eyes helped the sick feeling from being unable to focus, so I opted to relax and let Sebastian do whatever he had in mind.

A moment later, I heard the distinct rip of plastic and then what sounded like him slapping meat. The curiosity got the better of me.

"What are you doing?"

"I told you, getting ice packs. They have to be activated."

"Did it occur to you we have all the ice we could want right outside?"

"Yes, but it also occurred to me you probably wouldn't like when all that ice melted on you."

"Fair point," I agreed.

"Here." His gentle hands lifted my head tenderly, then set it back down on a lovely cooling sensation that eased the ache.

Sighing heavily, I conceded defeat. "Thank you, that really helps."

"You're welcome, Stella." His voice was as gentle as his fingers, and a moment later, another ice pack began easing the pain in my knee. "There is some tylenol here, but you'd have to sit up to take it."

"I'll take it later," I breathed. "Right now, this is good."

CHAPTER
SEVEN

SEBASTIAN

W

hen Stella dozed off again, it surprised me how well that encounter had gone. Despite some initial sass, she'd actually listened and allowed me to treat her.

I should have known it wouldn't last.

I barely had time to assess the supplies in the cabin before she woke up again. One minute I was adding more wood to the fire and she was resting peacefully; the next, she sat up and climbed out of bed.

"Stella, stop! Your concussion-" I shoved the last piece of wood into the stove.

"I'm fine, Sebastian. I told you I've had worse," she retorted irritably. "I just need to pee." She pulled the covers back and moved the ice pack from her knee.

"Let me help you-"

"I got it," she snapped, standing up and taking a step in her stockinged feet.

Fortunately, the cabin was small, and it only took me two steps to cross the room and catch her as she tumbled to the floor.

But instead of being grateful that I kept her from hitting her head yet *again*, she took her frustration out on me. "God, Sebastian, I'm *fine*. I don't need your help!"

I pulled her back on her feet and glared down at her ice-blue eyes, ignoring the stubborn set of her jaw. "Now isn't the time for your Miss Independent act, Stella," I snapped back. "You've got an injured knee and a serious concussion, let alone your previous injuries. There's no one here to impress, so just let me fucking help you."

She glared back up at me, but there was no way I would back down. Her eyes narrowed slightly, and then she snorted, casting her gaze to the tiny bathroom. "Fine, Nurse Delacruz. Take me to the toilet."

I pulled her arm up around my shoulders and pressed her against my side, conscious to avoid squeezing too tightly on her ribs. There was no suitable spot to place my hand, however. Too high I was grazing the side of her boob, too low I was squeezing the surprisingly soft flesh of her hip. She was just in her long underwear, and I was suddenly aware of how thin the fabric was that separated her skin from mine. It all felt super inappropriate.

I settled for hooking my elbow below her other arm and avoiding the mine field altogether. Stella leaned heavily against me, avoiding putting weight on her left leg as we hobbled.

Fortunately, it was only a couple of steps to the toilet.

Unfortunately, she couldn't maintain her balance long enough to undress to use it without help.

I tried releasing her to lean against the wall, but she began tipping forward and I had to step in and catch her. After two more tries and a frustrated growl escaping her lips, I sighed. "Just let me help you."

"No fucking way," she snarled. "I can do it."

"Stella, you can't even see straight, and you can't balance long enough to pull your own pants down."

"I'll figure it out. This isn't going to be some kind of twisted peep show, Sebastian."

"Trust me, I have *zero* interest in looking. But I don't see this getting any better anytime soon. Just... brace your hands on my shoulders, I'll pull them down and help you sit with my eyes closed."

"Yeah, *sure* you will." She was trying to tug the fabric down herself with one hand against the wall and me propping her up, but her body was stiff and the tight-fitting fabric was damp with sweat and clinging to her.

"Stella, for fuck's sake already. Just let me help."

"Fine!" she snarled. "But no copping feels and you keep your face turned up to me. I don't trust you to keep your eyes closed."

"Fine!" I snapped back, settling my gaze directly on her eyes. She was clearly in pain, and angry, but there was a softness to her expression, a deep vulnerability she was trying to bury.

Prickly exterior hiding inner pain? That I understood.

I drew in a deep breath and softened my tone. "Okay, my eyes stay on you. Hands on my shoulders." She complied without comment. "I'm going to feel for the waistband without looking, so don't accuse me of copping a feel, alright?"

Stella nodded, and I reached out, my fingers running delicately from her rib cage, past her narrow waist, to the bulge of fabric she had been tugging at. She pulled in a deep breath and held it as my thumbs hooked on the inside and pressed against her flesh. That vulnerability flashed in her eyes again, but I kept my promise and focused only on her gaze as I worked the fabric down to her knees, crouching as I went.

Stella lowered herself onto the seat and gasped.

"What hurts?" I asked immediately.

"I'm fine, it's just cold." She had both arms crossed over her body defensively.

"Ok, I'll just... step over here, I guess. Let me know when you're done."

There was no door, not even a curtain, to provide privacy. I supposed we ought to be grateful that it was in an alcove of sorts, but there was still nowhere in the room that I could be and not see her, so I faced the stove and stared hard at the fire.

Just as I was wondering if she'd finished, Stella released a long, frustrated sigh. "It's not working."

"You mean you don't need to go after all?"

"No, I mean, I can't go with you standing there listening."

"I swear I'm not listening."

"I know, but you can't help but hear all the same. This is impossible."

Grabbing the kettle, I poured some water from my bottle into it and banged it around, making as much racket as possible to provide her some cover. Then I placed it on the stove and pulled a couple of apple cider packets from the cupboard.

"It's still not working!"

I struggled to maintain my patience. "Well, I'm sorry. What do you want me to do? It's not like I've got a lot of options here."

"Can you sing?"

"What, you want me to provide entertainment while you pee now?"

"No, just something loud enough that I know you won't hear me over yourself."

"Jesus, Stella, you really are impossible."

"Come on, Sebastian, please? I really need to go. It's not like this is the most humiliating moment of my life or anything." Her sarcasm was easy to hear, and I couldn't blame her. Certainly, needing someone to pull her pants down just to pee was a tough pill to swallow.

Sighing once more, I scrambled for something to sing but drew a blank.

Stella was impatient. "Dude, I already said please. Do you seriously want me to beg?"

"I'm trying to think of a song, okay?"

"I don't care what it is! Sing 'I'm a Little Teapot', or 'You Are My Sunshine', anything."

Grumbling, I took her suggestion.

"You are my sunshine, my only sunshine..."

I focused on opening the packets and dumping them into a battered pair of aluminum camping mugs while singing as loudly as I dared.

Apparently, it wasn't loud enough.

"Are you gonna start singing or what?"

My patience was definitely wearing thin with her demanding tone.

"I *am* singing!"

"Well I can't hear you, so it's not working. Louder!"

I sang at the top of my lungs. "YOU ARE MY SUNSHINE, MY ONLY SUNSHINE, YOU MAKE ME HAPPEEEEEEE, WHEN SKIES ARE GREY!" Ok, so perhaps it was petty, but she *said* louder.

"Yes!"

I wasn't sure if her enthusiastic shout was because of relief or if she was simply praising me for being suitably noisy, but either way, it seemed to be a good sign.

"YOU'LL NEVER KNOW, DEAR, HOW MUCH I LOVE YOU, PLEASE DON'T TAAAAKE, MY SUNSHINE AWAAAAAAYYYY!"

The kettle whistled on the stove, so I grabbed the wooden handle and carefully poured the steaming liquid into the mugs.

I waited for further instruction, but when she didn't speak again for several long moments, I grew concerned.

"Stella, are you okay?"

"Gah, I'm fine! Just mind your business!"

"Sheesh, okay!" I busied myself with rifling through the scant food offerings in the single cupboard. Fortunately, there was actually more here than Gary made it out to be. Someone had left several packets of dehydrated camping food. It was a couple of years past the 'best by' date, but all it required was hot water, which we had in abundance. It would definitely be better than cold power bars.

I dug the few provisions I brought out of my pack—a couple of granola bars, a packet of beef jerky, and a handful of chocolate kisses—and added them to the collection.

Without glancing over my shoulder, I asked, "Do you have any food in your bag?"

"Um, I might. I think I ate most of it. You can look."

I tugged her pack over and started digging. Several reusable plastic bags—obviously from Reece—were empty, but there was a bag of some kind of rolled oat balls in the bottom, along with a huge flask. It had to be at least sixteen ounces, and from the weight, it was full. I unscrewed the cap and took a sniff.

"Why the hell do you have this giant bottle of whisky in your pack?"

"I like to drink, so sue me. I'm legal."

"While you're out there playing the daredevil and speeding down double-blacks?"

"I don't recall signing up for your judgement, asshole."

"Christ, forget it. Are you almost finished?"

"Yes, I'm done, and my ass is frozen. Let's go."

I rolled my eyes and drew in a deep breath, then crossed back to the alcove where Stella was still hunched over. She brushed a hand over her eyes and resumed glaring at me.

Was she... crying?

With a softer tone, I said, "Okay, we're going to do the same thing in reverse order, right? I'll help you stand—yes, keeping my eyes on yours—and then I'll help you get dressed."

"Fine, let's just get it over with."

Her eyes were definitely watery and red-rimmed, but she still managed to stare at me fiercely. I crouched to help her up, then repeated the process to replace her clothing. Once I had her top pulled down over the leggings, I turned sideways to help her hobble back to the bed.

When she was safely seated, I rearranged the pillows so she could lean back but still be mostly upright, and helped her get covered back up before I brought her a steaming mug that filled the space with the aroma of tart apples and cinnamon.

Stella accepted it stiffly with a curt, 'thank you,' so I considered that progress and retrieved my mug, then occupied the single rickety chair.

"You never answered my question," I murmured, blowing on the surface of my drink. "Why do you have that enormous flask in your pack?"

"Why do you want to know so badly?" She countered.

"Let's call it curiosity."

"Doesn't sound like a need-to-know reason to me."

"What if I guess?"

"You mean like, twenty questions?"

I shrugged. "Sure, pretty much. I'll make guesses and you tell me yes, no, or close."

Her eyes narrowed as she regarded me. Then she sighed. "Fine, ask away."

Even though I was fairly certain I knew why, I decided to make more of a game out of it.

"You carry it in case you come across a lost skier, like those Newfoundland sheepdogs with the barrel around their necks."

Stella snorted. "No."

"You have it to sneak alcohol to your teenage buddies in the terrain park."

"Definitely not."

"You use it to clean your tools when you adjust your bindings."

"Okay, now you're not even trying."

I said my real guess without lifting my gaze from my hands. "You have it because sometimes you can't face the world without it."

There was a long, pregnant pause; all I could hear was the howling wind outside and the crackling logs in the fire.

Stella's voice was very low when she answered. "Close."

"Will you tell me?" I raised my gaze to observe her and caught an expression so vulnerable on her face my heart clenched. "I promise I won't judge you or tell anyone. Believe me when I say I have my own demons."

She watched me for a long moment, studying my face as if she were trying to decide if I meant it or not.

"If you tell me," I added, "I'll tell you something about me that no one here knows. Especially not Reece."

Stella took a sip of her cider, then wrapped both hands around her mug. "Sometimes—and it's not all the time, but *sometimes*—I need it."

"Need it for what?"

"Sometimes I can't go through with the tricks if I'm sober."

"Why don't you just skip them that day, if it's too much?"

She shook her head. "I can't skip out on practicing. If I skipped every day I didn't feel like doing a trick, I'd never do it at all. Some days are just... harder than others. So the whisky helps."

"What do you mean, you can't go through with it?" I probed gently.

She shrugged as if it were nothing. "I dunno, sometimes I get scared, and my hands shake, and I can't breathe, and the pipe seems to stretch on forever, the sides grow impossibly high, and all I can think about-"

"Is when you fell," I finished.

"Yeah."

"And you're afraid it'll happen again." It wasn't a question.

"Yeah."

"Stella, you know that's a sign of trauma, right?"

"Everyone goes through it. I mean, every boarder I know has had the jitters after a big fall."

"This doesn't sound like normal jitters. It's not unusual to be extra cautious after an accident, but what you describe sounds like a panic attack."

"It's not all the time. Sometimes I don't feel anything at all, and I can do it just fine."

This was all sounding incredibly familiar. "That's also a trauma response, Stella. Have you seen anyone for this? Like getting any sort of counselling?"

She shrugged. "Not really. I mean I talked to my coach about it, but he just told me it was normal and gave me some breathing exercises."

"That's definitely a good coping skill, but it doesn't help you work through the issue."

Abruptly, her tone shifted. "Well, I just have to deal with it. There's no time to fix anything before regionals. Now, you promised to tell me something. Your turn."

A lump formed in my throat. It was one thing to use the hint of a truth to coax her to talk; it was another thing altogether to actually tell her.

"I won't judge or tell anyone, either," she added softly.

My heart rate picked up, like it was physically difficult to admit it, even though I knew it was all in my head.

"I got out because I couldn't do it anymore."

"Got out... from the Army? Couldn't do *what* anymore?"

"The job. I couldn't do the job anymore. Not without something to numb my feelings and make it easier."

It took her a minute. "So you really do understand why I have the whisky."

"Yes, I do. And when it started feeling like there wasn't enough alcohol to numb it, and I needed something stronger, that was scary enough to force me to change. I knew I couldn't keep on like that, and I'd end up getting kicked out for making dumb decisions. So I got out."

"What made you that way?"

"I promised you one truth, and you got it. We're not doing a deep dive into my issues, not when you've got plenty of your own to deal with here. How's the knee?" I was deflecting and from her thoughtful expression, Stella knew it. Still, she didn't push.

"It's better. The ice definitely made a difference."

"Good, and your head?"

"Still have a headache, but my vision isn't blurry any more. The world seems pretty stable at the moment, so that's good."

"Agreed. I think the best thing for you is to keep resting. How's the cider?"

"Not great, but not bad. Is there any coffee? It's likely that part of my headache is caffeine withdrawal."

"Nice try. I'm going to get you some tylenol and food. Do you want," I checked the packages, "quinoa and beans, fettucini Alfredo, rocky mountain scramble, or three bean veggie stew?"

———

STELLA

———

SEBASTIAN RETRIEVED my phone for me before heating water for the food, but he warned me it was no use and he was right: there was no service in the storm. Even on clear days, it was spotty back here, but I couldn't let go of the hope until I saw it with my own two eyes.

Now I knew without any doubt that I was all alone with Sebastian Delacruz, with nothing but the howling wind to keep us company.

To be fair, he was being okay, all things considered. Despite my attitude, I was grateful that he rescued me and brought me here. I still didn't remember any of it, particularly how I ended up facedown in the snow.

But when the fog cleared, I went immediately into full panic mode. A severe concussion, a knee injury? Either of them could keep me off the hill for *weeks*, and I didn't have weeks. I had regionals to prepare for, and then hopefully nationals, and so on.

It was stupid; I knew it was stupid. But I figured I could just tough my way through the dizziness and *make* myself better. And when that failed miserably, and Sebastian had to practically carry me to the toilet and literally undress me to use it, the dam broke. I had no idea where those tears came from, but they burst out of me in an effusion of emotion I couldn't control.

Obviously I had no problem with him hearing me pee—if he even could over the storm—but having him listen to me cry... well, there was no way in hell I'd allow that to happen.

Sebastian Delacruz had drawn his last tear from me six years ago, and there was no way I'd even let him *think* he had that power over me anymore.

But he'd been surprisingly gentle, and far more understanding than I expected. It was still hard to reconcile this Jekyll and Hyde persona of his switching from insensitive prick to concerned caregiver.

I turned stiffly in my bed to watch him. He still wore his snow pants and hard ski boots that clicked with every step—the floor was icy cold on my stockinged feet so I could understand that part—but he'd stripped his upper body down to a thin black long sleeve shirt that clung tightly to his muscled chest and arms. Probably merino wool, like mine, for a moisture-wicking base layer. His red ski patrol pants hung low on his hips, just baggy enough for effortless movement without being excessive. Of course, his hair was slightly messy, and a rosy tint was visible even on his warm brown skin, either from the biting wind outside or the heat inside the cabin. His eyes were serious, focused on pouring the steaming water into the packets.

Huh, that part surprised me. All throughout school, Sebastian had never been serious. He joked and prodded, flirted and teased. He was every part the high school heart throb that took nothing seriously, for whom everything was a simple game he was bound to win.

A blossom of nerves bloomed in my chest, and I was suddenly extremely concerned about the tragic state of my hair. I untied the braids and raked my fingers through the snarls before I realized why I'd done it.

Certainly not. While I could admit he was still objectively handsome—okay, seriously hot—I shouldn't have to remind my rebel hormones that I hated this man. Sure it was kind of him to rescue me—although that is technically his job and he'd do it for anyone—but it didn't change what he did, and it certainly didn't change the fact that he'd had zero remorse about it.

My unbidden sexual thoughts about him when he was checking me for injuries came back, suddenly clear as day, and heat instantly warmed my cheeks. I comforted myself by knowing that I didn't have full brain function in the immediate wake of a concussion and couldn't be held accountable for wandering thoughts.

Still...

Despite how aggravating it was to have him bossing me around and treating me like a toddler, I found his no-nonsense Nurse Delacruz persona... kinda hot. Somehow, when he was examining me, there was no hint of sarcastic ass Sebastian, just this new, concerned and commanding soldier I found it difficult to argue with.

And his eyes, when he was helping me, didn't hold a trace of derision. He was practically a different person.

CHAPTER
EIGHT

SEBASTIAN

"Here." I stopped next to Stella's bed and held out a steaming plastic packet with a spoon sticking out of it. "There aren't any forks."

She jumped as if I'd startled her, then accepted the rehydrated food. "Thank you," she murmured, her eyes trained on her lap.

I resumed my seat on the rickety wooden chair and focused on my own packet. It tasted a little stale, but was certainly better than the power bar alternative. Way better than MREs. I shoveled the spoonfuls into my mouth, ignoring the burn from the hot mush. It wouldn't taste any better cold, and my stomach had been rumbling for hours. The tremor returned to my hands, and mental images of Stella face down in the snow overlapped with images of another body, one covered in brown and red. I squeezed my eyes shut and tried to force the images out of my brain, drew in three deep breaths, then returned my focus to my food.

Expecting to eat in silence, Stella's tentative voice surprised me. "Which one did you choose?"

I glanced up, freezing in the middle of bringing a spoonful to my mouth. "Huh?"

"Which meal? I got the Alfredo. I was just wondering which one you have."

"Oh." I looked at the label, my mind immediately going blank and unable to process an answer. "Three bean veggie stew."

"Is it good?"

"Not bad, all things considered. How's yours?"

"I haven't tried it yet. It's too hot. But it smells good."

"Good." I pushed another spoonful into my mouth.

Stella heaved a sigh, as if she was about to face something extremely difficult.

"Thank you."

"No worries, I just had to boil water."

"No, not for the food. I mean, yes, thanks for that too. But thank you for rescuing me."

I shrugged, keeping my eyes down and ignoring the way my ears warmed. "It's my job."

"Well, I can still be grateful. And for all of this, too. I think it's safe to say you've gone above and beyond the requirements of ski patrol."

"Mmmph." The non-committal grunt was all I dared make, and Stella apparently took it as a dismissal, sighing again and focusing on her meal.

Honestly, I didn't know how to take it. This all sounded shockingly friendly, coming from Stella. Considering that all she'd done since I returned was snap at me, it was definitely an improvement.

Not that I didn't deserve her hatred; I one-hundred percent did. She would be well within her right to hate me for the rest of her life, and I couldn't blame her for it.

Of course, I regretted it now—I regretted it before it even happened. But I'd been toeing a dangerous line between Stella and Reece, and I couldn't risk losing my best friend over a slip-up with his sister.

So I did what had to be done, ensuring she'd keep her distance, and we'd never get too close again.

Or so I thought. Because here we were, alone in such incredibly close quarters, and if it was possible, I wanted her even more now than I had back then.

She put up a good front of being the badass snowboarding bitch, but I'd seen enough in the last couple of hours to realize that the sweet, intelligent girl was still in there somewhere. Sure, packed away behind layers of armor—for which I had to accept at least some of the blame—but she was there, nonetheless.

Despite her extensive training, her body was still surprisingly soft and curvy in all the right places. But even when she'd been a skinny rail of a girl, she still had those wide, vulnerable eyes that could hold me prisoner if I wasn't careful to look away. She'd always been sweet and still bitingly sarcastic, a combination I'd enjoyed far too much from a girl I professed to love like a little sister. The last couple days I'd had far more of the sarcasm, but just now... just now she revealed a tiny peek of that sweetness.

And she still had that thick, pale blonde hair that was somewhere between silver and gold. She'd loosed it from her braids and it now lay in a wild tangle over one shoulder. It was far too tempting; *she* was far too tempting, in this room so small her spicy floral fragrance had filled my senses despite a myriad of other, stronger odors.

Realizing I'd stopped eating and was staring at her despite my down-turned face, I quickly resumed scooping the meal into my mouth.

It didn't matter; none of it mattered. I'd buried my feelings for her back then, and there was no reason to dig them up now. This was nothing but a temporary truce. And when we got out of here, I'd go straight back to being the asshole she loved to hate.

An icy sweat spread over my body, and the meal I'd been shoveling down was threatening to make a reappearance. I took a long drink of water and forced myself to finish the last few bites—in this situation, we couldn't afford to waste any food. I turned my thoughts to Stella's injuries to draw myself away from my own problems.

My biggest concern was definitely her concussion. It was a good sign that she was feeling slightly better, but she was out for a long time. I had no idea how much the cold might have played a factor in the length of time she was unconscious. I'd read that a body slows down its function as it cools to preserve life, and people who die of exposure to cold sort of just go to sleep and never wake up. Even though I doubted it could have been that long, I really didn't know how long she was out there. But she'd seemed warm enough in her snow gear.

Not to mention the breathing—she'd been face down in the snow, so lack of oxygen could also be a factor.

"How's your head?"

Stella glanced up in surprise, but then her expression turned thoughtful while she considered. "Better," she replied slowly. "The tylenol definitely helped with the pain, and I feel like my vision is pretty clear."

"That's good to hear. How's the knee?"

She moved her leg around. "Definitely better. I probably just tweaked it. That happens from time to time. It should be better tomorrow."

"Well, don't make any predictions just yet. Sometimes it can take a day or two to feel the aftermath of a tumble, and we don't really know what happened. Considering you were probably going pretty fast, it was likely the equivalent of a car crash on your body." Standing, I placed my spoon on the counter and stuck the empty packet into a bucket I'd designated as trash. "Let me check your head."

Stella made no comment as I probed gently around her skull, searching for excessive heat or swelling. I fought back the desire to toy with the long strands of spun gold and focused on treating her like any patient. "Feels pretty normal," I agreed, lowering my gaze to meet hers. "Now I want to check your eyes. Just follow my finger back and forth." I held up one index finger, moving it left to right while I watched her eyes intently.

They slid back and forth easily, and each pupil was equally dilated, revealing the same amount of crystal blue. "Okay, it looks good. Did that bother you at all?"

"No, it's fine."

"That's all positive. You should still take it easy tonight, and we'll check how you're doing in the morning."

"Okay."

"Are you done?" I gestured to her dinner.

"Yeah." She held up the packet, and I disposed of it, then returned with her water bottle.

Faced with an emergency, my training had kicked in, filling my body with an eerie sense of calm while I focused on the issues at hand.

Now, when Stella was calm and seemed stable enough, I was suddenly on the verge of falling apart. My heart raced, adrenaline surging through my veins like I was in immediate, life-threatening danger.

"Sebastian... are you alright?"

I'd frozen in place, my eyes closed to combat the return of the nausea, and didn't realize Stella was watching me.

"Fine," I choked out, spinning to my left and adding more wood to the stove. I didn't want her to see my face; I knew what it looked like.

"You don't look fine," she stated, a note of concern in her voice.

The rage bubbled up without warning. "What are you, a fucking doctor now?" I snarled. "I think between the two of us, I trust my opinion over whatever hillside medical advice you picked up in the terrain park. Stick to your lane, got it?"

"Fine, excuse me for giving a shit about you for two seconds," she retorted. "I really should know better. Forget I said anything."

"Already forgotten."

The tiny part of my brain that was still me knew this wasn't right; she'd merely asked about my wellbeing and I'd bitten her head off.

But the rage was in control, and when that happened, I simply didn't care.

STELLA

Asshole. Of course, the *second* I started to believe he could almost be a normal human being, he switched right back to Mr. Hyde.

It was always the same with him. Even when we were younger, there would be times when my immature teenage self really believed there was something between us; something more than the relationship a guy has with his best friend's little sister. We had moments that developed my school-girl attraction to a full-blown, heart-melting crush. Moments that I thought were special. In those moments, I witnessed a different side of Sebastian, one where he was gentle and sweet, completely different from how he acted in public.

Of course, it never lasted long. Reece would come in the room and they'd turn into loud, obnoxious boys who teased me mercilessly for my braces and crazy hair. The moments with Sebastian had been a tender secret I held close to my heart; he was *different* around me. Only I got to see the *real* him... or so I thought.

After Homecoming my sophomore year, I was

no longer deluded about who Sebastian Delacruz was. If he cared about me at all, there was no way he could have done that.

Even so, this flip-flop seemed different from the old Sebastian. I was genuinely concerned about him; he looked like he was about to pass out. In the wake of his outburst I shut my mouth, but I didn't stop watching him.

His face was oddly devoid of emotion now, his back and body stiff as he tidied the miniscule space. I had no earthly idea what was going on, but I certainly knew better than to ask again.

Instead, I returned my focus to my phone. I had no signal, and I knew I should probably save the battery, but I couldn't stop myself tapping into my favorite social media apps and watching the little circle spin as it tried to connect. I thought doing something familiar would help, but it was actually making it worse. It felt like the walls of the tiny cabin were closing in on me, smothering me with all the fears I combated daily, now combined with fresh new ones in the wake of today's events.

Is my knee actually injured?

Do I have a concussion? David warned me to be careful because even a small amount of disorientation would throw me off my jumps. A concussion could mean I wouldn't be cleared to compete in my two best events.

Did I just ruin my chances of making it to the Olympics?

My heart began to pound, the pressure between my ears building and my breaths became rapid and shallow. My thoughts drifted to my flask, but there was no way I'd ask Sebastian to hand it to me. I knew what this was, and fortunately, I had a way to deal with it. I opened a different app and started a guided meditation to help me calm down.

A soothing woman's voice instructed me to breathe at a measured pace, backed by some synthetic wave sounds combined with pipe music. I didn't cross my legs, but I closed my eyes and tried to follow her instructions. I centered all of my focus on that voice and let the worries fall away.

Mercifully, Sebastian didn't interrupt my meditation with a smart-ass comment. In fact, it worked so well I forgot he was even in the room for a moment. And when I finished, my pulse was back to normal and my head felt fine, aside from the residual throb of my injury.

"Do you do that often?" Sebastian's voice was rough and low, without a hint of sarcasm.

"As often as I need to," I replied carefully.

"Why?"

"It helps me manage stress."

"Stress, like you have a paper due?"

"Stress like the world seems to close in on me and every fear or worry comes screaming into my face to convince me I'm not good enough." I turned to face him, daring him to lob an insult my way for being weak, or a dippy hippy, or who knows what else.

Sebastian's face was solemn. "I tried meditation, but it didn't really work out for me. I couldn't clear my mind. I'd just keep finding new things to think about."

"Yeah, I can't do it without the guide, either. That's why I like the app. The voice gives me something to focus on."

"Makes sense."

He didn't say anything else, and I didn't know if I was supposed to reply, or ask him a question, or just drop it. The silence between us grew so thick that the wind whistling through the tiny cracks in our shelter became deafening. A sudden shiver licked up my spine.

"Is it just me, or is it cold in here?"

Sebastian seemed to consider the question. "It feels cooler than it was an hour ago. What time is it?" He nodded at the phone in my hand.

I lit the screen. "Six oh three."

"Hm. It's after dark, and the temperatures have obviously dropped. The furnace can't stay on full blast because it has such a tiny fuel tank. I want to reserve it in case we run out of wood. I can throw another log in the fire, but the heat is probably pouring out of this place nearly as fast as we produce it."

"Could we actually run out of wood? I thought they kept this place stocked."

"They keep the stack on the east side of the cabin, and the door is on the west side. With the amount of snow piling up out there, I may not be able to even get through to reach it. While you were passed out, I brought in all of this and made a second stack next to the door. Hopefully, it's enough to get us through the storm."

"If it's snowing that much, shouldn't the snow insulate us, like an igloo?" I hadn't exactly taken winter survival courses, but it sounded reasonable.

"Yes and no. The snow piling up outside protects us from the wind down here, but there're lots of places the cold seeps in. Just because the snow blocks the wind doesn't mean it's not cold against the outside walls. The ground is frozen, so the floor is freezing cold. And the toilet—that's just a hole in the ground. The roof of this place can't be well insulated, because even through the storm, I saw some pretty large icicles all around it. Plus, that whistling sound means wind is getting in somewhere. It's fortunate this cabin is so small, since it's easier to heat. But there's not much space to get away from the cold, either."

As if suddenly spurred into action, Sebastian crossed to my bed and squatted down. He pulled out two bright red sleeping bags and a spare blanket. "Here." He held one bag out. "These are rated to negative 32 degrees, so they'll definitely help. Might as well settle in."

He folded the thin blanket in half and spread it on the wooden floor in the narrow space between my bed, the toilet alcove, the cupboard, and the stove. It took up nearly all the free space. After unrolling the second sleeping bag on top, he glanced at me awkwardly, then headed for the toilet closet.

It took me a second to catch up, but then I realized what was going on. I cranked up the volume and put on another song from the meditation app, this one fully instrumental, and busied myself with my own sleeping bag. Now that I was really paying attention, it was much cooler than I had even realized. My sweaty base layer had mostly dried—thank god for merino wool—but it wasn't meant to insulate, just wick moisture away from the body. So with great care, I shimmied my battered body into the mummy bag and waited for my heat to warm the material.

For some reason, my heart rate had elevated again, and I took a moment to consider why. I didn't want to believe it, but eventually I had to face the truth: despite everything Sebastian did to me in the past, and his shitty attitude now, I was still impossibly attracted to the man. Apparently, a simple, non-hostile conversation was all it took for those teenage hormones to come screaming back, and knowing we were about to spend the night together had kicked my subconscious imagination into overdrive.

Okay, we weren't exactly 'spending the night together', but we'd be sleeping mere inches apart. I didn't know whether to be insulted that he chose the cold hard floor over sharing the (admittedly small) bed with me, or impressed at his chivalry. It didn't look remotely comfortable, and even though he could be closer to the stove, I wondered if it would make a difference when combined with the freezing cold seeping in from the floor.

Sebastian finished his business and washed his hands in the icy cold water in the sink—no hot water heater, of course—then stepped across his bed and crouched to add more wood to the fire. The light dimmed briefly, then flared as flames consumed the new fuel. The potbelly stove put out a limited amount of light, being mostly self-contained, with an iron grate on its door. Sebastian had two lanterns lit, hanging from hooks on either end of the cabin that were clearly there for that purpose. Even so, the cabin was filled with a comfortable amount of light.

"Should we put them out?" I asked, then realized I had verbalized my train of thought without him being privy to what I was thinking. "The lanterns, I mean. At least one? I don't want to run out of gas or whatever."

Sebastian glanced up. "They're actually oil lamps, and we have two gallon jugs of oil plus a box of clean wicks, so we're definitely good. But you're right, there's not much sense in having them on if we don't need them."

He stood and turned a knob on first one, then the other lantern, extinguishing them. The light in the cabin reduced drastically; now Sebastian's dark features were cloaked in heavy shadows, lit only by the warm glow from the stove.

"Do you want a hat?" He asked out of nowhere.

"Huh?"

"To keep your head warm while you sleep. Do you want a hat? I have a spare in my bag."

"Oh, no thank you. I actually have one tucked in my jacket, but I think I'll be okay. This sleeping bag has a hood."

"Okay." He crouched and started arranging his bed.

Guilt at hogging the single bed swirled in my chest. "Hey, do you want a pillow? I feel bad that you're on the floor."

"It's nothing I haven't done before," he replied in a dry tone. "But you should keep them so you can stay propped up. Just in case you have swelling in your head, it'll help; at least a little."

"Well, that's a cheery thought. But no, seriously, I'm fine with one."

"It's fine, keep it."

"I said I don't need it."

"I don't either."

My frustration bubbled up again. "Why are you making such a big deal of this? It's just a pillow. I have two, and you have zero, so it makes the most sense to share. Here, I'll make it easy for you." I pulled the top one off and tossed it onto his makeshift bed. "Just take it."

Sebastian let out an exasperated groan. "You're impossible, you know that?"

I snorted. "If that isn't the pot calling the kettle black."

That drew a surprised grunt from him. "Touché."

I settled back into my bed and pulled the sleeping bag up to my chin. It was warm and cozy in the cabin now, with the lower light and the fire putting out more heat thanks to the fresh fuel.

But it was too early; I wasn't anywhere near ready to go to sleep. My body was used to running from one thing to another until I was tired enough to pass out, and it didn't seem to understand that I couldn't do any of that right now. The restless energy crept up my legs, spreading across my body, making my hands fidget inside my sleeping bag. The fire crackled and popped, the wind outside howled and occasionally whistled somewhere overhead, and Sebastian made zero noise.

Even though I knew I couldn't, I almost imagined I could hear him breathing, and for some reason that quickened my pulse again.

"Sebastian?"

"Yeah?"

"What did you do in the Army?"

A heavy sigh. "I was a medic."

"Oh, so you actually *are* some sort of doctor?" I felt bad for teasing him about it before.

"Not exactly. More like a combat nurse. My job was mainly to patch up injured people so they would survive long enough to get to the actual doctors."

"So, you were in combat?" I'd just imagined him marching back and forth, driving a green jeep around, and sitting at a desk. All while looking positively delicious in his uniform, of course.

"Yeah." His tone had turned distinctly sad.

"Was it bad?" I asked, my voice nearly a whisper.

His response was almost inaudible, but the pain was crystal clear. "Yeah."

"Is that why you got out?"

"Partially."

"I'm sorry I said that they kicked you out yesterday. I didn't mean it."

"I know."

"You seemed kinda hurt."

This time, he sighed heavily. "It's still pretty raw, I think. A lot of stuff happened really quickly and then I had to decide, basically on the spot. They offered me an honorable discharge a few months before my actual separation date, and I took it. I guess in some ways it sort of feels like I failed."

"I'm sorry." I didn't know what the appropriate response was. I was dying with curiosity, but something told me it would be a bad idea to probe him about it. Instead, I offered him some answers of my own. "I quit for over a year."

"Taking time off to heal is not quitting, Stella."

"No, I legit *quit*. I got through physical therapy and they said I was ready to go back. I could have taken my free pass to the World Cup—they give you that if you qualify and then can't compete because of injury—and been right back in it. But I refused."

"If you weren't ready, there's nothing wrong with that."

"I told my parents I was still in a lot of pain," I admitted in a small voice. "I knew they'd overreact, and I used them as an excuse to wait."

His response was slower in coming this time. "Why do you think you did that?"

Now it was my turn to be nearly inaudible. "Because I was afraid."

CHAPTER
NINE

STELLA

Sebastian was quiet for a moment, and I worried I'd said too much. "That's not surprising, Stella. From the sounds of it, you were seriously injured. Reece said you could have been paraplegic, and it was sheer luck you didn't. Trauma like that would make anyone second guess their life plans."

His soothing voice brought tears to my eyes, and I was grateful he couldn't see from his position on the ground. I'd admitted this to a few of my friends and they'd said the same thing, but I couldn't admit it to my family. They would *never* have let me compete again if I told them the truth. Sebastian's validation was the next best thing, and one that I didn't know I needed.

As if realizing I would not speak again, he followed with, "but you're doing it now. So it's gotten better?"

I swallowed the lump in my throat. "Do you want the correct answer or the actual answer?"

"Truth, always."

"I'm not any less afraid than I was two years ago."

"So, why are you doing it?" The question was reasonable, not harsh or judgemental. It gave me the encouragement to continue being honest.

"A lot of reasons. Because I feel like I have to prove I can. Because I've worked for it my whole life and I fell weeks short of going to the Olympics. Because I don't know what to do with myself without it." At the last part, my voice grew frail as I attempted to prevent the emotion building in my chest from leaking out.

"What do you think you have to prove? Or maybe, to whom?"

"Everybody." I sighed. "The whole town is invested in my career, like I'm some kind of global spokesperson for Aspen Ridge. But most particularly my parents."

"I thought your parents were always very supportive of your goals."

"It's hard to explain. They are, but at the same time they're so worried, and they've been pressuring me to take on responsibilities at the resort."

"That doesn't sound so bad. Few people have families that care that much, or are in the position you're in."

His response was reasonable, but I wasn't in the mood for it. My voice became a little clipped. "Look, I know I'm lucky. I'm not trying to pull the spoiled little rich girl card. But I don't think they'll let me do what I want to do with Aspen Ridge, and so it feels like my life will never be my own. They'll decide to stick me in some office and I'll end up bored to tears every day because 'it's a family business' and I have to 'do my part'."

Sebastian waited a long moment before replying. "I can see why that would concern you," he said carefully. "But why do you think that is? What do you want to do at Aspen Ridge?"

My eyes narrowed, even though I knew he couldn't see my expression. This felt like one of his old tricks. Get me to admit something and then mock me mercilessly for it.

But then again, there was something this time that just felt... different. Maybe it was the two of us locked in this cabin in the semi-darkness, but it felt safer somehow.

"Fine, but promise you won't laugh."

"I can't promise that. I might laugh if it's funny."

"Then promise me you won't make fun of me for it."

"I promise."

"I want to be a winter events coordinator."

A brief pause. "Like snowman building contests, that sort of thing?"

"No, like competitions, expos, features. I want Aspen Ridge to host big televised ski and snowboard comps like the X Games or Red Bull. Maybe even regionals some day."

"That's a cool idea. Why haven't you told your parents? I can't see why they'd say no."

"That's just it, they *have* said no. I was working on bidding for the X Games a couple years back when I was considering not competing any more, and they shut me down. Last year, Snowshoe Ridge hosted the games. That should have been us."

"What was their reasoning?"

"They said this is a family resort and it would attract the 'wrong crowd.' Basically, they don't want the place overrun with people like me." The hurt in my voice was palpable, even if he couldn't see the wounded expression on my face.

"I doubt that, Stella. Your parents are super proud of you."

"No, it's true. My parents think snowboarders are all assholes and they don't want Aspen Ridge to welcome them in droves. They opened the terrain park at my insistence, but only because they knew people were leaving here to go to Snowshoe for theirs. They just don't see the opportunity it would create to keep Aspen Ridge a global destination."

"You've obviously put a lot of thought into it. I'm no resort mogul, but I think it's a great idea. What else would you do?"

"I think we could have theme weekends, more comps, maybe some festivals of our own or work with the town and incorporate theirs in the resort. I feel like we sort of sit here and expect people to just come to ski, but we could do so much more. Especially since the hills close down at sunset, and people still want to be doing stuff. They're on vacation. We should provide more entertainment."

"I mean, I've never run a ski resort, but that all sounds smart to me."

"Yeah, well, maybe you can convince my parents for me. I've given up."

Sebastian didn't reply for a while, and I started to wonder if he fell asleep. Despite my frustration at the topic, chatting with him had actually calmed the restlessness in my body, and a wave of drowsiness drew a yawn from my lips.

"How often do you use that app to help you calm down?"

The question was kind of out of nowhere, and it took me by surprise.

"Um, maybe a couple of times a week."

"How do you feel when you're stressed to the point you need it?"

"Like I can't catch my breath. My heart feels like it's going to pound out of my chest. Sometimes my hands shake. It passes really fast though," I added quickly. "It's no big deal."

"Have you seen a doctor for it?"

"My coach told me what to do. He says it happens all the time."

"Stella, you know you're having panic attacks, right? While it is common, it shouldn't be something that happens to you multiple times a week doing something you love."

I'd suspected as much, but I preferred how David described it as a 'stress episode'. 'Panic attack' sounded like something that got you dumped in a room with padded walls.

"It's no big deal," I repeated. "I just have to work through them. I'm not about to quit now," I added sharply.

"I'm not suggesting you quit." Sebastian's voice was measured and soothing. "I just wonder if there's more to it. Maybe talking to someone would help."

"I'm talking to you right now, not sure it's helping."

"You know what I mean. Just... maybe it's not something you have to push through for the rest of your life. Just a thought."

"Yeah, so everyone thinks I'm crazy because I'm seeing a shrink? No thanks, life is hard enough as it is being the black sheep."

"You're not the black sheep, Stella, far from it. Your family loves and supports you. Maybe they aren't as good at showing you as they could be, but it's there. And no one would call you crazy for getting therapy."

"Says the tough guy war hero," I snorted in response.

His voice switched from low and soothing to a razor-sharp bark. "I'm *not* a hero. And there's nothing wrong with therapy. The military isn't what you think it is, Stella. I don't pretend to know anything about the Olympics, so stop assuming you know everything about what I've been through."

I recoiled instantly from his shift in tone, the almost savage way he denied being a hero. It took me a minute to put two and two together, but it did eventually hit me. "You've gone to therapy?"

"Yeah," he grunted. "There's a lot of terrible shit out there, Stella. And a lot of it happens to good people. People who don't deserve it. The world doesn't work the way we want it to."

"What happened to you while you were gone?"

"Nothing I want to talk about. Just don't call me a hero again. Alright?"

"Alright."

The wind howled, the fire crackled, and Sebastian didn't say another word, so neither did I.

But just before I dozed off, I realized that he hadn't called me Estrellita once today.

SEBASTIAN

THE FLOOR WAS HARD, but I'd slept on worse. The cold, however, was brutal. Even with my hoodie, snow pants, and sleeping bag, it still permeated all of my layers and keep me from being comfortably warm.

Not that I'd tell Stella. The last thing I needed was for her to insist I climb into bed with her. I could almost guarantee I wouldn't be able to keep my hands to myself.

It was bad enough that she'd insisted I take this pillow. Now my senses were truly filled with her, the fragrance of her skin clinging to the cotton. I buried my nose in it, the spice and warm amber notes penetrating deep into my layers of armor and rendering them useless.

It was easier to behave myself when she hated me. Far easier to close her out of my mind with continents between us and all the urgency and distraction of a deployed location. I'd even dated someone for a while; a pretty blonde girl, petite with big blue eyes.

Well, dated was probably inaccurate. We enjoyed each other's company from time to time, when we could get it. But I never really *saw* her for who she was, never quite let her in, and it eventually fizzled out.

It took me a while, but I realized that when we

were together, I didn't see her; I saw Stella. So I didn't have any interest in what she liked or what she had to say. She was just a surrogate, no matter how I tried to convince myself otherwise.

And it was easy to get distracted. So many tours into dangerous locations, very little time to rest and reflect on my feelings. No one wanted anything permanent out there, since we all knew it was too risky to get attached.

And yet here I was, right back in the same spot I'd been six years ago. I'd convinced myself it was an enormous mountain and even if I occasionally ran into her with Reece, well, he was there to act as a buffer. Besides, I made sure she hated me years ago.

Fate, however, apparently had its own plans.

Scarcely two weeks after arriving here, and I was *literally* locked in a cabin with the girl who was the most untouchable of all girls, and naturally the only one I wanted.

It was too late to wish that I hadn't taken the job. My parents were gone, and I had nowhere else to go. Reece threw me a lifeline, and I accepted it with gratitude. Of course, he didn't know about me and Stella, or he definitely wouldn't have invited me back.

Sighing, I shifted from my right side to my left, facing away from the fire and away from her.

The floor was not any softer on this side, nor any warmer.

Unable to shut down, my mind drifted back to high school, as it often had since I returned. That conversation I had with Reece changed so many things it was impossible to forget.

We were finishing up football practice, both of us starters our senior year. Reece was already big and burly, so he made a great lineman. I had the quick mind, powerful arm, and deadly accuracy, which was why I'd made quarterback for the third year in a row.

I'd known Stella had a crush on me since middle school. I never thought about it much; she was my best friend's kid sister. I didn't even know how it happened at the time, but somehow, when she started ninth grade, our relationship shifted. Stella had big dreams, big ideas. In school she was this bizarre combination of nerd and punk snowboarder, which only worked for her because of her family—no one dared make enemies of the Blackwells. Outside of the school hallways, she talked about interesting things. Her sense of humor was wicked. She made smart observations about people we knew. I genuinely enjoyed her company.

It started out with talking for a few minutes at their house when I came over to hang with Reece. Then I ran into her in town, and we ended up talking for almost a half hour before I even realized it. We started making plans to hang out on our own, away from school or Reece, just the two of us. It was easier to be ourselves without the complication of other people. It wasn't a secret, but... we never told anyone. We'd hang out at Bear Paw, or Tony's for pizza while we did homework. During the summer, we'd go for hikes or swimming in the crystal blue waters of Aspen Lake.

At first we were just buddies, but at some point, the tone changed, and even though I tried to feign ignorance of it, I was well aware. I figured as long as I never made a move, there was no reason to admit anything. Not to Reece, not to Stella, certainly not to myself.

That day after practice, Stella was watching us from the stands. It wasn't entirely unusual. She did it from time to time.

This time, however, she ran up and hugged me, her eyes bright and cheeks flushed with cold while she chattered on about the plays we'd run. The pompom on her hat tickled my nose, and I embraced her before I remembered where we were. Instead, I patted her awkwardly on the back and waited for her to disengage. To her credit, she then hugged Reece and commended his footwork, not making her treatment of him any different from how she'd approached me.

But Reece was no idiot. He waited for her to leave before he said, "Dude, what was that?"

"What was what?" Playing dumb, the best defense for someone in an absolute panic.

"That," he pointed at Stella's retreating form. "Why'd she hug you?"

I shrugged with a non-committal grunt. "Don't ask me. She does weird shit sometimes. Remember when she caught that squirrel and let it loose in your house?"

Reece didn't take the bait. "Is there something going on between you two?"

My blood began racing through my veins, my throat so thick it was suddenly hard to speak. "Going on?" I practically squeaked. After coughing to clear the blockage, I gave him my best innocent grin. "Of course not, man. We're just friends. She's practically a little sister to me, you know that."

"Yeah, well, there *better* not be. You always do your thing, and I may not agree, but it's not my business if you're the school player. Just don't play my little sister. Got it?" Reece took on that steely-eyed expression I'd only seen a handful of times, the one where he practically seemed like a different person from the laid-back guy I knew.

"Dude, there's nothing, I swear. I'm not into her that way, like at all. She's practically still a little girl." She most definitely was not. I'd seen her in a bikini plenty that summer, and although she was skinny she wasn't without curves. But I'd say just about anything to convince him I wasn't interested.

Reece was still watching me doubtfully.

I forced out a nervous laugh. "Come on, man, it's *me* you're talking to!"

He narrowed his eyes, then sighed. "Alright, I trust you. Just don't think that trust extends to my sister. Got it?"

"Got it."

We continued toward the locker room, chatting like normal, but inside I was panicking.

The reason that day was different was because I'd asked Stella to homecoming the night before. I finally admitted to myself that I liked her, as *more* than a little sister, and I thought we'd have a chat with Reece before our big surprise reveal at Homecoming.

And then he told me in no uncertain terms to keep my hands off.

Guilt bubbled in my chest just remembering it. I shifted, rolling onto my back and too damn aware that Stella was practically inches away.

I'd been an immature high school kid, stuck in an impossible place. I was going to upset one or the other of them, and I had to choose.

Of course I'd chosen wrong. It was kind of my signature move, if I was really being honest with myself.

But the average seventeen-year-old boy is an idiot, and in that capacity, I was incredibly average.

CHAPTER
TEN

STELLA

My dreams were filled with panic and the overwhelming sense of failure. I woke again and again, actually relieved to find myself snowed in a tiny cabin with a possible concussion and the man who humiliated me so thoroughly six years ago that I still bore the scars.

Because in every single dream, I failed my life's ambition.

I was too slow; I didn't make the podium.

I went too fast and crashed.

I did all the tricks but didn't score enough points.

And worst of all, I fell and broke myself completely.

When I woke and groggily realized one of the lanterns was lit, I figured that meant it was time to get up. The wind still howled outside, but the cabin had no windows, so I couldn't actually tell if it was daytime. And even if there were windows, it was likely they'd be covered with snow, anyway.

Bracing myself for the pain, I lifted myself into a sitting position. My entire body was stiff and incredibly sore, just like I'd been in a car wreck, as Sebastian had warned. My knee didn't seem too bad, and I could turn my head left and right without making anything worse. So that was a positive.

"Good, you're up," Sebastian's voice was surprisingly cheery, and he spoke rapidly like he was nervous. "It's about eight in the morning. I'm heating water for hot cocoa, and there's a few packets of oatmeal. Although, no bowls. I suppose we'll have to do one at a time. But first I'm going to test the radio, see if we can get through at all. I just didn't want to do that while you were sleeping."

He crouched by the radio and flipped some

switches, then began speaking into the handset and waiting for a response through the static.

I eased my legs over the side of the bed and contemplated the few steps to the toilet. I felt fine, but the last time I'd thought that, I ended up needing Sebastian to do everything for me.

His back still faced me, so I chanced putting one foot down, then the other, and braced myself against the bed. The floor felt like ice, even through my thick wool socks, and I couldn't help wondering how he slept on it last night. Of course his sleeping bag was already rolled up and tucked under the bed, along with the blanket. Drawing in a deep breath, I took one step and waited, then another.

Surprisingly, I felt almost normal. Of course achy, but only slightly light-head, not dizzy like yesterday. I was already finished using the facilities when Sebastian realized I had moved.

"Stella!" He wasn't visible thanks to the alcove, but the anger in his voice was tough to miss. "Why didn't you wait for me? What if you fell?"

I washed my hands with the icy water in the sink. "Because I feel loads better and didn't need your help to pee."

"I'm glad you feel better, but I'd prefer to be safe either way." His tone was still gruff, but he seemed to calm down a bit when I walked out and claimed the janky wooden chair without tipping over once. "Would you prefer cocoa or oatmeal for your first course?"

"So many options. How's a girl to choose?"

"Yes, only the finest here at Chez Shack."

"In that case, I'll start with the *chocolat chaud, s'il vous plaît.*"

"*Bien sûr, mademoiselle.*"

"Glad to see you haven't forgotten your high school French," I commended.

"Oh no, I definitely have. That was the extent of my skills."

"It works."

Sebastian didn't reply as he fixed the cocoa. The floor was so cold I put my snowboard boots back on for warmth and noticed he was still in stocking feet.

Of course, because his only other option was ski boots, and those things were almost as dangerous as they were uncomfortable.

"How did you sleep last night?" I asked lightly, as if I were just making conversation.

"Fine," he grunted.

"Were you warm enough?"

"Uh-huh."

"The floor is freezing."

"Yep." He turned from the stove and passed me a steaming aluminum mug.

I would have preferred coffee, but in this case I was just happy to have something hot.

Sebastian stood awkwardly with his cocoa for a moment, like he was unsure where to go since I'd taken the one chair.

"You can sit on the bed. It's not like I own it."

As if he couldn't help himself, he set his mug back down and straightened the covers before sitting gingerly on top. "How'd you sleep?"

I shrugged. "Fine. Probably as good as expected. Do you know how long this storm is supposed to last?"

"When I got Gary on the radio yesterday he said at least two days, so I wouldn't expect a rescue today."

"Great. I guess it's not like I have anywhere else to be. I certainly wouldn't be able to practice even if I were home. Although I could lift weights or swim. God, wouldn't a hot tub be amazing right now?"

"Seriously." Sebastian's feet were piled one on top of the other, as if trying to avoid touching the floor as much as possible.

"Are your feet cold?"

"I'm fine."

I did my best impression of the look Reece and Dad do, the one that cuts right through my excuses. "Don't bullshit me, it's freezing. I had to put my boots on."

"Fine, it's cold. Not much I can do about it," he growled.

"Just stick your feet in my sleeping bag. It's probably still warm."

"It's your bed. I'll be fine."

"Or you'll end up with frostbite."

"It's not that bad."

"God, why are you so stubborn? This is a survival situation, Sebastian, if you haven't noticed. Protocol and social norms go out the window."

"Yeah, I'm not telling Reece I took the first opportunity to climb into your bed, Stella."

"Do you even hear yourself? It's not *my* bed, and there's no one else here. You can hardly rescue me with your toes frozen solid, so stop being a stubborn ass and stick your damn feet under the covers!"

He glared at me, but I gave him the evil eye right back until he finally sighed and stood, pulling back the top of the sleeping bag and sitting fully in the bed with his feet covered. "There, you happy?"

"Yes, you're fucking welcome."

We both turned back to our cocoa, nothing else to say in the wake of our bickering. Why did every conversation with him turn out this way? I didn't mean to be combative, but something in him brought it out in me every time. Like I was tinder, and he was the match that set me on fire.

That analogy was certainly true in the physical sense. Even annoyed, I was supremely aware that my attraction to him just didn't give me a break. Hair mussed, the shadow of a beard on his chiseled jaw, his lips still supremely kissable and not at all chapped. His long deft fingers wrapped around his mug, those warm brown eyes focused on the billowing steam. God help me, even arguing with him turned me on. There was something incredibly sexy about how his eyes flashed and his voice dropped when I pissed him off. Maybe that's why I did it so often.

Down, Stella. He made it perfectly clear years ago that he did not, and would not, ever be interested in you. It was up to me to rein in that infatuation so I didn't get myself hurt, because I'd only have myself to blame if I fell for it again. Hurt me once, shame on you. Hurt me twice, shame on me.

I wished for the relief of exhaustion. If I were tired, I could try to sleep away the day and spend as little time interacting with him as possible. Unfortunately, that didn't appear to be in the plans. I felt wide awake, and it was early; my inner clock was very precise. Normally I'd be heading out to hit the slopes right now.

Despite all appearances of ignoring me, the second I finished my cocoa, Sebastian climbed out of the bed and collected my mug, rinsing both quickly in the sink then setting about preparing the instant oatmeal without a word.

This was all so incredibly confusing. On one hand, we could scarcely speak to each other without fighting, and he certainly held no warmer feelings for me than I had for him.

On the other hand, all he'd done since we got stuck in here was tend to my every need with great care. It had to be just instinct, something he would do for anyone. He was a medic in the Army, after all. His job was to take care of people then, just like it was to take care of people now as ski patrol.

It had nothing to do with me.

SEBASTIAN

WE GOT through the rest of our breakfast in silence before I cleaned up and checked Stella's head. There didn't seem to be any change, and she insisted she was better, so I turned my focus to our provisions. We had plenty of instant cocoa and cider, a handful of energy bars, and two more freeze-dried camping food packets, plus the assorted snacks from our packs and Stella's flask of whisky.

It was plenty for one more day, but I started considering how we could stretch it to two. I hadn't been able to reach anyone on the radio, so we were completely blind as to the situation outside. I leaned against the cupboard as I thought about our situation.

On the plus side, I'd barely burned a quarter of the wood I stockpiled in the cabin yesterday. Depending on what my supply looked like this afternoon, I might have to bundle up and dig into the pile outside. The fuel tank was about half full, and the generator had full bars since I'd only powered it on twice for a few minutes at a time.

If we had to, we could spend several more days in here before things got dire.

Dire in the survival sense, that is. Things were already dire for me in terms of sharing the cramped space with Stella.

Right now she was sitting on the bed, finger combing the snarls from her hair. Blood rushed through my veins as I watched her, unable to rip my gaze away. Her eyes were closed, face neutral, as if her mind were a million miles from here. The warm light from the lantern overhead cast her in a golden glow, and her cheeks were lightly pink, her lips glossy.

My brain was full of little moments like these, when she was completely relaxed, completely herself in my presence, before I fucked it all up. Now she couldn't even look at me without the disgust clear on her face.

I'd done it for a reason, and I knew it was for the best in the long run. I'd been friends with Reece since elementary school. I was practically part of the family growing up.

And family doesn't *date* family. Reece was the last bit of family I had left, and there was no way I could lose him, too.

It would break me.

But now we had an entire day stretching before us in this cramped little space and nothing to do. Not a tv, not a book. I had a few games on my phone, but nothing that would entertain me for hours, and I didn't want to waste the battery.

I decided to do another rummage of the cabin

to see if there was anything, *anything*, we could use for entertainment. Anything that I could use as a distraction from my completely inappropriate thoughts about my best friend's sister.

There weren't a lot of hiding places other than the cupboard, so I took my time using the lantern to see clearly to the back of the bottom shelves.

Nothing besides the lamp oil and wicks I'd found earlier.

Then the empty shelf where the mugs and spoons had been, and the shelf that held the medical supplies I'd already searched thoroughly. Then the upper one where I'd found the food and drink packets. There was one more up high that appeared to be empty, but I couldn't see all the way to the back from this angle.

It was unlikely anything was there, but it was worth being thorough.

After hanging the lantern back on its hook, I grabbed the chair and carefully placed a foot on it, testing for stability before I trusted it with my entire weight.

"What are you doing?" Stella had apparently finished her grooming.

"Checking the top shelf."

"For what?"

"Anything that could be there."

"Are you sure that's safe?"

"Absolutely not." I lifted my second foot onto the seat and crouched, keeping one hand on the cupboard and waiting for the entire thing to collapse.

"Do you want my help?"

"Absolutely not."

"Fine," she huffed. "If you fall and break your neck, don't blame it on me."

"Duly noted." Finally standing up straight, I peered at the back of the dark wood-paneled shelf. Unsurprisingly, there wasn't anything earth-shattering on it. But there, in the back, was a small, palm-sized rectangle.

I reached in, the chair creaking under my feet as my weight shifted, and grabbed the dusty box. I knew without looking exactly what it was—the shape was unmistakable.

Triumphantly, I pulled it out and held up the deck of cards. "Hah! We'll have to see if it's complete, but now we've at least got something to do." Just as gingerly as I stood up, I lowered myself back down and stepped off the chair. The box was dusty, but it felt full.

"Cards?" Stella asked dubiously.

"Yeah, cards. There're a ton of different games you can play with cards. This might just be the find of the century." I grinned at her. "I can't tell you how many hours I spent playing cards in the sandbox."

"Glad to see my tax money was well spent."

"Ha ha, as if I've never heard that one before. Come on, it's better than nothing."

"I don't really know any card games, aside from like, Go Fish and War."

"Lucky for you, I know a ton." I gestured to the bed. "Mind if I sit?"

She sighed, but pulled her feet back and sat cross-legged so there was room for both of us.

"What should we play first?"

"Doesn't matter to me, mister card-player extraordinaire. You pick."

I pulled the cards from the sleeve and gave them a quick count. They were worn, but all of them were there. "What about Gin Rummy?"

AFTER TEACHING STELLA THE RULES, we played several rounds of Gin Rummy. It was a pleasant distraction, although I'd still find myself admiring her brilliant eyes, or thinking about the way her long, silky hair felt between my fingers when I probed her head.

Eventually I had to take a break and walk around—sitting cross-legged was surprisingly hard on the back when you were no longer a kid—and I fixed us some more warm drinks before we continued.

We had all the time in the world, so I had nothing but patience in teaching Stella new games, and she seemed happy to learn. Somehow we settled into a comfortable companionship once again, like she forgot she hated me and I did my best to forget how very much I liked her. It was hard; unguarded, she graced me with joyful smiles that reminded me so much of how we were *before*. They pierced my heart and warmed my soul at the same time. We were both competitive, so I didn't let her win, but I could hardly be upset watching her celebrate, either.

We broke for lunch, sharing one of the remaining hot meals, then dove straight back into it, taking occasional breaks to feed the fire.

While we played, Stella kept shifting and rolling her neck, a pained wince occasionally crossing her features, but she said nothing.

I ignored them for a while, but eventually asked, "Are you doing okay? You look like you're in pain."

"It's just my shoulders. They're always really

tight, so it makes my neck hurt. Usually David rubs them out for me a few times a week so it's not an issue, but with the accident and everything," she shrugged, "I don't really have the option."

"I can rub them for you." My heart beat faster at the thought of it, and I knew I was setting myself up for a problem, but I couldn't stop myself.

"That's alright, I'll be fine. Maybe the next time you're up, you can grab me some Tylenol?"

"It's not a problem. I really don't mind. And I've been told before I'm pretty good at shoulder rubs. It's actually better for you to relieve pain naturally instead of taking Tylenol; that doesn't actually solve the problem, just masks the sensation in your brain so you can't feel it." I was rambling awkwardly like a fourteen-year-old kid who'd never touched a girl before, and I couldn't stop myself.

"I *know*, Doctor Delacruz. Right now, I'm happy to settle for not feeling it." She lowered her brows and stared at me, as if she was questioning my motives.

I could hardly blame her for it.

Sighing, I threw my hands up. "Fine, Tylenol it is. I just thought I could help." I turned to slide off the bed.

"Wait," Stella huffed a breath. "You're right, a massage would be better, and I would really appreciate it."

"Okay." Even though I had offered, I was suddenly more nervous. "Why don't you turn around and face the fire?"

She obliged, and I moved the cards aside to slide closer. I was contemplating her mane of hair, wondering if I should push it over one shoulder or just let it hang between my hands while I worked, when Stella said, "Wait!"

She gathered it up, the strands almost hitting my face while she whipped the tail back and forth, finishing with a large knot on top of her head. "Okay, continue."

I'd momentarily short-circuited; the fragrance from her locks forming a cloud around my head. Shaking myself free, I rubbed my hands together to warm them and lightly set them on her shoulders, using low pressure with my thumbs.

"Mmm," Stella moaned, and I bit on my lip to maintain my focus. "That feels good, but can you go any harder?"

Gritting my teeth, I dug in further with my thumbs. Her shoulders felt small, almost breakable, under my hands. Even so, her muscles were like mini boulders, so I pressed and pushed, trying to rub out the tension and bring her some relief.

I knew it was working because her head dipped back, her shoulders slumped slightly, and a heavy sigh slipped from her lips.

I continued squeezing and rubbing, feeling her muscles gradually soften. Meanwhile, my blood pressure rose, and I had to keep swallowing because of the saliva gathering on my tongue. I imagined myself leaning forward, pressing my lips to her pale neck and running my fingers along her throat.

Why did I do this to myself? I shook my head, trying to clear the images out of my brain. I could have just handed her the pills and avoided it, but clearly I couldn't be trusted to keep my hands to myself. Jaw clenched, I forced myself to continue.

Gently working my fingers up the column of her neck, I squeezed delicately, releasing the tightness there as well. When those two areas relaxed, I forced myself to stop and lean back. "Better?"

Stella rolled her neck, releasing a deep breath. "Yes, so much better, thank you."

She turned back around and smiled at me gratefully. "I'm impressed. You should thank whatever girl taught you that move."

I cleared my throat, my eyes dropping to my hands. "It was my mom."

"Oh," her voice rose, obviously surprised. "Well, tell her thank you, then. When we get out of here."

"She... she passed away a couple years ago." The lump in my throat grew impossibly large.

Stella took a moment before answering in a softer tone. "Sebastian, I'm sorry. I probably should have known."

"Nah, I wouldn't expect you to." I busied myself with collecting the cards and shuffling. "My parents moved out of Aspen Ridge after I left, so no one here knows. They died within a year of each other."

"God, I'm so sorry," she said again, the sympathy in her voice making my eyes tingle. "Were you able to come back for the funerals?"

"For my dad's, no. They would have had to wait weeks for me to get back stateside, so I told my mom to hold it without me. I thought I'd have time to see her soon, but..." I swallowed, then drew in a deep breath before I continued. "She passed before I made it home. I had to come back and take care of the arrangements myself. There was no one else to do it."

"Wow, Sebastian, I'm... I'm sorry."

"Stop saying you're sorry," I brushed her off gruffly. "It's not your fault."

Unlike normal, she didn't snap back at me. "I know, but it's the best way I know how to sympathize."

"Well, I don't want your sympathy. I'd rather just not think about it." Holding up the cards, I finally met her gaze. It was soft, her eyes wide and shining. Every trace of her armor was gone, and the last thing I needed right now was her vulnerability; it would tear me apart. Instead, I forced my signature grin.

"So, what about King's Corner?"

CHAPTER
ELEVEN

STELLA

I didn't know how to react to his revelation, but Sebastian clearly didn't want to talk about it anymore, so we went back to card games.

The afternoon wore on, and eventually we both grew tired of the cards. Sebastian kept monitoring the fire, and even though he continued feeding it wood, the room grew continuously colder. When it was feasibly dinner time, he heated the last packet of camping food for us to share with a power bar, and made us another round of hot cocoa. We had a bit of light conversation, but ignored the heavy cloud that was gathering between us.

Clearly, he regretted telling me about his parents, because he'd been acting weird ever since. For my part, I regretted he told me, too. Because my heart broke for him, and I didn't want to let him in again but now it felt almost inevitable. He'd done a horrible, shitty thing to me in high school, but he'd suffered a lot of horrible, shitty things since then. Perhaps karma had already repaid him that debt, and I should let it go.

Sebastian was good at hiding his feelings, acting like he was normal; but I saw it in the set of his shoulders, how his jaw flexed and his knuckles cracked. This stoic 'can't be bothered' attitude was a facade that he put up because he didn't want to let me in, either.

We were both sitting on the bed silently, my sleeping bag and blankets spread over our laps, and I knew another five minutes of this would drive me absolutely insane.

Resolved, I climbed out of bed, ignoring Sebastian's protest, and snatched my flask from the food stash. I avoided eye contact with him completely, only meeting his gaze when I'd taken a long pull of the burning liquor. "Here, want some?" I held out the open flask.

"Are you crazy? No. One of us has to keep our wits about us, and I guess that's me by default. You absolutely should *not* be drinking alcohol with a concussion." He frowned at me disdainfully, as if I were a misbehaving teenager.

I was not in the mood for his superiority. "Oh, get off it. We haven't confirmed I have a concussion, number one. We're trapped here for at least another night. We have plenty of firewood, and we're bored out of our skulls. Not to mention this," I waved a hand between us, "is driving me nuts. So let's have a drink and lighten up already."

"What's driving you nuts?"

"This tension, whatever the hell it is. You're all wound up, and I don't know the entire story because you clam up the second you feel something. So I propose a new game: Truth or Dare."

He snorted derisively. "What is this, middle school?"

"No, we're two people who obviously have some shit to sort out—don't give me that look, you know what I mean—and since we can't even seem to manage it locked in a cabin together, I figure some alcohol to grease the wheels can't hurt. So take a drink and stop acting so superior."

A sudden look of fear crossed his expression,

181

but then, with a sigh, he reached out and grabbed the flask, taking a long pull.

"There, that's what I'm talking about!" I crowed. "Welcome to the party, Sebastian."

"Yeah, yeah," he grumbled. "Are we jumping right into this, or are we getting drunk first?"

"I vote for drunk," I answered, snatching the flask back and taking another sip. If I was going to get down to the truth, I'd need to be at least a little tipsy to even bring it up.

"Drunk it is," he sighed, downing another pull, then sniffing the top. "I have to say I'm impressed. I expected it would be some cheap whisky that your terrain park friends would mix with coke, but I'm pretty sure this is scotch."

"Well, look at you, Fancy Pants, you know your liquor. Yeah, I raid my dad's collection to fill my flask. He's got more than he can drink in a lifetime, so he doesn't miss the occasional bottle." The warmth from the alcohol had spread to my limbs now, and heat was rising in my cheeks. "Okay, I'll start first. You ask me."

"Alright, truth or dare?"

"Truth."

"What happens if you don't make it to the Olympics?"

Of course he went straight there; probably to

punish me for suggesting this stupid game. My heart thumped painfully just thinking about it. "You mean like I get injured again, or I just don't make the podium?"

"Either, you pick."

I breathed in deeply, then released a heavy sigh; I asked for this. "I think either way, I'll be done. If I'm not good enough to compete any more, there's no sense in deluding myself any longer. If I get injured and I'm not completely broken, I won't risk it a third time." My fingers found a stray thread on the blanket and fiddled with it. Anything to distract myself from actually considering the alternative. It didn't matter. I was going to make it.

Sebastian nodded. "Fair enough. So what'll you do then?"

I took another sip from the flask. "Then I'll try to make a place for myself at Aspen Ridge that doesn't suck."

That drew a snort of a laugh from him, and I passed him the flask. "Sounds fair."

"Okay, your turn. Truth or dare?"

Sebastian eyed me dubiously. "Truth."

"Why'd you leave the Army? Really?"

He sighed heavily, then took a long sip of scotch. "I couldn't do it anymore."

"Do what anymore?"

"The whole thing. I didn't have any hoorah left in me. I couldn't do my job, and I just didn't want to be there anymore."

"Why?"

"Nope, I answered your question. You don't get unlimited follow-ups, Estrellita. What'll it be, truth or dare?"

Since he didn't say it with malice, I ignored the nickname. "Truth."

Sebastian's voice was low, his expression neutral, when he asked, "On a scale of one to ten, how much did you hate me after homecoming?"

I swallowed, suddenly nervous. There was no good reason, he already knew; but some part of me really didn't want to verbalize it. "Eleven," I whispered.

He blew out a slow breath, nodding to himself. "Yeah, that sounds about right."

I took the flask back. "Your turn, truth or dare?"

"Truth." He suddenly wore a resigned expression, as if he already knew what was coming.

"Why did you do it?" My voice was low, but he winced when I asked, as if I'd struck him.

"I didn't have a choice, Stella. At least, I felt like I didn't."

"That's not an answer," I growled, emotion gathering in my chest. "You could have not asked me at all. I would have been perfectly fine staying in the unrequited love zone. What you did was cruel and sadistic, and I didn't deserve it."

"You're right."

"So tell me the truth. I think you owe me that much."

He drew in a deep breath, then released it slowly. "Reece."

"I don't understand."

"Do you remember that practice, the day after I asked you to homecoming? You ran up to us on the field and hugged me."

"Sort of..."

"Reece knew something was up. He asked what was going on and I panicked, so I told him there was nothing, but he didn't believe me. He told me I was a player, and I had better not play his little sister."

My eyes started prickling, and I jutted my chin out. "So that was it? You were going to play me, but Reece stopped you and you humiliated me instead?"

"No, Stella... dammit. Reece didn't want me to *date* you. He was my best friend. I'd do anything for him. And if he didn't think I was worthy to date his sister, then I certainly would not convince him otherwise."

"So it was *his* idea to humiliate me in front of the entire school?"

"No, that one was all me." A heavy sigh.

"You still haven't told me *why* you did it, Sebastian."

And just like that, he lost his temper. "Because I was an idiot and a chicken shit, okay? Is that what you want to hear, Stella? I had already asked you, and I didn't want to take it back. I didn't know how to cancel without crushing you completely, and I didn't want to face your disappointment. Some stupid part of my brain thought that I could just ignore it and the problem would go away. I tried giving you the cold shoulder, being too busy to hang out, being indifferent when you talked about it. I suppose I hoped you'd get pissed at me and tell me to go fuck myself, but you didn't and I didn't have the heart to tell you.

"I also couldn't tell Reece that I had asked his sister out after he told me so clearly to stay away. So when Brittany asked me to be her date, I just said sure."

My eyes were welling with tears now, my vision distorted. "You're horrible," I whispered. "I *worshipped* you. We were *friends*. I considered you one of my *best* friends. You built me up with your talk of keeping it all a secret until Homecoming where we'd surprise everyone, like it was a big prank we were playing on Brittany, Reece; all of them. Like some cheesy high school movie. I loved every second. Instead, I ended up being the punch line."

"I know," he sighed in defeat. "It was unforgivable."

"You should have *told* me. I would have accepted it even if I didn't agree, and I didn't need the public humiliation to make it real. When you won Homecoming King and asked your date to meet you on the floor, that was supposed to be *our* signal. I was so excited I practically ran out there. It was my moment, *our* moment. And then, with everyone watching, you took Brittany's hand and laughed in my face. You left me standing there like some delusional dork with a crush on the homecoming king."

"I did."

"God, I hated you so much."

"I deserved it."

"You know, I went home and cried for *hours*. And the irony is, no one believed me because I hadn't even told them, like we agreed. Reece thought I'd misunderstood something and my parents thought I made the whole thing up. It was humiliation after humiliation. Only a couple of my friends knew, and it was their idea to deface your float."

"I deserved that, too."

His absolute acceptance of my anger pulled the wind right out of my sails. I could hardly keep after him when he owned every single thing I threw in his face. It felt cruel, somehow, to continue. I got my answer after six years, and somehow it wasn't nearly as satisfying as I expected. Now, finally, I had to find some way to move on.

So I sighed and took another drink. "Okay, your turn."

"Truth or dare?"

"Truth."

"Tell me how you really feel about competing in a few weeks. You said you were still afraid. Are you excited at all, even a little?"

"Honestly? It doesn't feel like fun anymore. It feels like an obligation."

"Do you feel that way about all the events?"

"No, just the half-pipe and slope style, really. The ones with tricks. It's the flipping in the air that freaks me out, since that's where everything went wrong last time."

"So slalom and snowboard cross are fun?"

"Yeah, actually. I like the speed, it's still a rush and my feet don't leave the ground. At least not for long. Probably most importantly, it's new. I don't have any bad memories from whizzing down the hill."

"But you're not sure you'll win in those, so that's why you're still doing the other two."

"Yeah."

"Okay, your turn." Sebastian stretched out to the side, resting his head on his hand, and waited for the question.

The alcohol in my veins was making me extremely brave at this point. "Truth or dare."

"Truth."

"Why did you get upset when I called you a hero?"

I didn't expect the venom in his tone. "Because it's a bullshit made-up thing, calling people in the military heroes for doing the shit we do."

That made zero sense to me. "You don't think your job was heroic, saving people's lives?"

A derisive snort. "It would be, if I actually did that."

"What does that mean?"

The dam burst. His eyes were red and glassy, and his voice cracked when he yelled. "They all died, okay? They all died, and I'm the only one who survived, and that doesn't make me a fucking hero." Sebastian rolled over onto his back and stared up at the ceiling.

My heart raced a mile a minute, and I didn't want to press him any more. He looked an inch from breaking completely. "Okay. You don't have to tell me any more. I won't ask. But if you *want* to tell me, I'll listen. And I won't judge. Promise."

Sebastian ignored me, his eyes never straying from the roof above us. I kept my word and didn't ask. The silence between us thickened, only broken by crackles from the fire and the storm outside.

My eyes dropped to my hands, and I picked at the chipped black nail polish on my thumb. The cabin was so small I couldn't go anywhere to give him space. But I could sit silently and wait.

"We were dispatched to help a patrol that ran over an IED." He launched into his story with a flat, emotionless voice. "There were four of us in my team, and two survivors that had radioed in for help. We were just minutes away, and we raced in. When we arrived, there was one humvee flipped over, on fire. The second was still on its tires, but the front end had obviously taken some of the blast. The driver was dead, the passenger had radioed. Someone had been thrown from the vehicle. He was injured, bleeding from his legs, but he was trying to guard the truck with the one other survivor.

"It felt wrong. I don't know how to explain it. There was no one around. Usually when they got us with an IED they were there, either because they triggered it remotely, or they'd run in quickly to scavenge tech, weapons, anything. Take a hostage if we let them. So it felt wrong that the road was completely empty, nothing but two burning humvees and a shit ton of sand."

My heart throbbed for him. Obviously he was getting to the part where something went wrong, and my body stiffened in anticipation.

Sebastian's voice was crumbly, weak with emotion like a wall made of sand. "I tried to tell the others to wait, that we should get a K-9 unit in, wait for EOD. We all knew the protocol. But we'd had an awful week, and I guess all they saw was this guy bleeding out, and they *knew* we could save him. We couldn't see the chick in the passenger seat, but she hadn't reported herself as seriously injured. So the best I could guess was they just got tunnel vision and went straight for him, like they trained us to do.

"Of course, I hung back and radioed to find out

when another patrol would arrive. They were telling me to order everyone to wait—I was the staff sergeant. It was my job to protect them.

"And then the second bomb detonated. It took them all out: the undamaged humvee, the guy on the ground, and my entire team. Poof, in a second, all gone. It threw me against our vehicle; I got hit by some shrapnel, but dragged myself into the truck and pulled out my sidearm. Good thing, too, because they all appeared after the second explosion. Half a dozen enemy combatants popped up out of the ditch. We had no idea they were there."

My god, he'd literally been hit by a bomb, and survived. Emotion welled behind my eyes, and I restrained myself from reaching out to comfort him; I wasn't sure if he would like it.

Sebastian continued, every word sounding like it was difficult for him to push out. "They came for me, and I held them back with my sidearm until Delta Squad showed up and took them all out. I passed out after that; I'd gotten pretty cut up, lost a lot of blood. I have a brief memory of being on a helicopter, strapped to a gurney, but then it goes dark again. I woke up in a hospital in Germany, all bandaged up and disoriented. Some Captain I didn't know showed up to give me a medal and call me a hero while I was still in a hospital gown wearing a catheter.

"They gave me a purple heart and called me a hero, because I was the only one who survived. I can't tell you how little I felt like a hero for letting my entire squad die." Sebastian's glossy eyes remained focused on the ceiling the entire time; I wasn't sure if he was still relating this story to me, or just saying it out loud to himself.

"There was smoke, and dust, and bodies on the ground. Andrews, face down, her uniform more red than brown. She was small, like you. We were... close. All of us; we were like a family. Then, in a second, they were all gone."

The tears I'd restrained for my own pain unleashed now, running down my cheeks. "I know you don't want to hear it, but I'm sorry, Sebastian. That sounds so horrible. I don't know how to relate. But I can understand why you don't want to be called a hero. And I understand why you had to get out. I can't imagine staying, after that."

His voice turned bitter. "*It's war*, that's what they tell you. They have therapists. Everyone walks on eggshells around you for a while. You go to physical therapy, people congratulate you on being able to walk... they're trying to build you back up, you get it? When you join the military, they like to say they break you down to build you back up. You go through all this dumb shit at boot camp to bond with your platoon and you come out the other end as a functional team. So when you get broken down by the job, they have an entire system to build you back up again.

"But it doesn't work the same. And at some point everyone stops having sympathy and they just expect you to move on. There's a job to do, a war to fight, and they don't have time to coddle you any more. So it's get up and shut up. And I did it for a while, but I was still on a profile. I still couldn't run normally. My arm hurt. In the end, they decided I was injured enough I could get out without repercussions, if I wanted to. I never imagined it before, but at that point I was happy to accept an early discharge."

"And then Reece invited you here," I murmured.

"Yeah. The one friend I have left in the world. Couldn't ask for a better one."

I didn't know how to respond to that—I knew they'd kept in touch, but I never asked my brother about Sebastian. However, it didn't surprise me they'd remained that close.

Searching for another topic of conversation, I asked, "So, have your injuries healed up?"

"No," he sighed, sitting up. He gave me a ghost of a smile, his eyes heavy with sadness. "It's my turn. Truth or dare."

I was definitely over the truth portion of the night. "Dare."

"Show me one of your scars from when you fell. I'll show you mine."

"Oh... Um, okay." I tugged down on the collar of my shirt, revealing the narrow scar along my left collarbone. "It didn't break the skin, but it was busted pretty bad. They had to put in a plate so it would heal right. Then they went in again and took the plate out."

"Damn, cut you open twice, huh?" He leaned in close, the sweet scent of scotch mingling with his spicy fragrance. He ran a delicate finger along the scar, and a tiny shiver of heat licked up my spine.

"Okay, here's one of mine." He tried pulling up the cuff of his sleeve, but it was too tight, so he tugged the shirt off completely and pointed at a raised scar on his biceps. "This one was a two-inch piece of shrapnel; they think it was a piece of the humvee but they aren't sure, could have been the bomb itself."

I tried to ignore his exposed torso and chest and focus on the indicated scar. Taking his lead, I touched the shiny mound. His skin was incredibly warm, and much smoother than I imagined. "How many pieces hit you?"

"Over a dozen," he answered, almost cheerfully. "A bunch of them hit my vest, but I had metal in both my legs and my side. Here," he grabbed my hand, lifting his arm to reveal his torso. A long, jagged scar lay in the space between his pec and his back, and he pressed my fingers to it. "This was actually several pieces that hit. They cut me up pretty good, right down to the bone."

"Reece's comment about my ribs." For some reason, that conversation came back to me lighting fast, embarrassment flooding my chest when I remembered how I'd acted just a few days ago.

"Yeah. Mine weren't broken, but they're still painful sometimes."

"Here." I pulled my arm out of my sleeve and faced away to show him the scar on my shoulder. "They had to do surgery to repair the socket so they could put it back in place."

He released a low whistle. "I have to hand it to you, Stella. When you decide to break yourself, you do it well."

"Go big or go home, right?" I chuckled, suddenly jittery at our closeness. I felt exposed, the air freezing on my bare skin. My breathing grew rapid. I had on a pretty significant sports bra, of course. But when Sebastian ran his warm fingers over my flesh, goosebumps prickled along the path. His hand trailed down along my side, and his breath was suddenly warm on my neck, warning me his face was inches from my body.

Then I felt his pillow soft lips press to my shoulder, and I melted completely.

CHAPTER
TWELVE

SEBASTIAN

The alcohol had done its job; The guilt was gone, and I was free of the inhibitions that weighed me down. Now I wanted nothing more than to see how her skin tasted, and there wasn't a single reason in my head why I shouldn't.

My blood was pounding in my veins, my heart about to burst from my chest, but I lingered, watching her breaths grow shallow the more my fingers dragged along her silky skin. And when I kissed that scar on her shoulder, she released a delicious sound, somewhere between a moan and a shuddering sigh.

"Sebastian?" She turned to me with those wide, bright eyes full of uncertainty.

I let my hands slide down to wrap around her ribcage, just below the band of her bra, where her delicate skin pebbled at my touch. "Yes?"

"What are we doing?" The question was a whisper, as if she were afraid of the answer.

"Only what you want to do, Stella. If you don't want me, just tell me now."

"I..." she hesitated, her eyes conflicted. "I want you, but I'm not sure I want you like this."

My thumbs rubbed circles against her ribs. "What do you mean, 'like this'?"

"I plied you with alcohol and got you to confess painful memories to me. I don't want you if it's a moment of weakness."

It was a moment of weakness, but not how she imagined it. "Stella, I don't want you because I feel weak *now*. I've *always* wanted you, but I was afraid to act on it because I *was* weak. I'm not afraid anymore."

Her lips parted, pupils dilating as she finally heard the truth I'd concealed from her for so many years. The hope in her expression almost broke my heart. "Always?" She breathed.

"Always," I answered, stroking her jaw with my thumb as I moved in to claim her lips. Her eyes closed in anticipation, head tilting back, and when I finally kissed her, it was just as I'd imagined. Her lips so warm and welcoming, so soft against mine. She shuddered, and I pulled her against my body as much to share my warmth with her as to feel her against me. When I drew her lower lip between my teeth and sucked, her arms twined around my neck and she pulled herself even closer, using my shoulders for leverage.

Within seconds, she was on my lap, and she pulled away to whip her top completely off before diving back in for more kisses. Her fingers ran up the base of my skull, sending delicious sensations down my spine. Even though we were both half undressed, the heat between our bodies made the cool air pleasant. However, we were so bundled up on the lower half with snow pants and long johns, it was as if I couldn't feel her at all.

My fingers splayed across her back, searching for the hooks on her bra, before I remembered it was a sports bra and those things required a magic spell and a full moon to remove. Instead, I ducked my fingers under the band, just trying to feel every inch of her skin.

Stella pulled back and smiled wickedly at me.

God, she was so beautiful like this, all rosy cheeks and swollen lips and brilliant blue eyes. "Looking for this?" She teased, then pulled at the hidden zipper on the front of her bra.

I sucked my lower lip between my teeth and watched the tiny piece of metal descend aggravatingly slowly. Of course Stella would draw this moment out, letting the anticipation ramp me up to a ten.

Not that I didn't love every second.

When the zipper finally released, the tight, stretchy fabric pulled back and revealed two beautifully round breasts, topped with deliciously pink nipples. My hands immediately rose to cup them, lifting them together so I could kiss first one, then the other perfectly taut pink tower. Stella arched back and her hair tumbled free of its knot; suddenly I was living the scenario I'd imagined so many times I'd lost count. I drew a nipple into my mouth, first sucking, then scraping it lightly with my teeth. The moan of pleasure that escaped her lips only encouraged me. After I did the same for its twin, I worked my way back up to claim Stella's mouth once more.

Her kisses were no longer exploratory; now they were deep and claiming, and she pressed down on me with a force that set my pulse into overdrive.

My hand rose, tangling in the thick, silky mass of her hair, before I fisted it and tugged her head back gently. Stella released a surprise gasp, fingernails scraping over my shoulders as I dragged my lips and teeth along her neck. Her chest heaved with rapid breaths, fingers trailing down my arms.

When I released her hair, she pushed me back on the bed and leaned over me, the wild tangle of hair brushing my forehead. "I dunno about you, but I still have way too many layers on," she purred.

I couldn't have said it better myself.

I reached up and held her to my body, then flipped us both over so she was now on the bottom.

"Allow me to help you with that, Miss Blackwell."

My instinct was to rip her clothes off and pound into her with all the speed and strength I possessed. It had been ages since I even desired someone like this, as opposed to just wanting to get off.

However, that simply would not be good enough for Stella, not by a long shot. There was no way to make removing several layers of snow gear sexy, no matter how I tried. Instead, I pressed a soft kiss to her lips and promised her I'd be right back, then set about stoking the fire and lowering the flames in the lanterns, leaving us with warm, romantic lighting.

When I returned to the bed, Stella had settled herself on the pillow, propped on one arm and watching me with glossy eyes. "Is this your attempt at mood lighting?" She asked slyly.

"I've always heard that making love by fire-light is the thing. Never tried it personally, but there's no better time to try it than now." My eyes drank her in, every inch of her creamy skin in the warm light from the fire, her eyes practically glowing as she smiled up at me.

I didn't break that eye contact when my hand slid down her belly, unsnapping and unzipping her snow pants. With another soft kiss, I moved to the end of the bed and tugged them off, then peeled back her woolen socks.

I shed my snow pants and socks as well, then joined her on the bed and straddled her body, kissing my way down her stomach before I hooked two fingers in the remaining barriers and freed them from her body.

And of course, her smart mouth just couldn't

be stopped. "Not to ruin the moment, Sebastian, but it's fucking cold in here with no clothes on."

"Allow me to take care of that for you." I slid into the narrow bed beside her, then pulled the covers up over us both. Now our kisses were deep and slow, passionate instead of frenzied. I leaned on one elbow and allowed my free hand to roam over her body, determined to caress every inch of her silky skin. Stella reached up to pull my head to hers, and when I could take it no longer, I let my fingers navigate between her legs.

She gasped lightly when I first ran the pad of my finger over her, her legs spreading automatically in response. I couldn't help the groan of desire that ripped from my chest, my roomy pants now uncomfortably tight. I allowed my fingers to dip further, slipping easily through the wetness, before I moved back to my target and started working firm circles on the spot guaranteed to bring her the most pleasure.

Her breath grew more rapid, and her hips lifted, pressing against my hand, begging wordlessly for more pressure. If we were going to do this, I was determined she should get her pleasure first. After waiting so long, I didn't want our first time to be a disappointment.

It reached the point where she pulled away from my lips and threw her head back, eyes closed, with throaty moans pouring from her lips. My hand worked faster, and I drank in the image of her in this moment of pleasure, searing it to my memory. When the dam finally broke, her body went rigid, her moans silenced, and I worked a few more moments until she relaxed completely. Only then did I withdraw my hand, sliding my fingers into my mouth to taste her.

STELLA

LIKE A HIGH SCHOOL fantasy come true, I found myself naked in bed with the quarterback, my body still tingly in the wake of a climax so overdue I'd practically seen fireworks.

But even as I came down from that high, my body craved more.

My eyes fluttered open to catch Sebastian, eyes closed, licking the fingers that had so recently been inside me. Something about that moment, seeing him so reverent and passionate about experiencing me, stoked the furnace of my desire. My hand found its way between us, and I stroked his considerable bulge over the thin fabric of his remaining clothes before I slipped my hand under the waistband.

Sebastian's eyes popped open at my initial touch, but then rolled back in his head again when my fingers wrapped around his hot, silky flesh. I only managed a couple of firm strokes before his hands pressed me back into the bed and he kissed me with renewed passion.

Now I could feel him against me, his hardness pressed to my softness, and my legs wrapped around him, squeezing him closer.

"Stella," he pulled back, his gaze heavy with desire. "Are you sure this is what you want?"

I couldn't help the eye roll... could I possibly be clearer? "Yes, I'm a hundred percent fucking sure, Sebastian. Do I need to spell it out for you? I'm naked and just had my hand down your pants."

"I don't have any condoms."

"*What?* I thought ski patrol was prepared for anything?"

At that, he chortled. "Well, I don't exactly plan to get it on when I'm rescuing old ladies who've fallen and lost a ski."

"Fair enough. I'm on the pill, anyway. You have nothing to worry about from me."

SASHA PIERCE

He hesitated, his voice taking on a slightly embarrassed tone. "Me too, in case you were wondering. I mean, I know everyone thinks people in the military are fucking like bunnies, but that's not me." His eyes were wide and sincere.

"I believe you," I assured him, then lifted my head to kiss him gently. My hands traveled down his sides to tug at his waistband, and he finally pulled back to remove the clothing completely.

Seconds later, he pressed against me, now barrier-free. The hot skin of his erection was almost painfully hard on my pelvic bone, and I wiggled to shift it to a more comfortable position.

Sebastian, meanwhile, gazed down at me with clear adoration. My pulse quickened, the intensity of his gaze doing strange things to my insides. I wanted him—I'd always wanted him, and something about suddenly finding out he wanted me too brought up a well of emotion I hadn't expected.

"Stella, I-" he started, but I interrupted with a finger to his lips.

"Stop. No more talking, Sebastian. I think we've had plenty of that tonight. I want this, I want you, I'm not that drunk and I have no doubts. Can we proceed?" For emphasis, I reached between us again, fisting him and sliding his tip against the wetness I'd created for him.

Sebastian's eyes closed, his jaw flexing, as he allowed me to tease him. Finally, he took charge, claiming one of my hands with his own and positioning himself. He held my gaze intently as he pressed, slowly and deliberately, inside of me.

The sensation was too much and not enough all at the same time. My head arched back, legs spreading further to accommodate him, and he watched me with that hooded gaze the entire time.

We started slowly, and I wrapped my legs around his hips, reaching up to pull his mouth to mine. It was sensual and romantic and I couldn't get enough of him.

Eventually, our desire for more couldn't be ignored, and our bodies moved faster, our passion growing. Sebastian changed angles, leaning back for better leverage, and he grabbed one of my hands to press it between us.

"Help me," he groaned, and I obliged, adding more stimulation for myself and increasing the intensity even more.

It didn't take long; I was already primed and ready, and the feeling of him combined with my skill at getting myself off soon had me clenching and shuddering around him. That was apparently the tipping point for Sebastian, who finished while I was still floating among the stars of my own release.

I pulled him down to me, wrapping him in my legs once more and running my fingers through his sweaty hair, pressing kisses to his forehead as our racing hearts gradually slowed.

This felt *huge*; our history went back a long way, and even though it had seemed impossible, now this moment felt inevitable. My chest swelled with a warm, glowing feeling, and I squeezed Sebastian tightly to my body.

I couldn't tell him, of course, but I loved Sebastian. I'd loved him since I was fifteen, and now, seven years later, I discovered that love was still here, just buried under all that hurt for so long I'd forgotten it existed.

But now he was back, and we had nothing but possibilities before us.

CHAPTER
THIRTEEN

SEBASTIAN

After recovering from the first round, I realized that the winds outside had died down. Since I was butt naked and definitely not interested in putting clothes on right now, I decided to forgo poking my head outside and instead flipped the generator back on, powering on the radio. There was still only static in response to my tests, so I turned it low but left it on. If the weather was clear, they'd be trying to get ahold of us in the morning, and I didn't want to miss them.

After that, I turned the lanterns off completely, and with Stella's help, hastily zipped the two sleeping bags together so we could stay warm, next to each other.

There was no talk of me sleeping on the floor tonight.

And when we made love again, it was slow and deliberate, our bodies in sync as if we'd done it a hundred times before.

I finally fell asleep with Stella wrapped in my arms, her body curled up and mine right behind her.

I slept like the dead; I didn't wake once, not even from my usual nightmares or the alternative —no apparent reason at all—which happened disturbingly often. I had a completely dreamless sleep, and for once I felt rested and content.

Stella was still asleep when I woke, and I lay perfectly still, burying my face in her hair and breathing her in. I had no desire to wake her; we had nowhere to go, anyway. Until rescue came, we were stuck here regardless, and in contrast to yesterday morning, now I had absolutely zero desire to leave.

It was at that moment the radio squawked to life. "Delacruz, do you read me? This is Patrol Command. Patrol Command to Delacruz."

I jumped in surprise at the intrusion of Gary's voice, and Stella startled awake.

"Sorry, sorry," I kissed her forehead and unzipped the bag, slipping out into the freezing room and diving for the radio. "Patrol Command, this is Delacruz. We read you."

"Great to hear you've pulled through, Delacruz. How's your patient?"

My eyes darted to Stella, and she grinned lazily at me from the nest of covers. "Patient is doing remarkably well, considering."

"Excellent. The snow died off at about two am, so the cats have been out working ever since. We sent a patrol team to help dig you out. They should be there soon. They'll make an assessment and determine if we need to send the helo or if she can return for treatment on the lift. We can all meet at the top of the mountain with a snowmobile, in that case."

"Roger, sounds good. We'll prepare for rescue."

"Copy that. See you soon, Delacruz! Patrol Command out."

I threw a couple of pieces of wood into the stove, then rushed back to bed and slipped into the covers, shivering.

Stella yelped at the touch of my chilled skin. "Jesus, Sebastian, you're freezing."

"Tell me something I don't know, Stella." Fortunately, the sleeping bags held heat well, and I warmed up pretty quickly. Never one to waste an opportunity, I pulled Stella in to my chest; I just wanted to stay in this perfect moment a bit longer, before the rest of the world crashed in and changed everything.

She sighed and wrapped her arms around my back, pressing her face to my chest. "Would it be weird if I said that I'm not actually all that excited about getting out of here now?"

I chuckled. "No, actually, I was thinking the same thing. Even though we never asked to be stuck out here, somehow it didn't turn out so bad."

"Yeah," Stella agreed. "It was like a break from real life, but now that life is coming to get us."

"Exactly."

We lay in silence for a few more minutes before I pressed a kiss to her hair. "Why don't I fire us up some cocoa so we can get dressed before our rescuers arrive?"

She groaned. "Yeah, that would probably be a good idea."

"No time like the present, I suppose." I slipped out of the bag and pulled on my shorts, pants, and wool socks, then handed Stella her clothing before I put on the rest of mine. She stayed under the covers and got dressed horizontally, not emerging from the cocoon until she was ready for snow pants.

Once we were both decent for rescue and I had water on to boil, we set about tidying up. I unzipped the sleeping bags, so it wasn't obvious we'd slept together, and once the cocoa was ready, we sat down to drink it in silence, waiting for the crunch of footsteps on the snow outside.

Stella appeared relaxed, and I knew my face was calm, but inside I was already panicking. My inhibitions had definitely been lowered last night, but now I was quite aware of what I'd done and what the repercussions would be. I didn't know what to do; on one hand, I was so relieved Stella and I were on the same page. My chest swelled with joy just thinking about it; happy didn't do this feeling justice. After all this time, we were finally back on the path it seemed we were meant to walk all those years ago.

On the other hand, the problems hadn't gone away. Stella was reckless; she insisted on participating in a dangerous sport that could get her killed, and even though she knew the danger, she wasn't willing to be talked out of it. I'd already lost so many people, I didn't know if I could open myself up to the chance of that kind of loss again.

And it wasn't like the issue with Reece had disappeared, either. He was my lifelong best friend, who'd literally thrown me a lifeline and given me this job when I had nowhere else to go. He knew how messed up I was, and he certainly would not find me any more suitable for his sister now than he did *before* all that shit happened.

I was once again in the position of having to choose, and I was no better at this than I was six years ago.

Fortunately, I was saved from further depressing thoughts by the arrival of muffled voices outside. "Hey Delacruz, you in there?"

The voice was familiar, but I couldn't put a name to it. "Yeah, we sure are," I called back. "How bad is it?"

"It's some snow, but nothing we can't handle. Give us a few minutes. We'll start digging you out."

"Thank you!" I downed the last of my cocoa and stood. "Well Stella, I guess we'd better gear up."

She observed me for a moment while I busied myself with retrieving our gear from all the nooks and crannies I'd stashed it in. The voices outside talked to each other, and the steady crunch of shovels scraping through snow grew louder.

I was rinsing our mugs in the sink when a hand stopped my movements.

"Hey," Stella looked up at me with bright, knowing blue eyes. "It'll be okay, Sebastian. All of it. You don't need to stress."

"I'm not stressed," I countered sharply, instantly regretting it. "I mean," I added more gently, "I don't know what's going to happen when we leave here, that's all."

Her warm eyes cooled slightly, sadness crossing her features. "Don't you?"

Panic rose in my throat. "Stella, I-"

A heavy knock at the door startled us both. I glanced at her once more, then threw on my coat and turned the knob.

"Rescue has arrived!" Two of my co-workers clomped into the tiny room, trailing clumps of powdery snow across the hard wooden floor. The guy in front pulled down his black mask, revealing a face I recognized.

"Paul, hey thanks for coming, man."

"Sure thing. Rick brought the med kit." He turned his attention to Stella, who'd moved back by the stove to make room. "How are you feeling, Ms. Blackwell?"

"Fine," her reply was almost surly, a challenge, but Paul didn't take offense.

"Great! We'll do a quick assessment to make sure, but what do you think about riding back on the lift if we clear it? It's definitely faster and cheaper than sending in the helo, not to mention a lot less embarrassing."

"I think I can manage it."

"Great. Why don't you have a seat? We'll get this exam over quickly. I'm sure you guys are champing at the bit to get out of here."

Stella and I exchanged a long glance, but she broke it off and smiled brightly. "Definitely, I can't wait to go home and have a shower."

I clipped on my ski boots and finished gearing up while Rick checked Stella out. He proclaimed her well enough to take the chairlift, so she got ready too. I powered down the generator, rinsed the dishes as well as I could, and threw some snow on the fire to put it out. We cranked the thermostat down to make the cabin just warm enough to keep the interior from freezing, and then with nothing left to do, we trudged single-file back outside.

The light hurt my eyes, and I quickly pulled on

my goggles to adjust. The air was so cold it felt as if my skin were freezing, and everything was blanketed completely in sparkling white. Massive trees drooped under the heavy weight of it, and the only thing moving aside from us was a chairlift a short distance away.

Paul and Rick had dug a deep channel from the path to the shack, where the snow piled on either side was nearly as high as the door.

I threw one last sad glance back at that little cabin, sending it a silent thank you for keeping us alive, and trudged on.

Rick had claimed Stella as a patient, so he went up in the first chair with her and Paul and I took the second.

"What a crazy time, eh?" Paul asked with a chuckle. "We don't get people stuck back here that often, but just when we think we may not need that shack any more, something like this happens and we're all reminded how important it is."

"Yeah, it was certainly a lifesaver for us," I agreed quietly.

"And to think, your first year barely started, and you got to christen it for the season."

I nearly choked. "Christen it?"

"Yeah, you know, you're the first one to stay overnight this season. I mean, most seasons, it's nothing more than a warming shack for the chair workers when they need it, of course."

"Of course."

"But when there ends up being a year it's used, it always seems like it happens a few times more that year. Like bad things come in threes and all that."

"Right. Hey Paul, do me a favor?"

"Yeah, sure thing."

"Please tell Gary I do not want to be the last sweep on the bowls for the next blizzard."

Paul threw his head back and laughed. "You got it, man."

THE RIDE to the top of the mountain seemed to take forever, but when we arrived, I wished it had taken longer.

Waiting at the top was Stella's entire family, along with several snowmobiles and a half dozen ski patrol.

As soon as they saw us appear over the edge, the group of them burst out cheering. Panic swelled in my chest, my breath growing rapid and shallow. My hands began to shake, and I squeezed them tightly around my poles to make it less obvious.

"Well, look at that," Paul grinned, oblivious. "Looks like you're the new local hero."

My throat grew thick, and I couldn't answer. He obviously meant well, just didn't know why that would bother me.

Stella dismounted the chair lift ahead, sliding one-footed on her board down to her waiting family. They flurried around her, switching off for hugs and shooing her to the nearest dark snowmobile.

My stomach churned, and as we approached the dismount, I wished hopelessly that they'd all turn and descend with her and forget me completely.

It was a vain wish, of course.

I pulled my mask all the way up, concealing my face completely and hoping I could disappear into the crowd of matching uniforms. But when we skied toward the group, Paul announced me. "Here he is folks, two weeks in and already a hero!"

Despite the frigid temperatures outside, my body was soaked with sweat. I didn't want this. I didn't want *any* of it. It was too many people, too confusing, too reminiscent of the last time with the bright light and people congratulating me, thanking me, for doing my job.

Reece cut through the crowd, and bear hugged me so tightly I couldn't breathe. Surprisingly, the tension in my chest eased, and when he released me, I pulled in a slow, deep breath.

Tapping his helmet to mine, he said, "Thank you, brother. How are you?"

"I'm good, man. I'm in desperate need of a shower, of course, but other than that..." I joked feebly.

"Well, I daresay you earned that, and a lot more," he chuckled. "Come on, let me give you a ride down the mountain. You can come to my place and clean up."

"Aren't you going to go with Stella?"

"No, my folks are taking her straight to the ER for an MRI. She says she's fine, but you know how she is. Anyway, they won't take no for an answer, so it'll be a couple of hours until she's home."

"Okay. Thanks for the offer, but I think I want to take the scenic route down. I'll meet you there?"

"Sure thing, Sebastian. You know how to find me."

"Yep. I'll see you soon."

Reece slapped me on the shoulder, then turned and mounted one of the dark green snowmobiles with the golden Aspen Ridge logo on the side. He followed two others, one with his mom, and the other with his dad and Stella. She turned and looked in my direction, but with her goggles down, I couldn't read her expression.

She stared for a moment, then turned her head the other way and squeezed tightly to her dad's back as then began the descent toward the resort.

CHAPTER
FOURTEEN

STELLA

O f course I had a concussion, albeit a very minor one. Other than a few bumps and bruises they deemed me fine, but in need of a new helmet thanks to the divot I'd given myself in my favorite one.

But my mind, which should have been mentally preparing to catch up on my competition prep, was fully occupied with thinking about Sebastian.

I'd been so certain of everything, so *sure*, right until the moment Sebastian said he wasn't.

Then it was as if the entire gingerbread house I'd built in one night had crumbled around me.

He didn't know what was going to happen? *He didn't know?*

Everything seemed crystal clear to me. He confessed that the reason he fucked up in the first place was because he was scared, and now he wasn't any more.

Isn't that what he meant? Or was I reading too much into it?

When I got home I took a quick shower, then drew a hot bath and soaked the ache out of my body while my mind raced.

I started picking every moment apart, word by word, and scrutinizing it.

A sick feeling grew in my stomach. Despite all of his talk about the past... when he talked about not being weak anymore, did he just mean sex? He said he *wanted* me, he never said he *loved* me.

Oh god, the realization hit me like a school bus. This was *exactly* like before. He showed the smallest amount of interest in me and I ran wild with it. He offered sex, and I accepted love. No amount of tender kisses and sweet caresses meant anything more than what he explicitly said.

And he *never* said he loved me. That one was all on me.

I told myself I wouldn't cry, not this time. I was no heartbroken little girl. I was a grown woman who knew how to handle herself.

Besides, this grown woman had a lot on her plate. Way too much to worry about what was going on in the mind of one Sebastian Delacruz.

Before I went to bed, I stretched my aching muscles, working through an easy mobility routine. David already approved for me to be on the hill again tomorrow, so long as I took it easy and avoided the terrain park.

I needed to get my head back in the game, put my focus where it belonged, and give this run my all. Because I'd been honest with Sebastian; if I didn't get anywhere this time, I was done.

So it was now or never, do or die, whatever other sports cliche existed.

Starting tomorrow.

SEBASTIAN

I WAS STARTING to think this job might actually kill me.

In the wake of my 'heroic' rescue of the resort sweetheart, I was suddenly infamous around Aspen Ridge. Some idiot found out my name and dug my old boot camp photo out from the depths of the internet, publishing an article in the Aspen Ridge Star with my dorky head shot next to one of Stella's glamorous Branton Snowboards photos. The article made my teeth ache from clenching every time I thought about it. They made it sound like I was some unknown rescuer who swooped into town and saved the village sweetheart—there was not a single mention that I'd actually grown up here. It was as if Aspen Ridge had forgotten all about me the moment I was no longer on the football team.

To top it off, one of my lovely coworkers clipped the article and pinned it to the corkboard in the Ski Patrol office. In my heart, I knew they meant well; they were honestly proud of me, and this was their way of showing appreciation.

But it reminded me too much of the last time people thought I was something special, and I felt like anything but a hero.

Gary tried to give me a few days off, but I insisted on continuing to work. It was all I had to distract me, and even that wasn't doing a good job, because I was mainly following Stella.

I tried to keep my distance; I didn't want her to know I was watching. She'd probably think I'd turned into some kind of stalker.

But really, I was just incredibly, irrationally afraid that she'd hurt herself and no one would be there to help her. Reece and his parents were keeping pretty close tabs on her in the wake of her recent accident, so it wasn't hard to wheedle her plans out of my best friend to check up on my patient.

And I knew that with every day that passed, she probably hated me more. I should have talked to her, had some kind of conversation—*anything* rather than leaving it the way I did.

But I didn't know what to say. She was all I thought about, all I wanted, and I couldn't have her. Even if Reece was miraculously okay with the thought of me dating his little sister, I was so worried about her safety I could barely function, and we weren't even... well, *anything*. Finding her facedown in the snow like that had crossed some wire in my brain, combining her image with Andrews from my old unit, and now I kept picturing her covered with blood in the snow. It was like my head took two traumas and combined them into one super trauma. Now I found myself so worried that she'd end up dead or disabled that

I couldn't think about anything else, couldn't react or treat her with a clear train of thought; it was just panic.

And she didn't need one more person in her life standing in the way of her dreams. With everything I'd been through, and everything she'd been through, there was no way we wouldn't be toxic together. I had to tamp down on the warm, glowing memories of that last night in the cabin and focus on what Stella needed; there was certainly no place for me in her life, not in that context.

So I couldn't risk growing even more attached, and I certainly couldn't let her see just how messed up I truly was. It was one thing to confess to being messed up by some past trauma. It was another entirely to continue traumatizing myself about things that hadn't even happened, and to tell the object of that fear about it.

But there was no reason I couldn't keep an eye on her. Being concerned about her safety was a normal, brotherly thing to do. So it wasn't really trauma so much as concern for someone I cared deeply for.

I drew in a deep sigh and released it slowly.

Everything was fine; I needed to stop building

minor issues up to mountains. There was nothing wrong with my worrying about Stella's reckless-ness, and nothing strange about me wanting to check up on her.

It was totally normal.

CHAPTER
FIFTEEN

STELLA

In my head, it seemed so simple to avoid Sebastian. We'd never exchanged numbers, and I could hardly imagine him hitting Reece up for mine after what he said—which, now that I remembered it, I needed to have a talk with my brother about that one, too—but I assumed it was a big mountain and as we both obviously wanted to avoid each other, it shouldn't be too difficult.

The problem being that I immediately began running into him everywhere.

I promised David I'd stick to blue runs for a

few days until I felt recovered, so I was dutifully cruising a nice groomer when I paused at an intersection for a drink from my water bottle, and who should pull up a second later from the other trail but Sebastian.

He was with another ski patrol, and of course they wore helmets with goggles along with matching uniforms, but I'd recognize that jaw, those lips, anywhere.

"Hey, Stella Blackwell, how are you doing? Fancy running into you here so soon after you escaped captivity with my man here." The unknown ski patroller clapped Sebastian on the shoulder.

I smiled broadly. "Yeah, gotta get back after it, you know. Regionals are in a couple of weeks."

"Glad you made it through safe! We're all rooting for you."

"Thanks so much. I really appreciate the support."

Sebastian finally found voice enough to speak, although it was tense and awkward. "Hey, Stella, good to see you."

"Yeah, you too. Well, I'd better be off. Later!"

I cranked up my music and slipped away without looking back. My heart clenched at his emotionless greeting, considering that the last time I'd seen him we'd been naked together. He'd kissed my forehead.

But if there was anything I knew, it was that men didn't see things the same way women did.

So if he was determined to go back to being just acquaintances, then I wouldn't let him interfere with my plans, either.

It was a great idea, except he seemed to be everywhere. I saw him constantly on the slopes or at my brother's place. The first time I stopped by Reece's after the cabin Sebastian was there, and after my heart finally dropped out of my throat, I made an excuse to leave and avoid the entire confrontation. It was absolutely unfair that the one place I could go, the *one place* that had always been my refuge, was now a minefield of emotional torment waiting to blow. And even though I knew no promises had been made and no expectations set, it still felt like a betrayal to have him hold me so tenderly, apologize for everything he'd done, and whisper that he'd always wanted me... then act as if he didn't know me at all the next day.

Because he wasn't a stranger. He wasn't a random guy from the bar I'd never see again. So it was one thing to hook up and go our separate ways.

It was another entirely for him to remind me

constantly he existed in every space that was supposed to be my sanctuary. I didn't hate him any more, but everything that happened at the cabin had cracked me wide open to him again, and no matter how I tried, I couldn't seal it back up.

THREE DAYS after the cabin incident, David finally cleared me to do tricks. He planned to meet me at the terrain park for some basics to warm up before we move over to the half-pipe. We got it reserved for later in the morning, when I should be all warmed up and ready to go.

It felt like it'd been ages since I did so much as tail press on a rail, let alone a backside rodeo. Nervous energy zipped through my veins, making my hands shake as I laced up my snow boots.

While preparing my backpack, I couldn't help throwing in a few more snacks than I really needed. I'd done it every day since the back bowls, fearing that I could get stuck without food again and be in a worse situation than before. We were extremely lucky there was so much there to eat. In fact, my dad told me he'd had a case of camping food delivered there, just because I'd talked about what a lifesaver it was.

I hesitated zipping the pack, and after a few moment's indecision, I slipped my flask inside. For some reason, Sebastian's voice was in my head, telling me it wasn't normal to need a buzz to do something I loved. But it'd been a rough few days, and it wasn't like I'd be knockdown drunk. I just might need an extra hit of courage today.

My parents, if not encouraging of my need to keep training immediately after my fall, had apparently become resigned to it. "Have a good day on the slopes, Bug," my dad said as I headed for the door.

"Thanks Dad, have fun at work," I replied with a grin, giving him a sarcastic salute.

"Hey, it's always a great day at Aspen Ridge!" He called back.

I didn't reply, just made my way to the slopes, collecting my board at our condo locker on the way.

My heart beat relentlessly at my ribs while I rode up the chairlift. When I reached the terrain park, my blood was rushing so fast I was almost lightheaded. I sat in my usual spot and waited for David to arrive, putting the meditation app on in my headphones and working to calm myself down.

I turned it off when my coach rode up and plopped in the snow beside me.

"So, how you feeling today, Super Star?" David had a wide, easy grin, and for a coach he was pretty laid back. Not all that surprising, given that he was a snowboarding coach and a former Olympic medalist himself. Snowboarders just had a different vibe, which was one reason I'd sworn off skiing ages ago. The company was better.

"A little shaky," I admitted. "I haven't done a trick since I fell, and I still don't even remember what happened."

"No worries, Stell. Let's just take it easy, okay? We'll do a nice calm run down the terrain, do a few basics to get you warmed up, and go from there. Cool?"

"Cool." I nodded, even though I felt anything but cool.

"Alright, let's hit it. I'm going to give you free rein on this one. Just ride what you feel. Hit me with some excellent technique on the box and the rail. Try to do the small jump. You can pass on the big jump if you're not feeling it yet, alright?"

The pressure eased in my chest, just slightly. I didn't have to do any real tricks yet. "Sounds good." I pushed off and took the circuit down he prescribed, performing flawless tricks that I'd been working since I was eight. Impressive to the kids in the terrain park, but basic beginner stuff to anyone who considered themselves a pro.

However, it did what it was meant to do and reestablished my confidence. David cruised down the straight pass on the side, watching my technique.

After a quick indy grab on the short jump, I felt well enough to hit the big jump and pull a smooth Wildcat Weddle, easing into the landing and carving straight down to David.

"Alright," he exclaimed, holding up a mitten'd hand for a high-five. "Beautiful. How did that feel?"

"Great," I admitted, grinning. "Like riding a bike."

"See? You *got* it, Stella, you just gotta trust yourself. Okay, let's take the bar back to the top and do another run."

We ran a few more times, David assigning me more and more difficult tricks, until we were looking at some of my competition flips.

David lifted his goggles and regarded me seriously. "Okay, Stell, moment of truth. How about a Backside Rodeo 360 off the biggie? I'm thinking a straight shot down and just give it all you got."

My heart thumped, blood rushing through my

239

veins again. "I'm not sure, David. Shouldn't I save that for the half-pipe?"

"It's better to do it here, Stell. The angle is better, and you'll have more room to land if you don't get the timing perfect. The pipe isn't forgiving, you know that."

Even though I'd suddenly lost all the confidence I'd built up over the last hour, I knew he was right. This was a far safer place to hit those tricks than the pipe. I would have preferred the air bag for practice, but it got busted a few weeks ago and wouldn't be ready before the competition. Besides, David said we'd reached the point I had to stop using the bag as a crutch because I needed the confidence to know I'd land the trick.

"Yeah, you're right," I agreed. "Okay."

"Great, Stella. You got this! I'll see you at the bottom, Super Star."

I tried to breathe in and out slowly as I lined myself up for the big jump. Everyone in the park had long since taken a seat to watch me practice, and I could feel their eyes on me while I hesitated. The sudden craving for the whisky in my flask hit me hard, my mouth going dry just anticipating the burn it'd give me, the warmth spreading through my body and the dulling of the panic in my head.

But the flask was in my backpack with David,

and besides, there were a few dozen teenagers here watching me with starry eyes like I was some kind of hero. What kind of example would that give them?

The word hero stuck in my brain with derision, and like being struck by a lightning bolt, I understood Sebastian's aversion to the title. I felt like a fraud, having all these people think so highly of me and expect so much when I could barely keep my knees from shaking at the thought of facing that pipe. People called sports figures their heroes all the time, and if there was one thing I knew, it was that I didn't deserve to have anyone call me a hero.

I faced down the hill, planning my straight run to the high ramp with deep, deliberate breaths.

This is no big deal, Stella. You've done about a thousand of these, and landed them just fine. This fear is in your head. Your body knows what to do. Use the energy in your body, the energy of everyone here rooting for you, and execute.

With a last deep breath, I pushed off, crouching as I carved my way down to build up speed. The jump zoomed toward me, and I ran through the sequence of movements a split second before my body performed them, crouching even further and turning off my heel edge, springing at the last possible second as momentum carried me into the air and into the backflip. I kept my eyes open, monitoring for the ground, and on cue stretched my body out to slow rotation so I could land switch.

I executed the trick flawlessly, but the landing tweaked my knee and I crumpled to the ground, sliding the last several yards down. As disappointed as I was to end up on my back, I was relieved to have completed the 360 without losing my awareness of the ground. All in all, it was a success.

David, of course, saw what happened. "Yooo, what's up with the knee, Stell? The trick looked mint, but you crumbled on the landing."

"Yeah, I guess I should have told you; when I got the concussion I had some pain in my knee, but it went away after a day. Seems like there's still something going on in there."

He crouched by my side and probed the knee, causing me to wince. "Yeah, it's swollen. Dammit Stell, you should have told me, we could have been working that out these last few days. Now we're going to have to take another few off."

"Sorry, David, I honestly forgot about it. I iced it one day and then it was fine after." Relief and guilt washed through my stomach in equal measures.

"Yeah, I get it. Okay, lets-"

"Stella, what the *fuck* do you think you're doing?" I knew who it was, even before the bright red uniform appeared in my field of vision.

"Easy bro," David stood between us, defending me with his hands out. "She's not breaking any rules."

Sebastian pulled his goggles from his face, revealing dark eyes brimming with fury. "I don't give a fuck about her breaking rules, *bro*. She almost broke her *neck* doing that stupid trick. Are you *trying* to kill yourself?" He shouted at me around David.

"Man, you seriously need to calm down," David's tone grew sharper. "I'm her coach, and she's fine. I think you should go; you probably have somewhere else to be right now."

Another ski patroller arrived, whether because he saw the commotion or because Sebastian had left him in the dust to come yell at me, I wasn't sure. He took one look at the scenario and lifted his goggles to fix me with a direct stare. "Everything alright here?"

"I'm fine, Gary," I reassured him. "I just had a wobbly landing off a trick. David's got me."

"No the fuck you are *not* fine!" Sebastian's voice was so venomous I almost didn't recognize it. He moved to the left so he could see me clearly and continue his ranting. "You're going to *kill* yourself, Stella. I know death comes for all of us eventually, but you seem to be actively seeking it out."

"Sebastian-"

"But fuck everyone who cares about you, right? Because you've still got something to prove, and even if you die doing it, that's all that matters." Sebastian's eyes were so wild and furious that he almost looked like a different person. I didn't recognize the man I'd known since childhood in the one shouting at me; he was a complete stranger. My gaze was locked on his, and my pulse elevated. I realized that in this moment, I was actually afraid of him.

Gary slipped between us, drawing himself up to his full height and breaking our eye contact. I'd always known him as a rather serene person, but now his calm voice took on a sharp, commanding edge I'd never heard before. "Delacruz, that's *enough*. We've got everything in hand here, I want you to report directly to Patrol Command and wait for me there."

"But-"

"No *buts*, Delacruz, that was an order. *Now*."

Gary stood completely still and waited for Sebastian to comply. Even from here, with his back to me, I found his presence intimidating; I couldn't imagine what it was like on the other side.

Finally, Sebastian huffed loudly, then muttered, "Fuck this," before he pushed off and made his way down the hill.

Now that he was gone, I pulled in a few deep breaths, trying to calm my nerves. In the aftermath of his outburst, I was actually shaking.

David knelt by me once more. "Damn, that was wild. You okay Stell?"

"Yeah," I lied.

Gary clicked out of his skis and crouched by me as well. "Are you injured?" His voice was back to the soothing, fatherly tone I was used to.

"Just tweaked my knee. I forgot I hurt it when I fell a few days ago."

"Hmm." He probed my leg gently. "Do you think you can ride down to the aid station, or should we get a stretcher?"

"I'm fine to ride down. David will take care of me. I don't want to go to Patrol Command while he's there."

"Understandable," Gary replied calmly. "You

know Delacruz, right? Outside of the incident a few days ago?"

"Yeah, I've known him since we were kids. He's never acted like that before, though."

He ignored my last comment. "So, you know what he's been through in the last few years?"

"Yeah." The memory of Sebastian's story flooded my chest with guilt. I didn't want to think about it.

Gary's eyes remained trained on my leg as he worked his fingers gently down my calf, checking for any other problem areas. "People respond to trauma differently, Stella. Sometimes they're completely fine. Other times, they lash out at the people they care about for seemingly insignificant things. That doesn't make it okay, but I hope you won't hold it against him. Did any of that hurt, aside from the knee?"

I shook my head. "No."

He stood up, offering me a hand. "I think you're good to ride down, and I trust David to take care of you, but we're always available if you need us."

"Thanks, Gary. I really appreciate it." I accepted the pull and tested putting weight on my injured leg. It ached a bit, but wouldn't keep me from carving if I took it easy.

"I'll have a chat with Delacruz, see if I can figure out what's going on. Regardless, we'll make sure he's not interrupting your training."

"Thanks," I repeated. "He... I don't want him to get in trouble, though."

Gary shot me a small smile, and it softened his stern face. "He isn't in trouble. We just need to address a few things. But I'm sure he'll appreciate your concern."

"Thank you."

The older man nodded, then clipped into his skis and rode off.

I waited for David to strap into his board, and we carved a long, careful line down the mountain together.

Once again, my brain should be frantically calculating how this setback would affect my preparations for regionals.

But all I seemed to think about was what Gary had to say about Sebastian, and how I wasn't even mad at him for screaming at me.

I was worried about him.

CHAPTER
SIXTEEN

SEBASTIAN

My fury at Stella didn't survive the ride down the hill.

By the time I reached Patrol Command, guilt bubbled in my stomach, along with a healthy dose of shame.

I shouldn't have yelled at her like that. I knew it.

But seeing her flying through the air, then falling on the ground in a heap, flipped my switch from concerned to terrified in a nanosecond. When I saw she was alive, it transferred immediately to rage.

Because that didn't have to happen. She was putting herself in that situation again and again, despite everyone who loved her begging her not to.

It was one thing to have someone die because of something you couldn't control, couldn't expect. It was another completely to see someone die when you could have prevented it.

I racked my skis and marched into Patrol Command, resigned that I was about to be fired. We were absolutely not supposed to lose our temper on guests, and since I was still on probation, Gary was definitely going to hand me my walking papers. He'd been waiting for me to fuck up, and it finally happened.

After hanging up my coat, I grabbed a cup of coffee and took a seat by Gary's office, tipping my head back against the wall and allowing my eyes to close. If only I could sleep at night, I wouldn't be on edge all the time. I'd grown accustomed to working on a few hours of sleep, since that seemed to be all my body allowed me any more. The one night I'd had with Stella was the most sleep I'd had in months, but it didn't happen again since.

"Hey kid, come on in." Gary walked by, heading into his office and leaving the door open.

I took a deep breath and released it, then stood and followed him.

"Go ahead and close the door, Sebastian."

He used my first name. That was definitely not good. Nor was closing the door.

I did as he instructed, then took my seat. Gary had yet to look at me; he was removing his snow gear, hanging it on a stand in the corner of his cramped office.

When he finally sat down, he ran a hand through his mat of silvery hair.

"How are you doing?"

"I'm fine."

"Are you really?" Gary fixed me with his icy stare. It felt like x-ray vision that could see straight through my bullshit. "Because that out there didn't seem fine to me."

"I know I shouldn't have lost my temper on a guest."

"True, but she's not just a regular guest, is she? And that wasn't just losing your temper."

A ball of anger flared up inside my chest. "No, she's not just a regular guest, she's like family. And of course, seeing her be so reckless pissed me off. She almost *died* last time, and she gives zero thought about what happens if she actually succeeds this time."

"I may be confused here, but I'm pretty sure she's an adult in her own right. I don't think she needs anyone's permission to do what she wants."

"She is," I ground out between my teeth.

"And from what I saw, she was under the supervision of her coach, and performed the trick well, with minimal risk."

"Did you see the part where she fell?" I snarled.

Gary's tone remained neutral. "It's been my experience that snowboarders doing tricks fall often. As long as they're doing them in designated areas, it's really not the resort's concern. They undertake the activity at their own risk, and we provide aid if needed. Most do not have the benefit of years of training or a full-time coach like Ms. Blackwell does. She's probably one of the most qualified on property to do those stunts."

"That doesn't make it any safer."

"Why are you so concerned about it?" He continued in his calm, thoughtful line of questioning.

My response was regrettably not as calm. "Because I don't want her to break her neck!"

"What's it to you if she does?"

"I told you, she's like family."

"So?"

"So I care that she's okay."

"And what would you say to the fact that she's an adult who can choose for herself, despite your feelings about it?" His patient condescension only stoked my anger.

"It doesn't matter. I can't let it happen."

"You can't let what happen?"

"I can't let someone else die on my watch!"

He paused, then asked, "Why is it your responsibility?"

My eyes dropped to my hands, fingers clenching and twisting together, and my voice cracked with emotion when I admitted, "Because I can't live with another death on my hands. I can't... I can't take another one. I won't survive it."

Gary's voice took on that sage, ageless tone. "I know what you went through, Sebastian. I've seen your service record; those deaths were not your fault."

My tone became flat and robotic. "They were my team; I was responsible for them. They died under my command." It was a refrain I'd repeated thousands of times to myself.

"That's true, but it doesn't make it your fault that they're dead."

I raised my eyes to his in challenge. "How? If it

was my responsibility to take care of them, then it's failure of my duties that they're dead."

Gary's icy gaze softened. "You're twisting logic to take responsibility that's not yours to shoulder."

"No, my logic is faultless."

"Did your command find you guilty of dereliction of your duties?"

"No, but they always gloss over those things. They don't want to look bad."

"Do the families blame you for the deaths of their loved ones?" His tone was soft, steady, and extremely gentle.

That brought a lump to my throat, along with a prickling sensation at the back of my eyes. I clenched my jaw to hold the emotion back. They'd all called me a hero and thanked me for looking out for my troops. "No."

"So why do you blame yourself?"

I couldn't hold the emotion back anymore, so I buried it under a heavy layer of derision. "I already told you. This is fucking stupid. There's no point in sitting here talking around in circles all day. Just fire me and be done with it."

Gary sighed heavily, then templed his fingers in front of him. "Sebastian, I'm not going to fire you. Your outburst was unwarranted, but it's not a termination-worthy event. However, I think you would benefit from talking through some things in your past that are affecting you today."

My derisive snort was half-hearted. "I did everything they told me to do. I talked to the shrink. I did physical therapy. I went to meetings. I passed it all with a clean bill of health."

"I know, as well as you do, that what ends up on paper isn't always the reality. The military provides the services, and they can make you attend, but they can't make you participate. If you're not open to help, if you've already made up your mind about your own guilt, they can't help you. I also know that it's very easy to give them the answers they want to hear; their job is to get you back in service, so the easier you make it on them, the faster everything goes. I'd be willing to bet you showed up where they told you to, but you didn't really open yourself to the help they offered."

"You think you know me so well, huh?"

At that, Gary actually chuckled. "Kid, I *am* you. I served, I watched people die. People I cared about, people I was responsible for. I convinced everyone I was fine, so they kept sending me back. But I wasn't fine, and I got worse and worse. I started making poor decisions because I was afraid. I endangered my troops' lives because I was unfit to lead, since I never really dealt with my issues. I ended up getting kicked out with a less-than-honorable discharge after receiving enough awards to fill a wall."

That pulled me up short. "They offered me an honorary to get out early."

Gary nodded sagely. "Then you're already smarter than I was, on some level. I refused to admit I had a problem until I fucked up so badly they kicked me out. I have a lot of regrets in my life, Sebastian, and not addressing those issues earlier is one of the big ones."

"Look," I sighed, abruptly weary, "I appreciate that you're trying to help me, but I've got this under control. I swear I'm not a loose cannon. I just feel especially protective of Stella because we go back so far. I'll avoid her and keep my mouth shut, mind my business when she's training. Okay?"

Gary's eyes closed, and he breathed in deeply before pushing out a long, slow release. "You're your own man, Sebastian. I can't tell you what to do. But make sure you keep yourself in check or we'll have to address this again. And I'm always here if you change your mind about getting some help. I have someone who would see you right away. You just have to ask."

"Thanks, I'll keep it in mind," I muttered as I

stood. I had no intent of talking to anyone about it, but I'd say anything to get out of here.

"Alright. Well, I want you to take the rest of the afternoon off. No, that's not a request," he insisted sharply when I started to protest. "Go home and find your peace. I'll see you tomorrow."

My jaw clenched, fists balled at my sides, but I knew he wasn't going to budge on this one. I didn't bother saying goodbye, just showed myself out of his office and closed the door behind me.

The rest of the afternoon... I checked my watch. It wasn't even noon yet! What the hell was I supposed to do?

A crowd of ski patrollers were in the lounge area, shedding jackets and waiting for their turn to heat up leftovers in the single microwave. I pushed through them to retrieve my jacket, not bothering to register their faces.

"Excuse me, it's Sebastian, right? Sebastian Delacruz?" I turned to find a thin older woman with a long braid of thick grey hair tossed over her shoulder. Her tanned face had seen a lot of mountain sun, but she smiled warmly with perfect teeth. "We haven't met, but I've seen you a couple of times. I'm Doris."

I pulled my arms through the sleeves and accepted her proffered hand. "Nice to meet you,

Doris." If my flat tone was an indicator of my lack of interest in this conversation, she didn't seem to pick up on it.

"We were all very impressed with your rescue of the Blackwell girl, especially being so early in your first season. That was some really fast thinking, and you handled it all so well!" She beamed like a proud grandma.

"Thank you," I replied dully, zipping my coat and tugging my gloves from the pockets.

"I heard you actually grew up here, too! And after a stint in the Army you've returned and jumped immediately into hero mode yet again."

My pulse jumped and my hands curled into fists. It took all of my control to grind out, in a somewhat even tone, "I'm not a hero."

"Oh, nonsense," Doris beamed. "Hey Mitchell," she called over her shoulder, "the young man who rescued the Blackwell girl is over here. I was just telling him what a hero-"

"I'M NOT A FUCKING HERO!" The shout ripped from my chest, my throat raw from the force behind the words. It rolled across the room like a thunderclap, practically echoing off of the walls.

The group of people who'd been milling around and chatting amiably went completely still and silent. Their heads snapped in my direction, every set of eyes wide and concerned. Panic rose in my throat. My gaze traveled across them, a sea of red and black and frightened faces; frightened at me. And near the back of the crowd, standing in the hallway, Gary stared at me with a calm, knowing expression in his icy blue eyes. His gaze held a heavy weight of meaning, so clear I could practically hear his voice in my ear.

You're fine, are you?

With no idea how to salvage the moment, I turned on my heel and marched out of the building.

CHAPTER
SEVENTEEN

STELLA

Icy wind chased me down the busy sidewalk on Main, pushing me toward my final destination. When I eventually pulled the door open, the warm, comforting scent of pastries and coffee wrapped around me like a cozy blanket, and I hobbled over to the fireplace chairs in relief.

David had insisted that I wear a knee brace for a few days to get the swelling in my knee to calm down. He was an interesting combination of chill and concerned; chill because he was eternally laid back—I'd swear he could literally be on fire, and he'd just shrug and roll in the snow. Concerned

261

because we were only two weeks away from regionals now and I was in a leg brace.

Since I couldn't practice, I was an anxious mess, so I got Madison to meet me for another coffee date. Of course, having nothing to do while she was working meant I got here far too early, but I didn't mind waiting. At least I wasn't at home.

David agreed to keep the leg brace between us so my parents wouldn't freak out, which meant I had to be extra careful to hide it from them. The metal and velcro contraption was easy to conceal beneath baggy snow pants, but it took a lot of work to disguise my stiff-legged hobble.

I got a giant mug of steaming deliciousness, then reclaimed my seat and propped my leg up on a footstool. With nothing to do but wait, I whipped out my phone to check in on social media. I had an assistant who basically ran my accounts, but I liked to pop in and post something live every once in a while, interact with fans a bit. It always gave me a boost and right now I was sorely in need of one.

It shouldn't have come as a surprise, but when I tapped on a notification that someone named Dylan tagged me in a photo, I honestly had no idea who it was. Then the carousel on Instagram pulled up and I couldn't help it; I burst out laughing. I'm clearly in the middle of turning toward him, smiling, and his lips are pressed to my face. Somehow, he still managed an impish grin for the photo, and as I swiped through the rest, I saw he included several of the poses I took intentionally with him as well.

The comments were wild, naturally. Lots of people congratulating him on his luck, and Dylan admirably glossing over how he had met me by eating it hard on the moguls in the first place. The post itself was complimentary, in the awkward way only a thirteen-year-old boy could be, and I didn't even have the energy to be pissed at him. The admiration was clear, and I'd evidently provided him with the best day of his life.

Deciding to give him another thrill, I commented it was a pleasure to meet him, and then went back to reviewing my account.

Andrea, my assistant, did a pretty good job choosing images and replying to comments. I usually just forwarded her anything that David took while we were practicing—the man knew how to get action shots—and she had access to my imagery from Branton, so it was always a pretty good mix.

Finally, I snapped a photo of my mug with my feet up in front of the fire and made a little post about resting up before the big day. Immediately comments and likes started flooding in. People telling me I deserved a rest, others saying they were rooting for me or knew I'd kill it in qualifying. Each new heart was a tiny hit of dopamine, and a wave of warmth spread through my body to see these people, mostly literal strangers, who were excited for me.

Of course, the inevitable backlash came swiftly; the deep, aching hurt that these strangers were more invested in my career than anyone I called family. But instead of dwelling on it, I focused on replying to as many comments as I could until Madison arrived.

She eventually rolled in, still in her forest green Aspen Ridge employee uniform. When she had her drink in hand and shucked her heavy coat, she settled her focus on me.

"Okay, Stella. Hit me."

A wave of emotion caught in my throat. "Mads, I don't even know where to start."

"Well, why don't you start with being snowed in with that hot ski patrol guy? I've seen him around a few times, and *woof*. He's not your average ski patroller."

I snorted. "Yeah, that's for damn sure. So, I

guess I should tell you we grew up together, for starters. And he's a complete dick."

"What?!" She leaned in for the story, her light brown eyes wide.

"He was my brother's best friend. He left for the Army and when he got out, Reece got him the job."

Madison sipped her coffee and nodded. "Ah, that makes more sense. But why is he a dick?"

"I don't want to get into all that history, just suffice it to say that he was pretty awful to me in high school and I would have been happy to never see him again."

"Then he ends up here, working for your resort... and you get stuck alone with him in the back bowls." Madison's sympathetic gaze warms my heart.

"Yes, exactly. It wasn't the romantic scenario it sounds like, we basically spent the entire time fighting. I had a concussion—thankfully a minor one—and it was a one-room shack that didn't even have a door to the toilet—which is a compost toilet, by the way."

"Eww," Madison pulled a face. "What happened, anyway? How did you get stuck back there?"

"I don't know, exactly. I was tearing down the

hill, trying to make it back to the lift as the storm came in, and then... nothing. I don't remember anything. I guess Sebastian found me and took me to the cabin. The storm was so bad they couldn't come in for a rescue, and we were stuck."

"Honestly, that sounds horrible. Were you scared?"

"Not really. I was kind of out of it the first day." Then, begrudgingly, I added, "It did help that Sebastian was there. He managed the fire, made food... took care of me, really."

Madison lifted a brow. "But he's a dick, and you fought the entire time?"

"It's not as simple as it sounds," I snapped, then immediately regretted it and softened my tone a smidge. "He was a total jerk. He kept bossing me around, and he'd be fine one minute, then bite my head off the next. There was nowhere to go to get away from each other. We were just stuck in that one room, and he kept making a big deal about what I should and shouldn't do because I had a concussion. I couldn't even get a minute to myself to think. And then I was worrying about regionals because of the concussion and my knee, and he started lecturing me about that, too."

"That does sound shitty," Madison agreed.

"But maybe he was worried about you? If you've known him that long-"

"Sebastian Delacruz doesn't care about anyone but himself," I snarled.

"Woah, okay, easy Stell. I'm on your side, remember?"

I released a heavy breath. "I'm sorry, I know. I just-" I hesitated, not sure if I wanted to confess to the next part. But this was Madison. When most of my high school friends had moved away or moved on, she'd just arrived and started working at Aspen Ridge. If there was anyone I considered a best friend now, it was her.

She waited patiently for me to think it over, sipping her drink, and I caved. "Okay look, I'm gonna tell you something, but you have to promise not to tell ANYONE else. Got it?"

Madison's eyes lit up, and she leaned in closer. "Of course, Stella, you know I won't."

A bubble of excitement rose in my chest—to be honest, I'd been desperate to talk about it, but being so pissed at Sebastian I didn't want to tell anyone. It was so full of complicated feelings.

"So, the second night we were in the cabin, we were both bored and we started playing card games."

"Okay..."

This was going to require more explanation. "Look, the reason I hated him in high school was because I had a huge crush on him and he humiliated me in front of the entire school. I don't want to go into details," I cut off the question she'd opened her mouth to ask, "but the point being, yes, I've always thought he was hot."

"Go on," she encouraged, eyes sparkling.

"So eventually, I was so tired of the bickering and the tension I cracked open my emergency flask. We started drinking-"

"And you played strip poker?"

"No!"

"Sorry, go on."

"Okay, so we started drinking, and that turned into truth or dare, and somehow we got to talking about high school and... it got crazy from there."

"What does 'crazy' mean, exactly?" Madison asked suspiciously.

"He said he did what he did in school because Reece told him to leave me alone, but that he really liked me, and he told me some terrible stuff that happened while he was gone in the Army, and I dunno I guess it all softened me up and I thought we had this connection finally, and..." I had a difficult time finding the next words.

"... And?"

I shot her a meaningful stare. "And you know."

"I knew it!" She crowed, then glanced around the coffee shop and lowered her voice. "So... how was it?"

Finally getting my confession out, the warm rush of endorphins from the memory brought a smile to my lips. "It was pretty awesome, considering the situation we were in. And I thought we'd resolved things, that we were finally on the same page, but then the rescue came and he instantly switched back to being a complete asshole."

"No! Why?"

"I have no idea. It was like he regretted it and wanted to act like it never happened. So we reached the top of the mountain and went our separate ways."

"And you haven't seen him since?"

"No, that's the messed up part. He is *everywhere* I go. And yesterday I was in the terrain park with David and I landed a trick slightly off and Sebastian came out of nowhere and started ripping me a new one for being selfish and not caring about my family."

"That's fucked up. Why would he say that?"

"I dunno," I shrugged. "He's been toeing the family line this entire time, which is strange in itself. It's bad enough my parents don't want me

269

to compete and keep hounding me to take a job at the resort. Reece is slightly better, but he still agrees that I should cut back. And apparently Sebastian has settled himself right in with all of them and thinks he knows what's best for me, too."

"What do you mean, 'what's best for you?'"

"Well, you know how I'm doing the four events, right?" She nodded. "Somehow, adding the two that are more speed than trick events has made them all decide that I should drop the half-pipe and slope style altogether. Those are my *best* events. I've never competed in the others before. It's like they've all collectively decided what I'm supposed to do, and no one cares what *I* think I should do. It's coming at me from all sides and I'm sick of it." A momentary twinge of guilt twisted my stomach—I'd never told Madison exactly how *much* I struggled with doing the tricks since my accident, but it wasn't really relevant. She knew I had a hard time getting back into it.

"That's shitty, Stella. I'm so sorry. But you feel solid now, right?"

"Well, yeah. I didn't land the trick right because I tweaked my knee when I crashed in the bowls and I didn't realize it was still an issue, so I have a brace on now," I admitted.

"Oh no! Are you going to be ready for regionals?"

"David said I will, so long as I do exactly what he prescribes from here on out."

"What does your family say? Are they giving you a hard time?"

"They don't know about the knee. I can't hand them another thing to get on my case about."

Madison's gaze shifted to concern. "I know you're trying to avoid more lectures, but don't you think they should know? They're just concerned about you."

"Yeah, I'll pass thanks. I'll be fine in a couple of days and then it won't matter, anyway. No point in telling them and then hearing about it for the next six months."

"Okay, if you think so." Madison sat back and took another sip from her drink. "So, what about Sebastian? Are you going to talk to him?"

I snorted. "No, I'm trying to avoid him at all costs. I'm just as likely to get chewed out as I am to get a 'hi' from him. It's like he's bipolar or something, and I don't have the energy to put into figuring him out. I have a competition to win."

"That's fair."

"So," I said, a guilty feeling swimming in my stomach. I had launched right into my issues without even asking about her. Brightening my tone, I asked, "What's new with you? The last time I saw you, we basically talked about your cousin the entire time and you and I haven't caught up properly in ages. Are you still seeing that bartender?"

She snorted a laugh. "Hell no, he's long gone. Apparently, he 'just wanted to keep things casual' even though he *also* wanted to move into my apartment."

"What?!"

"I *know*. I don't understand the thought process there."

"So what else is going on? Still enjoying ski school?"

"Yeah, it's great," she beamed. "I get to be on the slopes all day, and I mainly work with kids. I'm getting hired for more private lessons than group classes, which is fun. That's kind of like hanging out with my younger siblings at home."

"I didn't know your siblings were that young. How old are they?"

"Oh, yeah, my parents had a weird gap in there. Josiah is twelve and Avery is ten."

"Wow, that is a big gap. So you used to take them skiing?"

"Yeah, before I moved here, anyway. It was fun, and basically how I got the job."

"Do you have any regular clients or is it all just tourists?"

"Mostly tourists, but I was going to tell you—James Tremont hired me to teach his kids."

"No way! That's awesome, I love Liam and Ava. And a regular gig is definitely good."

"Yeah, I thought I'd get the scoop from you, see if they're good kids. I'm supposed to start in a couple of weeks. He wants daily lessons for like an hour and a half after school, which is perfect. My weekends are still free for other bookings and my days are mostly open."

"Yeah, they're great kids. You'll have a lot of fun. They've been without their mom for a few years, so I know James hasn't spent as much time with them on the snow as he'd like. I think he kind of threw himself into work, if I'm honest. Just another reason I don't want my life to be all about Aspen Ridge."

"So you don't neglect your fictitious kids when your theoretical husband dies?" Madison asked in a skeptical tone.

"Not that, exactly, of course. I just don't want to end up feeling like it's all I have, you know? I want something of my own, something I can point at and say, "*I* did that, all by myself. That is *mine*."

"Makes sense," she replied agreeably.

"So circling back to you again," I grinned, "sorry we keep getting off the rails into my drama. I'm a shitty friend."

She beamed back at me. "Nah, you're a good friend. You just have a lot going on."

"Well, everyone does. So since the bartender is out of the picture, are you seeing anyone else?"

"You know, I'm kind of over it for the moment. I'm thinking being single for the season is the way to be. I just want to hit the slopes, have fun with my girls, and just live my life, you know?"

"Now that I understand one hundred percent. Cheers to living our lives!"

It was a relief to talk with Madison about normal girl things, and to finally confess to someone what actually happened in that cabin. I felt less crazy acknowledging the truth instead of just trying to pretend it never happened, as Sebastian seemed determined to do.

But acknowledging these things also opened me up to the feelings that came with them. Because even though I was a grown woman, I was still a girl who got her heart stomped on by the same guy who hurt her in high school. It was a terrible, shitty cliche, but apparently Sebastian Delacruz was the one guy I couldn't just sleep with and chalk up to an alcohol-driven mistake. I knew what I was doing, despite the drinking. And I wanted it—I wanted him.

And I thought he wanted me, too.

Impossibly, I felt like I was right back where I'd been six years ago, with no one to tell and only myself to blame. Madison meant well, but she didn't really understand, and there was no point unloading on her. This wasn't hooking up with some hot guy at a bar; this was the man I'd been half in love with for most of my life, even as a little girl. I'd buried those feelings under layers of hate after homecoming, but all it took was one night alone in a cabin to soften me right back up again.

And then he betrayed me, *again*.

Not as obviously, not as publicly. Somehow, this felt worse. It was more personal, more private of a rejection.

And so my feelings about it remained private, too. It was easier to give Madison the watered down version with a more ambivalent response. If I kept the worst of it under wraps, I could maybe pretend it never happened at all, just like him.

CHAPTER
EIGHTEEN

SEBASTIAN

I t had been a terrible week, and no matter how hard I tried to push them down, my feelings for Stella would not be repressed. Now, more than ever, I wanted to tell her how I felt —How I *truly* felt, with no exceptions or excuses. I knew she probably hated me, maybe even more than she had before and which, again, I had brought on myself. But if I were to have even a chance to fix that with her, there was something I needed to do first.

So when Reece invited me over for dinner, I swallowed down my anxiety and agreed. I'd harbored this secret from him for too long, and with as much as he'd done for me, he deserved to hear the truth.

Reece's text told me to come in when I arrived, so I didn't bother knocking. I shouted a hello, and once my gear was properly stowed away I made my way into the kitchen. Reece was concentrating on a large pot on the stove, which emitted billows of fragrant steam. His entire place smelled homey and comforting, and a pang hit my stomach at the thought. The last time I'd felt that way was my final visit home to my parents, before they passed. The knowledge that I was about to blow up the only place that still felt like home settled like a sour lump in my stomach.

"Get a drink and pull up a chair," Reece flashed me a grin before returning to his masterpiece.

Sweat broke out on my upper lip, and I wiped it away quickly. "Yessir. It smells fantastic, man. Thanks for the invite." I helped myself to a glass of bourbon and returned to the island, nervous energy making my leg twitch. "Um, is there anything I can do?"

"Nah, just relax. Something tells me you haven't spent the last six years improving your cooking, and I remember what you were like before you left." He swiftly chopped some herbs and sprinkled them into the pot.

His comment dredged up a memory and pulled a chuckle from me. "Yeah well, that's not exactly fair, considering you're like some sort of cooking prodigy. How many people can make cheesecake on a campfire, anyway? You should consider yourself lucky I managed the hot dogs."

"I don't know if I'd call that 'managed', Sebastian. They were black on one side and cold on the other. I think we're just lucky they were pre-cooked."

"Fair enough," I conceded. "Cooking isn't one of my strengths. I prefer to leave it to the professionals."

"I think we can agree that we're lucky you have the strengths you do, so I'm happy to be the chef in this friendship." Reece turned around and picked up his own glass. "Cheers to you, my friend. I just wanted an opportunity to thank you properly for rescuing Stella."

"You don't have to thank me," I replied gruffly, guilt roiling in my stomach. In the past week I'd spent far too many hours replaying the memory of being with her in a way he definitely would not thank me for, to the point I feared it was written all over my face.

Reece, however, didn't seem to notice. "I know, she's like a little sister to you too, and you'd have done it for anyone, but I'm still grateful."

The guilt turned from a low bubble to a full boil, to the point I had to set my drink down for fear the nausea would make me sick all over his counter.

"I would do it for anyone," I agreed nervously. "But I mean, Stella's not a little girl anymore, either. She's pretty good at handling herself." My hands trembled, and I clenched them where they were safely hidden below the counter from Reece's watchful gaze.

My best friend's eyes narrowed slightly. "She may be an adult, but she's still my little sister and I'll always worry about her. That will never change."

"Of course," I conceded quickly. "I'm just saying it's not like I did that much."

He snorted. "Didn't do that much? Aside from rescuing her from a snowdrift, hauling her to the warming house, tending to her injuries, and keeping the both of you alive for two days, you mean?"

"Yeah, aside from that," I chuckled, covering for my tight voice and hoping it didn't sound forced.

But Reece relaxed and went back to his cooking. "I guess that's what it's like being a hero; you don't think saving lives is a big deal anymore."

I bristled at the word, but tried to keep my calm. "Don't call me a hero, Reece. I just did my job."

"Why not? You clearly are, all those medals and-"

"Just don't call me that, okay?" It came out way sharper than I intended, and I sounded on the verge of losing it, even to myself.

This time Reece picked up on it, turning back around slowly. "Okay, Sebastian, I won't." Long pause. "Is everything... okay?"

"Yeah, I'm fine," I muttered, lying through my teeth. I was most certainly *not* okay. "It's just been a long week."

"Didn't they give you any time off? Especially after all of that, you should have had a break."

"I didn't want any time off." My bubbling nerves had transformed into annoyance at Reece's poking.

Reece regarded me seriously. "You may not have wanted it but you probably needed it, man. You won't get in trouble for taking time off here, you know that, right? Especially in this case. They wouldn't use your PTO. We're a family, you don't have to-"

The fury rose in my body like a tsunami. "I don't want time off!" I snarled. "I was just doing my job, and I'm not a hero for it. I don't want any kind of accolades, and I don't want time off. I just want to keep working, alright?"

Reece's face went completely neutral, and he studied me for a long, silent moment.

With no additional stimuli, the rage disappeared as swiftly and it had arrived. I drew in a deep breath and blew it out. "I'm sorry, Reece. I... I guess I'm still adapting, and it's harder than I thought. I shouldn't take it out on you."

He waited another moment, then finally asked, "Adapting to what?" His voice was low and even, and it reminded me of the shrinks I'd seen.

"All of it, really. Civilian life, being here, my parents being gone, life after... everything that happened. It feels like... like there's no place that's quite right anymore. Things are the same, but then they're not. And they may look the same, but they feel different. Or maybe I'm the one that's different. I mean, it's probably me. But I don't know what that means or what I'm supposed to do. I just feel... lost and frustrated a lot." I didn't know it until the words were out of my mouth, but that was certainly more thought than I'd given to my feeling in quite a while.

Reece walked around the island to stand next to me, and I kept my gaze on my glass. "I'm sorry you're going through that, Sebastian. I knew, even though you shared a great deal, there was still a lot you weren't telling me while you were away. I figured you'd tell me eventually, or it was something you didn't want to share, and either way is fine. But you know I'm always here for you, right?"

He waited, and I nodded without glancing up.

"Whatever you need, whether it's to talk or listen or to find a distraction, I'm here for you. Even if it doesn't make sense. I don't want you to ever feel you can't tell me something. Brothers for life, right?"

"Yeah, brothers for life," I repeated hollowly.

"Okay, come here." He slapped me on the back and I stood, accepting the half-hug.

The guilt returned, gnawing a hole in my sour stomach. He said I could tell him anything. He *said* brothers for life, but I still wasn't convinced that included his sister.

So I kept my mouth shut as he went back around the island to finish dinner. As if trying to make up for the tension earlier, even though it was entirely my fault, Reece became extra talkative while he cooked. I did my best to return his energy, but it felt false, hollow.

Because for as long as I kept this secret, I wasn't being the friend I promised him.

The plaintive cry of a cat drew my attention right before the furry beast leaped on the counter and nearly sent me diving for the floor.

"Ah, I wondered when Baxter would come out and say hi," Reece commented with delight.

Even though I hadn't dropped to my knees, I still shot back in my seat, as far away from the island as I could in one push. The cat, who obviously had no respect for personal space and did not get the hint, hopped on my lap and proceeded to rub its furry head against my chest.

"Aww, now see, Baxter missed you. Didn't you, Baxter?" His voice switched to his weird baby talk that was apparently reserved just for the cat. I still couldn't make it make sense with my beefy, bearded best friend.

"Yeah, great," I gasped, my heart still in my throat. The cat was either completely unaware or totally sadistic, because it continued to purr happily while my pulse raced.

My bet was on the latter.

Eventually, I calmed down enough to pet the damn thing, and then as if it knew the game was over, it dug its claws into my leg and pounced off. I released a silent scream from the sharp pain, not wanting Reece to know how little I cared for his beloved pet.

Fortunately, he missed the entire exchange. "Stew's ready; come over and grab a bowl, we'll sit at the island tonight." Reece pulled a tray of thick bread slices from the oven and held out a bowl as I dutifully hopped off my stool and approached.

I wasn't sure if this was a better or worse scenario for us to eat, honestly. The two of us sitting side by side was a lot more informal, but sitting across the table from him would afford me a second's head start if he decided to throttle me when I confessed the truth.

Through dinner I did my best to be some approximation of normal. Reece tried to catch me up on the happenings with people we knew from school. He rambled more than usual, and I suspected he sensed I wasn't really in the mood to talk.

We made it through the entire dinner, after which I helped him clean up the kitchen, and I still didn't manage to spit out the words. If all the people who called me a hero could see the real me, the one who couldn't be honest with his best friend, I had a feeling they wouldn't feel quite so strongly about my heroism.

When he invited me to hang out longer and have another drink, I realized this was my last shot. If I wanted even a chance to tell him without making it worse, it had to be now.

We took our glasses and settled in the living room. Reece sprawled on the couch with his trusty feline friend immediately claiming his lap. I chose a nearby chair and did my best to appear relaxed.

I realized there was no good way to start this conversation. I certainly wasn't going to open with the fact that I hooked up with his sister while we were stranded in a snowstorm and she was suffering from a concussion. I didn't think confessing that I had actually asked her to homecoming and then thrown her to the wolves was a great opener, either. And I really didn't want to tell him that the whole time we were in school, when I claimed to see her as a little sister, just like him, I was secretly fantasizing about her boobs.

But if not one of those options, what?

I rubbed my sweaty palms on my pants and wrapped a hand around my icy drink to help cool me down.

"So," I started awkwardly, "is Stella all set for regionals?"

"She says she is..." Reece's tone was dubious.

"I sense a 'but' coming."

"I dunno, she's been acting strange."

"Strange how?"

"Secretive. She avoids our parents, tells them as little as possible. I haven't even seen much of her the last week."

"Isn't that normal, if she's training and everything?"

"Maybe, I don't know. She's usually still around a lot. It's weird not to see her this much." His brow furrowed, and he seemed genuinely concerned.

"Do you think she's got a boyfriend or something?" Sweat trickled down my neck. Not the most subtle, but it was at least leaning in the right direction.

Reece unleashed a long, boisterous laugh. "No way, man. The only time I've seen Stella with a guy is in the off season, and they rarely last the whole summer. It's like she tries it out, decides it's not worth it, then goes back to snowboarding."

"Well, maybe she just hasn't met the right guy yet."

Clearly my attempts at being casual were failing miserably, because Reece leveled a flatbrowed stare in my direction. "Why are you so interested all of a sudden?"

My heart leapt against my rib cage, pure panic flooding my system. This was my chance to warm him up to the idea, and I still didn't know how to do it.

I hesitated too long, then coughed to delay a little longer. "Ahem, well, we talked a lot when we were stuck in that cabin. We had a lot of catching up to do," I hedged.

His tone darkened. "Wait, did she tell you she was seeing someone? Dammit, she promised she would tell me if she was."

Gah, one-hundred percent wrong direction, buddy. "No, nothing like that. I just meant it was nice talking to her. She's easy to get along with."

"My sister?" He guffawed. "Don't get me wrong, I love her, and we get along okay. But she's always got a chip on her shoulder, particularly around new people. I don't think anyone would say she's easy to get along with."

"I don't think that's fair," I argued. "I think you mostly see her in the context of your family stuff, so perhaps that colors your perception. But from what I saw, she was pretty laid back and fun, especially given the context."

Reece's eyes narrowed again. "What do you mean, 'family stuff'?"

"She told me about you guys wanting her to take a more active role in the resort, and why she's not ready to do that until she gets through this run for the Olympics."

"She did, did she?" His tone got gruffer. "Did she tell you why our parents are pushing for that?"

"Yeah, she said it's because they think it's time for her to have more responsibility. And that she's made suggestions about things and they didn't want to act on them."

"I see. And you got this straight from the horse's mouth, so in your book it's scripture, right?"

"Wait, I didn't say-"

Reece's cheeks took on a ruddy flush above his thick beard. "I don't know why you're championing her all of a sudden, but let me fill you in on something here: When Stella got hurt, it took a long time for her to heal. And you weren't there; I'm the one who saw her stuck in that bed for weeks, unable to move around, let alone get outside or on the snow. She did not handle it well."

This was the gruff 'older brother' voice that redirected my attention to the fact that the guy was a monster and had a good fifty pounds on me, if not more. Bigger guys in the Army had never intimidated me, but in this context, Reece's size and tone made my throat clench up.

"At first she put on a brave face, and people kept coming by with flowers and cards, wishing her a speedy recovery. Slowly, the visitors stopped, and the only thing that changed was she was now alone with nothing else to do. She had dedicated herself to that sport so thoroughly she had nothing else, you understand? All of that passion, that fire, just leaked away without somewhere for her to put it, and she became a ghost of Stella Blackwell. The pressure started for her to get moving, get back on the board, start doing tricks, posting videos smiling and performing and thanking the fans for supporting her.

"But it was like she faded away for a while. Once the doctors cleared her to do some exercises and begin rebuilding her strength, that's what she did. She still didn't recover her personality, you understand; it became moving from one goalpost to the next. 'Once I can pull ten pounds, then I can switch to fifteen. Once I can do small arm circles, I can switch to large ones.' And on and on and on."

My heart squeezed painfully, imagining what

Stella went through alone, too stubborn to open up about her feelings to anyone.

"It wasn't until she could finally get on the snow that we started to see Stella come back out again. And at the beginning she took it easy. She could only be out there for short periods of time, and supervised. So then she began reaching out to friends, going to movies, grabbing lunch, doing more social things. For the first time in ages, she actually had a pretty full life.

"But once she could go full bore once again and start training, she gradually stopped doing all the extras in favor of more and more training. I don't know if it's admirable or scary, to have that kind of single-minded focus. I definitely don't think it's healthy. But what do I know about what it takes to be a world-class athlete? I try not to judge and just support her the best I can."

Reece heaved a sigh and rubbed a hand over his face before taking a long sip of his drink. I mimicked the movement, still not sure what to say.

"However, that's why my parents have been trying to get her more involved in the business; they think if she has something else that she cares about, it might make it easier for her to recover if this all doesn't go how she hopes. We're all worried about her pushing herself too hard and getting injured again—what if she doesn't have a light at the end of the 'tunnel the second time around?"

My body froze completely. Reece's words hit hard, and I realized Stella and I really had more in common than we knew.

"So she's focused on the end goal, where she's standing on the podium, and you all are worried about the wreckage when she doesn't make it."

Reece scrubbed at his beard. "Yes and no. We worry about her, that's all. When she crashed last time... well, I think it could have been avoided."

"What do you mean?"

"She had been pushing herself too hard. Too many hours doing tricks, too much training, and not enough sleep. I think her landing was off because she doesn't know when to stop."

"You know, when we talked in that cabin, she told me some things."

"Oh yeah? About her accident?"

"Not exactly. It was more about now. She basically told me she feels like she has to prove to herself, but also to you and your parents, that she can do this. She thinks you don't believe in her anymore."

"Well, that's a hundred percent horse shit. Of

course we believe in her!" Reece was genuinely upset at that revelation.

"I didn't say it was fact. I said it's what she feels," I answered. "Can you see how she might have gotten that impression?"

Reece glared at me for a long moment, then sighed. "Like I said, I've done my best to leave her be. But I know my parents have been pushing her a lot. They're worried about her getting hurt, and they really aren't sure how to show their concern but also show her the support she needs. She's a fighter, she always has been. I think they try to keep the hard line like some kind of tough love that will eventually break through. But sometimes I feel like she might respond better to a softer touch. Maybe she just needs someone who understands what she's been through better than we do."

If I was looking for an opening, I wouldn't find something better than that. I tipped my glass and poured the remainder of my drink straight down my throat, like that act would give me courage.

"Reece, I haven't exactly been honest with you about a few things, and I feel like I need to come clean."

He looked at me with mild surprise, but no suspicion. "Okay, let's have it."

SASHA PIERCE

My mind blanked, and then I dredged up the memory of the very beginning of my downfall with Stella. "Do you remember, back in senior year, one day after practice Stella came to watch us and she hugged me, then you basically told me to stay away from her?"

Reece scratched at his beard, a hint of suspicion narrowing his eyes. "Not exactly."

My heart rate elevated—*he didn't remember?* "It was a couple weeks before homecoming. When I won homecoming king, and Stella tried to come dance with me, but I was there with Brittany?"

"I mean, I remember the dance, but I don't remember the other thing." He shrugged, taking another sip and settling back into the cushions.

His not remembering this made the explanation infinitely harder. "Stella hugged me and you said it was weird, and I kind of tried to play it off. But you told me you didn't mind that I was the town player, but I couldn't play your sister. That ring any bells?"

"Vaguely, but that was ages ago. What does it have to do with Stella and the Olympics?"

"Just hear me out." I wiped my damp palms on my legs. This was going to be the hardest part. Sweat trickled down the back of my neck. "The truth... the truth is," I stammered, my tongue

294

suddenly thick and useless in my mouth. "I had asked Stella to homecoming the night before," I finally spat out.

Reece just stared at me, eyes wide, from his seat on the couch.

I rushed to continue. "When you said you didn't want me to date your sister, I panicked. We'd been hanging out a lot, and it was all just friendly, but I felt guilty for not telling you. I knew even then that it was wrong. But I really liked her, and I'd decided just to go for it. It was supposed to be our big reveal on homecoming, but after you told me no, I didn't know what to do. I didn't know how to tell Stella we couldn't date, and so everything at homecoming... happened."

Reece was quiet for a long, painful moment, his jaw working as if he were clenching his teeth while he thought. I was keenly aware of his hands where they rested on his thighs, one flat and one clutching his glass. They were not forming fists... yet.

"So you mean to tell me that... when Stella was bawling her eyes out and none of us believed her, when she insisted she was supposed to be your date... she was telling the truth?"

"Yes," the word practically choked me.

"And you just acted like you had no idea why." His voice took on that scary-deep edge.

"Yes." This time is was barely a whisper.

"No wonder Stella fucking hated you."

"I deserved it," I insisted swiftly. "If I had been braver, less afraid of losing the only friend I had, I would have told you. But it was pretty clear you didn't think I was good enough for her, so I figured it was just better for her to hate me than to have her pissed at you and *you* pissed at *me*."

Reece's head turned sharply. "I never thought you weren't good enough for her. When did I give you that impression?"

"You were pissed when she ran up and hugged me, it was pretty clear. And then you specifically told me not to date her."

Reece set his glass on the table and leaned toward me, elbows on his knees. "I'm starting to remember that. But what you said I told you was that I didn't want you to *play* Stella, not *date* her."

I swallowed hard. "I mean, it was pretty much one and the same, right? I wasn't exactly the monogamous type, I didn't really go steady I just kind of... hooked up."

"Is that what you planned to do with Stella?"

"What? No, hell no. I asked her to be my date for homecoming because I really liked her. I wanted to seriously date her—we already spent a lot of time together anyway. We hadn't done anything, but... I wanted to. If I wasn't with you, I was probably with her. But I didn't want to lose my best friend over it. I felt like I had to choose, so I picked you."

Abuptly, Reece swiped a hand over his face and sighed deeply. "Sebastian, I never once thought you weren't good enough for my sister. I just didn't want you to break her heart, which apparently you did anyway. If you had told me how you really felt, I would have given you a stern warning to not be a dick, but I would have been happy for you."

A rock dropped in my stomach. "Really?"

"Of course, moron. You were my best friend. Still *are* my best friend. If I thought that poorly of you, I wouldn't have been hanging out with you, either."

My head swam with confusion. A good deal of it was relief, but there was also a sick feeling in my stomach knowing that I had screwed it all up for no reason. "I... wow, that's a lot to take in."

"Well, that's the only good news you're going to get from me, because whether or not you intended to, you did her dirty at homecoming."

"I know, and I can't tell you how much I've regretted it for the last six years."

"I'm not the one you need to be apologizing to."

"That's why I'm bringing it up—Stella and I hashed it out in the cabin. I apologized and explained everything. And we both... kind of realized we still like each other."

Reece stared at me, expressionless. The silence was deafening, and the lump stayed in my throat the entire time. It was almost painfully lodged there with a feeling akin to permanence, like I would never be able to swallow normally again.

"So you're dating... now?"

"Not exactly. I wasn't sure it was a good idea, with everything she has going on. And I wanted to clear the air with you, because, well, like I said, I thought you didn't want me to date her. So I've been trying to keep my distance from her, but..."

"But that's not what you want." Reece's voice was flat, definitely not a question.

"No, it's not." A heavy sigh pushed from my lips. "If I'm being really honest, she's all I've wanted this entire time, even since before I left."

"That's... that's a lot," Reece sighed. "Look, it's not my place to hold a grudge about homecoming, so if Stella has put that in the past, then I'll just set it aside, too." Reece shifted in his seat, and his tone dropped. "But I'm gonna be honest with you too: I know you're not at your best right now. I see the shadows in your eyes, and Gary told me about your outbursts—yes, they keep me informed. I know what happened to you. You're clearly battling your own demons, and you know what I mean." He leveled a stern gaze in my direction. "Stella has enough issues of her own, she doesn't need more problems—she needs someone who's going to be a firm, steady support in her life. So if you want to be her partner, you need to deal with your own shit and not expect my sister to make you whole."

"Hey," I protested. "You know me. I'm fine."

"Like hell you are. Don't lie to me, Sebastian. I can read your face like a recipe card. You are not the same man who left Aspen Ridge on an Army bus six years ago. You've suffered, and you're struggling. Don't try to tell me you aren't, I see it every time I look at you. I invited you back here because I thought you'd have the best chance at recovering from everything that happened to you at *home*. And I will advocate for you, and I will help you, and by god I'm going to tell you when you're being an idiot. Because you're my brother for life. And now, more than ever, I think you need someone to call you on your shit, so I'm doing that for you. You've got unresolved trauma from all those things you told me about in your emails. Yes, I read every one, more than once. I even educated myself on PTSD because they talk about it on the news all the time, and how it's affected our soldiers when they come back."

Reece leaned forward and set his heavy hand on my shoulder, trapping my gaze in his serious eyes. "I won't let you fall through the cracks, Sebastian. You're my best friend, and I'm here for you, whatever you need. If I need to sleep on your couch to make sure you don't do something stupid, I'll do it. Even if I need to babysit you twenty-four seven, I'll do what it takes. Gary gave me the name of a counselor that specializes in PTSD, and if I have to, I'll march you into that office every week myself. But I'm hoping you'll take the advice of the people who care about you, and just do what you need to do to get better."

This conversation had taken a much different turn than I expected. Emotion welled up in my chest; people had danced around it, suggesting I had issues, trauma, painful experiences in my past. Reece just bold-faced called it out as PTSD, and it sort of reminded me of the no-nonsense way my commanding officer had talked about it.

He'd been through some stuff of his own, and he was the only person at my last garrison that didn't give me a pleased nod when I said I was fine. He just leveled the same stare Reece gave me now; the same one Gary gave me yesterday. It seemed to say, 'I see you, you can't trick me. I'll wait as long as it takes for you to see it, too.'

Reece remained in the same position, reaching forward with his massive palm on my shoulder, eyes holding mine, waiting.

And finally, something within me unlocked. My hand reached up, covered his, and squeezed hard as my head dropped in shame. The sobs rose in my throat, and my best friend squeezed my shoulder harder, but still didn't move, didn't say a word.

"I can't control it," I whispered, sniffing. "I feel like I should just be able to shut it down, move past it, let it go. But it's like the more I try to push it away, the stronger it gets, and the worse it gets, worse every time."

Reece's voice was gentle. "Bottling it up, ignoring it doesn't work. The only way to deal with it is to face it head on. Even if it's hard. Even if it tears you apart to think about it. It's not going to get easier with time."

"When did you get so wise?" I sniffed, sitting

up and attempting to bring a lighter shift to the atmosphere.

"Psh, you know I've always been the smart one," he smirked. Reece stood, tugging me up by my shirt, and pulled me into his chest. No half-assed 'we're men we don't want to touch' fake hug; this time he wrapped his arms around me and squeezed, to the point my ribs hurt. "I'm here for you, brother. Always. You hear me?"

I nodded against his shoulder. "Yeah, I hear you," I gasped. "But will you let me go now? I think you just cracked one of my ribs."

Reece chuckled. "Weak sauce." But he released me and clapped his hand on my shoulder once more. "Why don't I make some popcorn and we can find some dumb movie to laugh at on TV?"

"Yeah, sounds good," I nodded, and he strode into the kitchen in search of the ingredients.

Even though the heavy weight of realization had finally settled in my chest, there was relief, too. Because now, for the first time, I'd finally acknowledged the skeleton in my closet, the demon that haunted me relentlessly. And the world didn't implode.

It was a start.

CHAPTER
NINETEEN

STELLA

After a few days in the brace, I passed inspection and was finally cleared to be on the snow again. David still didn't want me doing any tricks, but it was important for me to get in the physical work of riding at the very least. My knee felt fine, and restless energy had built up in my system to the point it felt as if I'd explode without an outlet.

There's only so much swimming a girl can do when she wants to be out carving down a mountain.

Once again, it was a beautiful, blue-bird day,

and I was practically the first person in line when the lift opened up. Of course I took David's advice and opted to start easy with some blue groomers. At the top, there were the occasional locals getting in a few runs before their workday started, and a handful of tourists who just couldn't wait another second to get their vacation truly rolling, but other than that, the mountain was empty.

I loved this. The sky was brilliant blue, nearly cloudless, the early morning sunshine sparkling on the freshly groomed ridges of snow, and miles of wide-open runs. From the top of Peak 6, the sky was so clear I could see the mountain ranges that were miles away. It took my breath away, forced me to stop for a minute and just admire it. This was the *life*. The thing people traveled across the world to experience; and it was *my* life, my backyard. My family's resort, and nowhere in the world I'd rather be.

My lungs filled with fresh, bitingly cold mountain air, and I released it in a breath of snowy vapor.

This was where I belonged. I knew it when I was a kid, and I knew it now.

After adjusting my goggles, double-checking my bindings, and selecting the right playlist, I turned the edge of my board and started a nice smooth carve down Grizzly Way. The competitive voice in my mind kept pushing me to go faster, carve harder, dig in more deeply. But the orders from David gave me an excuse not to push so hard; at least, not yet. Instead, I just flowed over the rivers of snow, finding that moment of Zen where my body and board were one and I could just enjoy the ride instead of pushing, pushing, pushing for more.

I missed this. I missed the pure joy I used to get from snowboarding, back when it was all just for fun. It'd been so long since there wasn't a task to complete, a time to mark, a goal to hit. When had it all gotten away from me? It was as if I'd long forgotten the passion for enjoying it and was left with the obligation to perform.

Granted I brought that on myself, I knew that. I got such a thrill from the ride and was so inspired by my heroes that all I wanted to do was push harder. And then after my accident, It became more and more about proving to everyone that I wasn't washed up or broken or stuck in a foolish dream. The entire point became *proving* I could, instead of just doing what I loved.

My mind easily swam through the sea of thoughts while my body controlled the action. Cruising like this was second nature. I didn't have to think about it. I did several mellow runs before I hit an easy black on Peak 9. I navigated the cross-peak trails like I had them memorized, which—to be fair, I pretty much did. I'd spent more time on these 'roads' than anywhere else in my life.

It wasn't until I got to the top of Peak 9 that I saw the Bowlivian Express and suddenly remembered the thing I was trying to avoid thinking about: Sebastian. Naturally, seeing the chairlift to the back bowls where we'd spent our time together brought all those memories and feelings screaming to the forefront of my mind. Internally cursing myself for choosing Peak 9 over ANY other peak with black runs, I turned my back to memories, literally and figuratively, and very bravely ran away instead.

More people were making their way to the hills now, but there was still plenty of space for me to cruise without giving it too much of my concentration. Even though I refused to let my head turn over the memories of Sebastian in the cabin, I couldn't make the feelings disappear as easily. *Why* did I have to fall for the same stupid shit over and over again? I knew who he was and how he operated. It was as predictable as winter snowfall in the Rockies that he'd soften me up, then push me away. There was no excuse, but I fell for it all the same.

And now, here I was, with my head focused on my hurt feelings instead of on my upcoming performance in the competition that could determine the direction of the rest of my life. And I knew the only thing that would change that: going faster.

So I crouched, lowering my center of gravity, and picked up speed, carving just enough to manage the pace without losing control completely, cruising around other people, whizzing between trees and their outstretched branches. Pushing pushing pushing once again.

I flew down the mountain, nearly out of breath by the time I carved a rooster tail at the bottom to stop myself from crashing into the nets separating the lines for the chairlift. Angling neatly into the solo rider line, I rode all the way to the front before I popped my rear foot loose from the binding, got my badge scanned, and mounted the next chairlift.

But on the lift, there was no distraction to keep me from my feelings, and they wasted no time in reminding me I had unfinished business. A thirst crept up the back of my throat, but I denied it savagely. I wasn't like him; I didn't need alcohol to numb *everything*.

Somehow, I had to get over this. Somehow, I had to figure out what the magic of Sebastian was so I could pack it away, beat it down, and make sure it never took over me again. He was just a guy, after all. There were millions of them in the world, and it wasn't like I was hurting for male attention. Being sponsored by Branton Snowboards definitely didn't hurt, but I'd learned ages ago that dudes were invariably impressed by a girl who handled her own on a board. Let alone one who was on my level.

That's right, I assured myself. *I'm* the catch here. *I'm* the one people gush over on the hill, *I'm* the one with the massive following and fan clubs, the one who gets asked for autographs and pictures.

Who was Sebastian Delacruz? *Just a guy that came back to his hometown after a stint in the Army who had nowhere else to go*, I thought savagely.

Guilt swiftly overtook the venomous thoughts, and I had to retract. It wasn't fair to think those things about him, no matter how he'd treated me. Obviously, the guy had issues of his own, and whether or not they were about me, it wasn't something I could change.

I needed to find some way to get over him, and I didn't need to do that by hating the guy. Although it was incredibly tempting.

When I reached the top of the run, I carved a slow line to the right, determined to refocus on the task at hand and really dig into my training. No jumps, no tricks, but my body had energy to burn, and I was determined to use it up.

As I was adjusting my playlist to something more energetic, a faint shout reached my ears, and two skiers went whizzing past shortly after. Once I knew which direction they took, I angled my body to the other side and started my run.

Crouching, carving, leaning into the turns when the run grew steeper. I was practically parallel to the ground at some points, just inches from wiping out completely. My focus was entirely on my path forward, never behind, never beside. So when a flash of orange appeared in my peripheral vision, I ignored it—just some skier who cut it a little close. The rule on the hill was that the downhill person had the right of way, and we all depended on this well-known rule for the flow of traffic to avoid accidents. Otherwise, it'd be complete chaos, and I needed all of my focus to be forward.

However, the orange appeared in my vision

again, and with a huff, I spun toward the right side of the run to give the jerk more space. Clearly, he couldn't be bothered to keep his distance. Incredibly, he followed me off to my side, and was keeping pace with me, remaining in my field of vision like an annoying insect that was determined to pester me until I swatted it down.

It wasn't good form; I knew he was close enough that he could feasibly crash into me. Being downhill didn't excuse me from being an asshole, but I kind of felt like he was already playing the jerk card, so I was within my right to reciprocate.

Instead of continuing my smooth carving downhill, I abruptly banked a hard left, directly into the path of the guy who'd been pacing me and forcing him to pull up short.

That was when I realized it was Sebastian.

To be fair, he wasn't wearing the Ski Patrol red today, and I'd never seen him in anything else on the hill. And somehow, despite his insistence at treating me like I didn't matter, he'd turned into my own personal stalker on the mountain after our time in that cabin. Granted, I hadn't been on the hill for several days, but I should have known better than to assume he'd just buzzed off.

I glared at him for a long second, knowing he couldn't see anything behind my goggles nor I behind his, and then I turned on my heel without a word and bombed down the hill.

If he wanted to follow me, he'd have to catch up. I built speed quickly, pushing myself even faster than I'd been riding before. My music was loud enough that I couldn't hear if he was trying to get my attention or not—and it didn't matter. At this moment, there was nothing I wanted to hear from Sebastian, anyway.

I had a few choice words for him, but I wasn't interested in engaging him in conversation to share them. Why the hell wouldn't he just leave me alone? He had no problem blowing me off whenever it was convenient for him, but when I was just minding my own business on the slopes, that's when he had to see me.

Figures.

He was probably chasing me down to yell at me if I wiped out again. Like it was some personal affront to his sensibilities for me to take risks; like he had any right to boss me around.

Wind of my own making ripped at my clothes, tearing strands of my hair from their braids and stinging the small amount of exposed skin on my face. But even though I was pushing the limits of my speed, that pop of orange bobbed in and out of my vision, a non-stop irritant to what was supposed to be a fun, relaxing day of getting back into boarding.

We were coming up quickly on the base of Peak 9, and I was going to have to slow down soon or risk bowling into a ton of tourists skating in from the slow zone on Bear Claw Way. With a frustrated sigh, I dug my toes in sharply, pulling myself into an abrupt stop facing uphill.

Sebastian had been right beside me, so my sudden stop took him by surprise and he traveled another hundred feet until he could stop completely. Since it was far more difficult to go uphill than down, I turned and dragged my heel edge, scraping my way down the mountain until we were face to face. At least the mountain had my back when it came to my short stature.

I yanked my goggles up on my helmet. "What is your fucking problem, Sebastian? I can't get an *hour* on the hill without you tracking me down and harassing me."

He held a gloved hand up. "Stella, that's not-"

"I don't want to hear it," I snapped. "I'm so tired of your hot and cold routine, and then this bizarre policing like you somehow have a right to tell me what to do with my body. You don't, okay? Being on ski patrol doesn't give you the right to do any of this. I can and will report you for it, and this is your last warning from me."

"Wait, Stella let me-"

"No, *you* wait. I'm tired of listening to you. It's time you hear what I have to say. You're a selfish asshole, Sebastian Delacruz. You were a selfish asshole in high school and you're a selfish asshole now."

A pair of skiers carved past us without pausing, and I waited for them to blow past before I continued.

"I should have known you weren't magically reformed. I thought your confessions in that cabin were an apology, perhaps some kind of promise that you wouldn't pull that shit again after you realized how fucked up it was in the first place. And just like when we were kids, you sucked me in with that gentle, surprisingly fucking self-aware bullshit and I fell for it again. And here's me, right? Thinking I'd learned this lesson and I wouldn't be anyone's sucker again. I did pretty well for the last six years, you know. I kept that lesson close to my heart and remembered how easy it was for someone to flip a switch and change their mind from one day to the next. And wouldn't you know, the master of that song and dance returned, and I fell for it all over again."

Sebastian pulled his goggles up and revealed angry brown eyes. "Stella, that's not-"

"I don't want to hear your excuses, Sebastian. I'm so fucking tired of them. You have this reason, or that, or the other to explain the way you act. Yeah, I know you've had some tough times and I am truly sorry. I understand having to deal with shit, although I won't pretend that I fully understand what you've gone through. I've been dealing with my own. But I don't deserve to deal with all of this, either. I have so many things hanging over my head, and my focus is anywhere but where it needs to be. So I'm over it. Just leave me the fuck alone."

While I spoke Sebastian's expression hardened, his eyes turning flinty when I kept cutting him off. I didn't miss how his jaw flexed like he was clenching his teeth, or how he kept stabbing one of his poles in the snow out of frustration. But all I could think was, *'Good. He should be frustrated. Lord knows I've been frustrated as hell. It's about time some of that went around.'*

When I didn't immediately launch into another attack, he spit out, "Is it my turn to speak now, or does the princess of Aspen Ridge have more to say?"

I glared at him with all the venom I could

muster, but crossed my arms and replied, "Sure, let's hear it. This'll be fun."

"First of all, you may have heard what I said, but you have no idea what I went through. So you're right, there's no way you could understand what the last six years have been like for me.

"However, it's complete bullshit to accuse me of stalking and harassing you. Yeah, so maybe I've been keeping a closer eye on you lately in the wake of everything that happened. So what? You insist on acting like you aren't interested in preserving your own life, and I happen to know you have a family who loves you and would be devastated if something happened. Seeing as, between the two of us, I'm the only one who's lost my family completely, I think I'm uniquely qualified to tell you how it feels. And you may not care, but I wouldn't inflict that pain on anyone, let alone my best friend in the world."

I imagined my fury rising off my body in visible waves of heat. "That still doesn't give you the right to tell me how to live my life," I spat.

Sebastian sighed heavily and nodded. "You're right, it doesn't. And that's not what I'm trying to do. You told me you were *afraid* of doing those tricks, that you worried you'd end up seriously injured or even paralyzed. You said you wished you could drop the two most dangerous events, but you felt like you had to do them. To prove something, to your parents, your brother, your fans, hell, even yourself. You told me your anxiety gets so bad you have literal panic attacks, and sometimes you get yourself drunk just to perform a trick. That's not normal, or healthy, Stella."

A blob of guilt dropped in my stomach, chilling the boiling anger. As much as I tried to deny it to myself, everything he said was true.

"You may not understand, but we have something in the Army, a sort of code. When you have a friend you're worried about, someone you know is hurting, you do your best to keep them out of trouble. You can try to get them to seek counseling, talk to a chaplain, get some sort of treatment, but a lot of times people in our position don't take any of that seriously. Or they're too stubborn and think they ought to manage everything on their own.

"Instead, you just try to be there, however they need it. Like Ambrose, my friend who loved golf. Now, for the record, I fucking hate golf. It's boring and pointless. But Ambrose needed someone, and I went. We didn't talk about our shit, at least not at first. I just went along with him, doing something he wanted to do, and didn't leave him to be alone, to *feel* alone. That was my mission; that was all I was there to do. Eventually, he opened up some more and started talking to me about deeper things. About his problems, about his guilt, his fear. And I did the same—we shared equally. He told me he'd been thinking about killing himself, Stella. That at one point, the only thing that stopped him from pulling the trigger was knowing I'd be at his door at oh-nine for our tee time. That I kept showing up made the difference for him."

My jaw clenched against the emotion that pricked behind my eyes. I wouldn't soften to him, not after everything he'd done. He'd fooled me far too many times for me to blame it on him.

Sebastian gestured widely. "So, yeah, I've been keeping an eye on you on the hill. After that time in the back bowls I was worried about you, worried you'd be off by yourself and something would happen, and no one would be nearby to help you. And yes, some part of it was concern about your family and what would happen to them, but more importantly, I was worried about everything you were going through; the fear, the panic, the pressure to perform. I wanted to show you support in the only way I knew how."

I snorted. "Yeah, shouting at me in the terrain park really felt like you had my back."

His head tipped back in frustration. "Look, I'm sorry, alright? I'm not perfect either, and I freely admit I'm dealing with my own shit. You're the third person to point it out in the last week, so trust me, I'm well aware. That doesn't mean I don't care about you."

My eyes narrowed, and I pulled up my best cutting tone. "Yeah, I know where this is going. You care about me like a *sister*, right? This game you play, this back and forth, is so *pathetic*, Sebastian. You're always one way with me, then another around everyone else. I knew it back then, but stupid kid I was, I thought you were being your real self with *me*. I thought, for some naïve reason, that the way you acted with *other people* was the mask, that I was special; that I got to see the real you."

Emotion threatened to close my throat, but I swallowed it down angrily. "And when you talked to me in that cabin, I fell for it *again*. You told me your sob story, and I thought, well he must really care about me, to trust me with something so difficult for him to say. But once again, you did a great job of making a fool out of me. I bought it hook, line, and sinker, and then the *very next morning* you reeled it all back in. You 'didn't know what was going to happen' when we left the cabin, but until that moment, I could have sworn I did.

"You avoided me, didn't follow up with a call, or a text, or a fucking smoke signal. You went right back to pretending everything was the same as it had been before, like that whole thing never even happened. And you know, from any other guy, that's exactly what I would have wanted. I've had no problem walking away with zero attachment.

"But for some reason, it's always been different with you. And I think you know that, too. And it's like you get off on it, pulling on that string that connects me to you. Using this apparent chink in my armor to dig at me again." My voice finally broke at the end, but I covered it with a cough.

Sebastian's eyes flashed, and he retorted, "Stella, that's *enough*. I'm not going to make excuses for my behavior in the past. I *know* that there's no excuse. But I think it's time for you to know a few things that I couldn't tell you before."

I snorted. "This ought to be good."

Sebastian released an exasperated sigh, but ignored my comment. "I did what I did at home-coming because I knew I wasn't good enough for you."

CHAPTER
TWENTY

STELLA

I snorted again. "Right. Mister homecoming king, football quarterback, who had girls shoving notes in his locker and texting him X-rated pics, didn't think he was good enough for *me*."

"There's more to it than that, if you'd let me explain." He paused, and when I didn't come back with a quip, he continued. "Looking back on it now, I see things a little differently. But at the time, I believed that Reece didn't want me to date you, because *he* didn't think I was good enough for you. Like, we were best friends, and that was cool, but I wasn't someone he wanted involved with his sister.

"And knowing how I was, and how I felt—like a guy who had no business being best friends with the kid who was practically a billionaire but still cool as hell—I believed it. And yeah, when I made the football team and then became quarterback sophomore year, it *did* kind of go to my head. Suddenly, I had girls coming at me from all sides. They didn't look twice at me before, since I didn't have an inheritance to my working-class name. But being tight with your brother got me into those circles, and being quarterback earned me some respect."

After standing so long on my heel edge my shins were screaming at me, so I plopped onto the snow. For snowboarders, this was easy; skiers either had to pop their skis off or do an awkward, controlled fall onto their side. Sebastian did neither, just remained standing. He observed me like he wasn't sure what I meant by sitting down. I gestured for him to go on.

"Look, it was a lot to deal with. I didn't handle it well. I'm the first to admit that. And while I had all the trappings of high school glory, the honest-to-god best part of my life back then was you."

As if he wanted to prove his sincerity, Sebastian managed the side-plop maneuver with some level of dignity before continuing.

"Being able to spend time with you was a relief; someone I didn't feel like I had to play a role for. Don't get me wrong, Reece and I were tight, too. But it was always different with you. And then the way Reece reacted when he saw you hug me— well, it felt like I was balancing on the top of some mountain and the slightest shift in the wind would send me toppling over. I didn't know what to do; it felt like no matter which choice I made, it was going to be wrong." Emotion crept into his voice, and for the first time, I finally felt some small measure of remorse from him.

He cleared his throat and continued. "So I did what I did, for better or for worse. It was a terrible, shitty thing to do, and I've regretted it every day since. But you should know I didn't blow out of town and just forget you. I thought about you pretty much every day. I followed your career, and I reached out to Reece when you had your accident. He offered to connect us or let you know I called, and I told him no. Not because I didn't want to, but because I didn't think I deserved it."

My heart lurched at that revelation. Reece had never said a word about it. It surprised me he didn't take the opportunity to try to get me to forgive Sebastian, but then again, I knew how loyal he was. If Sebastian didn't want him to say anything, he wouldn't. His insistence that he didn't deserve for me to know he cared, however, was mystifying. What did that mean?

He continued with no awareness of my inner thoughts. "And when I came back here, I somehow convinced myself that we wouldn't see each other very much. But honestly, I had nowhere else to go. It's not like I had zero options, but with my parents gone, I literally had no place that felt like it could be home. I'd been drifting with the Army, in and out of war zones and transferring to different bases, for six years. After all that, I just wanted some place that felt like home. Reece and I exchanged a lot of emails while I was gone, and one night I sent him a rather pathetic, long, drunken message about it all.

"The next day, he replied with an invitation to come back to Aspen Ridge. He promised to find a place for me and said that Aspen Ridge takes care of family. Stella, I can't tell you how it affected me to see that, to have someone calling *me* family."

That trace of emotion crept back into his voice and I shifted uncomfortably on the hill, drawing my arms over my knees. The occasional skier continued to swish past, but I'd long since lost the ability to focus on anything but the sincerity in Sebastian's eyes.

"So even though I wanted desperately to make up with you, I felt like now, more than ever, I had to keep my distance. It was better for you to keep hating me, so you'd stay away and it wouldn't be up to just me to keep us apart because I knew I would fail. And the second I saw you walk into Reece's house, I knew I was in trouble.

"Because I felt exactly the way I felt all those years ago. That here, with you and Reece, was *home*. And while I hoped that you might forgive me for what I did, I didn't believe *Reece* would forgive me if I went back on my promise to him. It was the one thing he asked of me, Stella."

My eyes prickled once more, the sincerity in his very being melting every bit of my fury even as I tried desperately to hold on to it.

"So anyway, that's what led us up to the cabin and what happened there. Obviously in that scenario, despite my best intentions, I could not keep up the act any more. But as soon as the outside world became real again, I went into a panic—I had done *exactly* what Reece asked me not to do. It was like I'd betrayed the trust of the one person who had been on my side since the beginning. And I panicked. I didn't want to keep it from him, but I didn't know how to tell him, either.

"But after everything, I couldn't take it anymore. I gathered up my courage and went to Reece's last night for dinner, and I told him. I figured he deserved the truth, and so did you. Even if it cost me that relationship, I didn't want to keep secrets from him anymore, and I didn't want us to be like this anymore. For better or for worse, I had to tell you everything, and just... *try*. Try to explain, try to earn your forgiveness, whatever it took. But in my mind, the first step was talking to your brother.

"And so I was shocked as hell when Reece told me I was a fucking idiot. Leave it to me to completely misinterpret what he meant because of my own damn insecurities. Reece hadn't told me not to *date* you, and he definitely didn't think I wasn't good enough for you. He told me not to *play* you, like the other girls I'd messed around with back then. He just didn't want me to date you if I wasn't going to take it seriously.

"Obviously, I misunderstood and pulled that stunt at homecoming. I confessed to that too, just so you know. Reece looked like he was about to kick my ass last night, realizing that what you'd said was true and he didn't believe you back then.

326

And I didn't give him details, but I told him we'd rekindled something in that cabin and I'd been trying, but I couldn't hold back how I felt anymore. And I wanted him to know, even if he was going to hate me for it.

"But he said he figured as much, and the only objection he had was that I have... that I have to deal with my PTSD," he swallowed thickly then continued, "and he didn't want me to pursue you if I wasn't working on myself, because you didn't deserve to get stuck with my issues."

If I hadn't softened before, the way his face broke when he actually put a name to his problems was enough to melt me completely.

"And so I'm here, after all of that, to tell you I'm sorry. I'm sorry for being a coward, for hurting you, for running away and never resolving anything, and for letting you think, even for a moment, that I didn't love you exactly as you are."

I was too stunned to speak. Sure, every girl dreams about an epic apology and a passionate declaration of love, but I guess I hadn't imagined it would take place in the middle of a ski hill with people whizzing past and spraying us with snow.

Although, honestly, it couldn't have been better for us. This was my happy place, my sanctuary; and while I was pissed at him initially for invading it, he came here to meet me where I was and lay it all out. That felt like a big gesture.

Not to mention that this was sort of where things had picked back up for us, with a few minor differences of situation. So it kind of felt... full circle.

My mind spun through all of this while Sebastian watched my face, his expression somehow both remorseful and hopeful. From everything he said, everything we threw at each other, there was one word that my mind kept returning to. "Did you just say you love me?" I felt safe asking, with my board between us like a security wall.

Because it felt like a trick. It *had* to be a trick. Who barely talks to a person without yelling at them, then comes back and declares love? I couldn't, *wouldn't*, let myself misinterpret him another time.

Sebastian's dark eyes sparkled, his lips curling into that wide smile that made both of his dimples appear. "I did, Estrellita."

My heart stuttered in my chest, but I managed to roll my eyes yet again. "Ugh, and you have to go and ruin it by using that nickname, of course. Why can't you just call me by my name?"

Despite my snotty tone, Sebastian's remained a hundred percent sincere. "Because it's who you are. You've always been a little star, Stella. I don't say it to make fun of you. I say it because I love you."

A warm, gooey feeling spread through my veins, but I was still annoyed. "And if you love me, shouldn't you do what I ask and call me what I want?"

He feigned considering my request. "Well, I *could*, if that's what you really want. But everyone in the world calls you Stella, and I like that Estrellita is just between you and me. If it helps, my mom had a nickname for my dad, that he acted like he hated, but we all knew he loved."

"Oh yeah? What was that?"

"She called him Jefe. It means 'boss'. He said it made him sound like a jerk, like she had to obey him. But when no one was around, when he didn't think anyone was watching, he grinned like an idiot every time she said it."

My stomach flipped. "You know, I didn't hate the nickname so much as how you said it."

"Ah," he smiled knowingly, "so if I say it differently, it's okay?"

I struggled to maintain my indifferent tone. "Maybe..."

Using the benefit of gravity, he pushed himself off the steep hill until he was standing, then reached down for my hand and yanked me to my feet. My board slid until my body crashed into his, and he wrapped both arms around me to steady me. Bending down to bring his face level with mine, he whispered, "Te amo, Estrellita." His voice was rich and low, and the gust of his warm breath caressed my cheek. This time, instead of the nickname setting my teeth on edge, it sent a shiver down my spine accompanied by a streak of heat. "Is that better?"

I gasped a breath. "'Yeah, that's better," I agreed in a falsely light voice. "'But if I'm going to let you get away with that one, I think we'll have to bring Buttboy McTool back."

Sebastian's head tipped back as he roared with laughter, pulling me even tighter to his chest. "If that is my penance, Estrellita, I will accept it with pleasure."

"Well, good, then. As long as you don't act like a tool, we can save it for special occasions." I smiled back at him beatifically.

"That's very generous of you."

"I'm a very generous person."

"Clearly."

Although I didn't want to move, I was suddenly very uncomfortable with just how many people were flying past us. "What do you say we take this downhill and go grab something to drink?"

"That sounds like an excellent idea," he agreed. "Are we talking about liquid courage or normal beverages?"

I shot him an incredulous look and glanced at my phone. "It's barely nine-thirty, kind of early for alcohol, wouldn't you say?"

"Don't you have some in your pack?" He challenged.

"Actually, no. Some jerk pointed out that it wasn't a healthy crutch to rely on."

Sebastian nodded seriously. "I see. Although I agree with this jerk, I don't think that applies to special occasions."

"Even for a special occasion, it's still hours before noon."

"That's what Irish Coffee is for." A devilish glint in his eye accompanied his dimpled grin.

"Okay, I never say no to an Irish Coffee. Wait, did you already know that?" I asked, suddenly suspicious.

Sebastian retrieved his poles and raised his hands, laughing. "I swear I didn't. I just know it's a popular ski hill drink, and doubles as an excuse for day drinking."

"That's fair," I agreed. "Then yeah, I'm down.

Grizzlies should be open and serving. Let's head there."

This time, we didn't race down the hill so much as cruise together. And almost as soon as we began moving, my brain finally caught up with everything he'd said, and everything he hadn't. So when we racked our skis and board and got our deliciously warm and alcoholic drinks, I followed up.

"Sebastian," I started, biting my lip. "I know you apologized for yelling at me, but it doesn't really change the context. You can think I'm reckless, but I'm an adult who can decide for myself, and whether you like it or not it isn't your decision. So if you want this to work," I gestured between us, "then you're going to have to accept that."

He actually looked surprised. "Stella, I do, and I'm sorry if I wasn't clear earlier. That was more about me than about you. I shouldn't have taken that out on you. The things I've gone through... well, I'm terrified of losing anyone else that I care about. I've lost enough people for ten lifetimes. But that's my issue, not yours, and I'm working on it. And I want you to know that no matter what you choose to do, I will support you."

I stared at him, unblinking, for a long moment.

He just... supported me? No redirecting, no bargaining, no negotiating?

"Now," he added quickly, as if afraid that he'd said the wrong thing, "that isn't to say I won't let you know when I think you should reconsider. But I promise not to hound you, not to scold you, and not to treat you in any way other than with the respect you deserve. I just want you to be happy, Stella. And if that means boarding at breakneck speeds and doing absolutely insane tricks in the air... well, I will suck it up and be the partner that you need me to be. Because I think you've got enough pressure in your life."

My throat grew thick with emotion, eyes tingling, and I covered by taking a long sip of my drink. It was everything I'd wanted to hear from my family: that they'd support me no matter what, even if they thought I was wrong, even if they didn't like it. Never in a million years did I think I'd be sitting here with Sebastian Delacruz saying he loved me, then unloading all of that. That feeling of nostalgia resurfaced again, like we'd been here before.

I popped up from my seat, glancing around the nearly empty restaurant as if searching desperately for something.

Sebastian looked around as well, confused. "Are you expecting someone?"

I lifted a fist and gave him my best mean mug. "I'm just looking for Brittney, because if that bitch comes in here and tries to swoop in again, I'm gonna straight punch her in the nose."

Sebastian released a surprised laugh, and I chuckled along with him but maintained my raised fist. "I mean it, she's not going to replace me again. I won't let her."

"Come here, Estrellita," he purred, tugging me down in my seat and wrapping an arm around my shoulders. His forehead tipped against mine, and when he spoke, it was in a voice so low his words were only meant for me. "No one can replace you; you've always been my number one."

"Always?" I whispered back.

"Always."

EPILOGUE

STELLA

Just breathe...

A year later, and I was staring down the most important run of my life. But I did it—I made it here, in the Olympic Trials. The sky was overcast, sort of universally grey outside, and that made for poor visibility. I prepared—had my hi-vis goggles on, and I was just waiting for the buzzer to sound and tell me to *go*.

It was like time had nearly stopped—the seconds counting down on the giant clock changed slower than molasses, and all I wanted to do was get moving. Adrenaline surged through my veins, my body absolutely thrumming with the need to *move*. It was enough to make me want to jump out of my own skin.

But I didn't. Instead, I took another breath. Sebastian was big on the breathing lately. His therapist gave him a ton of tools to manage his PTSD, and it's definitely helped him, so I was trying to follow suit.

Another glance at the clock, another deep breath. Just a few more seconds left. I didn't have time to question my choice to drop out of halfpipe and slope style—I still wondered occasionally if I would have done even better in those, but I was happy that focusing on snowboard cross and slalom had been successful. They'd gotten me here, at any rate. I was get that answer in another few seconds...

I crouched low, my body warm and ready. I felt like a coiled spring, just condensing down to a ball of pure energy. My opponent, to my right, did the same. I didn't look left, but I was sure we look like carbon copies of each other. And with one more deep breath, I pushed out of the gate, and flew.

SEBASTIAN

THE SHITTY THING about being at the gate, waiting for Stella to come flying through, is that I couldn't be with her at the top of the mountain. It made me anxious, but that's what she wanted. The giant monitors over the finish line showed her preparing to go, and her face, mostly concealed behind her giant goggles, gave nothing away.

"Just a few seconds now," Reece muttered. His hands were bare, even in this cold, and white-knuckled, gripping the barrier that keeps the spectators off of the course. A crowd surrounded us, comprising friends, family, and even some competitors in other events.

It was funny, because even though these people were competing against each other, there was no tension in the air. Like we were all part of the same thing, on the same side, and it felt far more cohesive than I expected. Of course everyone was desperate to see their loved one make the team, but there was an overall feeling of excitement for everyone—we all wanted to see the US do its best, whoever got selected for it.

I had an extensive course on competitive

snowboarding, the Olympic Trials, and everything involved with the whole production over the last year. I wasn't ashamed to admit that I knew pretty much zip about it before, despite feeling like I had a solid idea of how it all worked. But now I truly felt like an expert.

The last seconds ticked away, and a horn sounded over the loudspeaker. Stella and her competitors were off, carving over the rollers so fast the drones could barely keep up with them. Fortunately, they had cameras stationed at regular intervals down the course, and most people's eyes were glued to the screen. I kept glancing back and forth, watching her progress but also waiting to see when she'd appear from our perspective.

Reece was watching the screen, his hands so tight on the barrier that I was actually starting to question if he'd damage the thing—it's only plastic, after all. My eyes darted between so many places now: the faces of the spectators, Reece, the monitor, and the bend where Stella should come shooting around in seconds. The course took many dips, turns, and jumps, and each one made me nervous even though I knew it shouldn't. This was how Stella rode for fun—fast and controlled, but in such a way that it seemed reckless, weaving around other people and shooting around corners at breakneck speeds. I should know: I'd been trying—and failing—to keep up with her.

Another glance at the monitor—she was at turn five. One girl was ahead of Stella, and several close on her heels. Stella predicted this—Jayme Douglass, the girl in front, was fast on the rollers and straightaways, but slightly slower on the jumps and corners—so her strategy was to overtake her on the last three curves. They're all extremely sharp and turn seven has a jump right before, so Douglass should slow down just enough to give Stella the edge. Stella had been practicing keeping her curves extra tight and hugging the inner line to gain an advantage. Her experience with controlled jumps helped her; she kept her body compact and took advantage of the launch to land as far out as possible.

I glanced back at the course, but they weren't here yet. The turns were built up around the edges, almost like they were in a snow canyon of some kind. Then you'd occasionally see their heads pop over the surface when they were on jumps or rollers, like gophers emerging from holes. A quick check of the monitor and they were almost here; Stella and Douglass were practically neck and neck. Stella went flying over the jump, landing just inside the curve and making a smooth transition into the corner while Douglass falls ever so slightly behind.

To say I was a nervous wreck would be an understatement. She was so close, and one wrong move at these speeds could mean more than just a lost opportunity for a medal.

Everyone's head turned as they came flying around the corner, Stella crouched so low she practically looked like she was sitting on her board. She hit the rollers and her body extended and folded to manage them—it looked like her head stayed in the same place but her body was like a spring, coiling and uncoiling. Douglass started to gain on her by inches, but they were nearing the final jump and Stella was already preparing for it. She hit the jump and soared, throwing in an Indy grab in mid-air while Douglass fell further behind. When her board finally hit snow, there were just two rollers and then the finish line, and it was all over. Stella took first by a full half of a second and she came roaring into the finish with her fists in the air.

"Yes!" Reece shouted, his booming voice so loud that I might actually be deaf in that ear now. Stella kicked up a rooster tail as she slowed from her breakneck speed to a complete stop just inches from where we were waiting. The smile on her face was ultra-wide, even though she was obviously trying to catch her breath. The barriers were thick, extra padding in case the racers failed to stop completely. We couldn't hug her, but we could reach over and score a high five.

"You did it, Estrellita! I mean, I knew you would, but still. Amazing!"

"My sister's going to the Olympics!" Reece shouted at the top of his lungs.

Stella and I exchanged a glance, but couldn't help laughing; he was like an extremely proud father. A few nearby spectators smiled in his direction, but now that the race was over, many had to go find their own racer to support.

Jaymie Douglass came over to congratulate Stella on her victory, as did the other racers. As a group they pushed off for the exit, where they'd find a tent to remove their gear and rest a minute before coming out to face the world.

With the athletes retreating to their tent, the crowd moved as one toward the podium set up and took their places. I stuck closely behind Reece, given his size. The crowds always seemed to part around him, so I didn't have to push through. With the regionals, nationals, and world cup behind us, we'd had a lot of practice being spectators.

But this one was the most important one yet, and Stella had officially won her place on the Olympic Team. She still had to finish her slalom run tomorrow to qualify in that event, but now she was guaranteed a ticket to the Olympics either way.

It hadn't been easy on any of us. Every training session, every competition, my nerves were a live wire, filling me with worry that she'd get hurt. But I kept my promise and stopped trying to dictate her direction. It took a fair amount of therapy, but I was getting better at letting go of the need to control her in order to protect her. She needed me to trust her to make her own decisions, and support her, and just listen when she was upset instead of trying to solve everything. That last one was particularly hard—loving someone meant you never wanted to see them hurting—but I learned that wasn't what she needed from me. I wouldn't call myself a perfect partner, but I was trying.

A wave of noise rose around us as the announcer walked onto the stage and waved. She read off the alternates, then third, second, and finally first place. I'd seen Stella on top of so many podiums in the last year you'd think I'd become immune to it, but it still lit me up every time.

She'd always known she'd be here. Since she was a little girl she knew, and watching her wave and beam from that center box, I could still see that little girl in her wide smile. It didn't hurt that she was so much shorter than her competitors that, despite being on the highest box, her head was on a level with the third-place winner.

Her bright blue eyes scanned the crowd and landed directly on my face. Warmth bubbled up in my chest and I blew her a kiss, chuckling when she mocked catching it and slapping it on her cheek. Beside me, Reece used both hands as a megaphone to boom his pride for his little sister, then dropped a heavy arm across my shoulders.

"She's something else, isn't she?" Reece's voice was hoarse from all of his cheering.

I wasn't sure if that was rhetorical or not, but I replied anyway. "She definitely is," I agreed.

"Don't forget, this is only the beginning. From here it's the Olympic training center until the actual event in two months. If you thought she trained hard before, that was nothing compared to what you have coming."

"It'll be fine," I replied, nonplussed.

"I don't think you get it," Reece insisted. "Last time she didn't even talk to me during the week before she had her accident." He tightened his arm around my neck. "I'll keep you from going completely nuts, man. You're always welcome to hang with me, you know that."

"I'll be alright," I assured him. "I trust her to do what she needs to do. If that means she needs a week to focus exclusively on what she's doing, that's what she needs."

Reece's heavy arm dropped from my shoulders and he turned to stare at me incredulously. "Seriously?"

I nodded. "Yep."

"Wow. Well, I guess you're a better man than I, and that's saying something. I never thought I'd see the day."

"Thanks, asshole."

He nudged me with his elbow. "You know what I mean. I'm just surprised that you're so Zen about it. If I were you, I'd be freaking out. Hell, I'm not you and I'm freaking out."

I just shrugged. "Look, she needs me to not freak out. So if that's what she needs, that's what I'll be."

Reece raised an eyebrow. "Just like that? It's that easy?" He snapped his thick fingers.

"I wouldn't say easy, but..." I trailed off, watching Stella give one last beaming smile, waving furiously, before she stepped off the podium. My cheeks hurt from grinning with pride. "It's not easy, but she's worth it."

THE END

Would you like a sneak peek into
Sebastian and Stella's future?
Join Sasha's newsletter to get your free download!

http://www.sashapierceauthor.com/
thewrongplace

Book 3, The Wrong Nanny, is coming February
2025!

In the meantime, please enjoy chapter 1 of
The Wrong Girl.

THE WRONG GIRL - CHAPTER 1

A high-pitched voice carried down the hall. "Daaaad, where's my Spider-man book?"

I was elbows deep in a box full of loose tupperware, searching for something that resembled the dishes I still hadn't unpacked. "I don't know, Ethan; where did you leave it?"

"*I* didn't leave it anywhere. *You* packed it!" The reply was accusatory.

He sounded exactly like his mother, which immediately raised my hackles. I forced myself to draw in a slow breath and unclench my jaw before replying.

"Then check the boxes in your room, buddy. Anything that was yours went in there."

"There's like a hundred of them!" Oh man, here we go. "I'll *never* find it." I could practically hear the tears already.

I glanced up to spot Olivia silently watching me with wide brown eyes. "Honey, can you please go help your brother find his comic books? There should be a box in his room labeled 'books.'"

"Sure Dad," she nodded seriously, then took off down the hallway with the determination of a soldier headed into battle.

"Thanks Livvie!" I called after her, but if she heard me, she didn't reply.

Giving up, I scooped an armload of plastic wear out of the box and directly onto the floor, and I could finally spot the multi-colored dishes the kids liked at the bottom of the carton.

Olivia would eat on whatever I gave her—I'd swear she was easier than half the Airmen I led— but Ethan insisted they have the same. And if he didn't have his particular green plate and special blue cup, the world would implode.

The doctor agreed with me that his behavior was a little immature for seven, but he *also* agreed with my ex wife that our home life was probably a contributing factor. He said Ethan would grow out of it when he was ready.

So, in the meantime, I had to placate my own tiny dictator.

And they say America doesn't negotiate with terrorists.

By the time the kids appeared, I had two bowls of cereal, twin glasses of orange juice, and two slices of toast with peanut butter—cut into triangles, naturally—set out on the dining table. The house was still an absolute wreck from the move, but I managed to clear a space for them to eat.

Ethan's splotchy face and glossy eyes were a dead giveaway: he had definitely been on the verge of another meltdown, even though the comic book was clenched in one hand.

I purposefully made my voice extra bright. "Oh great, you found it. Thank you, Olivia!" I hinted.

My eldest gave me a silent nod, then steered her younger brother to their seats and pushed him in. He muttered a thank you, then inspected his meal carefully and compared it to his sister's. Once he was satisfied, he picked up his spoon.

Olivia followed suit, and when my eggs were ready, I slid them onto a matching plastic plate and joined them at the table with my coffee.

"Daddy, you can't use that. It's *my* plate."

Ethan glared at me with all the fire a seven-year-old could muster.

"I'm sorry buddy, but I couldn't find the norm —I mean, I couldn't find my plates in all the boxes. Do you mind if I use this one just for breakfast? I promise I'll unpack before you guys come back from Gramma and Grandpa's Sunday."

A sweat broke out on my back. If my troops could only see me now, pouring sweat in fear of an angry second grader.

Ethan seemed to consider it, then nodded seriously. "Okay, but *only* for breakfast."

"Thanks buddy," I smiled, but he'd already turned his attention back to his lucky charms and was busily scooping out the marshmallows.

Breakfast was always a quiet affair for us. To be fair, all meals seemed rather quiet, as of late. The kids and I... were still getting used to each other. It was Cheryl who knew how to lighten Olivia up or calm Ethan down with just the right words.

Which made sense. She was their mother. And while I was either working all day or deployed for months, she had seen them through every skinned knee and tantrum.

Of course, she had also just decided she was over it and left—not even pretending to want our children. She stuck around to see the divorce through and made some vague promises about 'having the kids to visit' once she 'was settled' and then disappeared. Over a year later and she hadn't even called them. She'd answer if we called, but they'd pretty much stopped asking for her.

It fucking killed me, but I knew it was a good sign that they weren't relying on her for emotional support any more.

I just wished I was better at giving that to them.

I glanced at my watch and sighed, then finished the last gulp of my coffee. "Okay guys, we have ten minutes before we have to be out the door. Just put your dishes in the sink when you're done, and make sure you've got everything you want for the weekend in your backpacks. Gramma and Grandpa have pajamas and everything already for you, but bring any toys you want."

"What about my toothbrush?" Ethan stared up at me stonily.

"Gramma bought you a *brand new* toothbrush to use just at her house." I grinned at him in encouragement.

"I don't want a *new* toothbrush. I want my raptor toothbrush."

"You know what? I told her how much you

loved it, so she bought the *exact* same one. Now you have *two* raptor toothbrushes, one for each house. What do you think about that?"

"It's not the same," he shook his head. "It's not *my* raptor toothbrush."

"Okay, buddy, if you want to bring your toothbrush to Gramma's house, that's fine. Just put it in your backpack when you're done eating. I need to finish getting dressed."

Ethan scowled, then turned back to his food.

"Olivia, make sure you both wash your hands and that he doesn't forget his toothbrush, please." I kissed the top of her head as I passed.

"Sure, Dad." Even though I used my gentlest tone and smiled widely, she replied with the stern expression of a hardened warrior taking orders.

Deflated, I placed my own dishes in the sink and headed for my room.

Experience had taught me not to wear my work clothes at the breakfast table, because accidents were bound to happen. I couldn't say how many times I ended up with jelly or coffee spilled on my pristine dress blues.

Since it was my first day at a new job in management civilian style, I figured it was a smart idea to dress to impress. I'd only worn the charcoal suit once—for divorce court—so it was still impeccably clean. Shirt bright white and starched, red silk tie spotless.

By the time I reemerged from my room, the kids were waiting silently by the door, faces clean and backpacks on. My heart pinched at their serious expressions—I hated they were so sullen all the time, but I had no idea how to change it.

Hopefully, this move to Aspen Ridge would be the fresh start we all needed. With my parents here to help and the beautiful mountain scenery, it was an ideal place to settle our family and put down some roots. It was a place the kids could make friends, settle in, and perhaps we'd all find some more joy in our lives.

I just prayed it worked.

MOM AND DAD were waiting on the porch when we arrived, eager to spend time with their grandkids. The tightness in my chest loosened, confirming that I'd made the right choice, moving us here. Military bases provide a lot of support for families, but they don't compare to living a few blocks away from your parents.

As soon as we pulled into the driveway, the kids were unbuckled and tearing toward the house with eager smiles. I followed up the stairs to greet my parents, relieved to see my two serious children joyful about something.

"I don't know who's more excited, you guys or the kids," I teased. Ethan had jumped into my dad's arms and my mom was already telling Olivia the itinerary for their weekend.

"Well, we've got to make up for lost time, son." Dad greeted me with a hug and a firm pat on the back. "This is the first time we've all lived in the same state, let alone the same town."

"I just hope you don't get sick of us," I chuckled. "They're old enough to ride their bikes here once I get them unpacked. I have a feeling they'll be over a lot."

"You're always welcome, Jake," Mom replied with a warm smile. "You all can join us for dinner any time, too. The house has been quiet for too long, and I know you'll be working all day."

"Nah, we wouldn't want to put you out, Mom. You should take more time to relax. Maybe you should come over to our house for dinner." Instinctively, I glanced down at my watch. "Speaking of working all day, I had better not be late. Love you guys. Call me if you need anything."

Dad waved me off. "We'll be fine. Tell JJ hello for me!"

"Will do. Thanks again, for everything."

"Nonsense." He shook his head. "You don't need to thank us for watching our grandchildren."

"All the same, they can be a handful, so call me if you need anything."

Dad just waved, so I climbed into the truck and took off. I used my GPS to get to the Aspen Ridge Lodging office, so I had no trouble navigating through the ski resort's downtown.

Of course, being the end of summer, there was no snow to be seen. The mountains were bald rock at the peaks, with bright grass-covered runs trickling downhill between swaths of evergreens. The town itself was an attractive cross between the charm of the old west and the sleek appeal of modern mountain style. It'd been a while, but I'd visited once on a ski trip and had always loved Aspen Ridge. When my parents retired here, I'd sworn we'd visit every season to ski.

That'd been four years ago, and this was the first time we'd come. But we were here to stay, hopefully, so I supposed that'd make up for it.

Despite the season, the small resort town was packed with visitors, thanks to warm weather activities like mountain biking, rafting, and horseback riding. I made a point to arrive at the tail end of summer. I wanted the kids settled before school started, and my boss wanted me on board before winter, their busiest season.

I navigated to the resort parking garage and inserted the card I'd received in the mail, granting me permission to park for free. Thankfully, since signs at the entrance proclaimed parking to be $35 a day.

After a final once-over, I grabbed my shiny new briefcase—which was empty apart from a few sheets of paper—and followed directions for the main offices.

My pulse raced, but I tried to focus on the important things.

One, I already had the job.

Two, training leaders was basically what I'd done for my entire career, culminating in a stint at the Air Force's prestigious Officer Training School. Turning one flighty woman into the successful CEO of a ski resort would be cake after whipping groups of sullen college grads into battle-ready lieutenants.

Three, this was the best opportunity I was likely to receive in Aspen Ridge, and for the kids' sake—and my own—I needed to be near my parents. JJ Tremont had promised that once his daughter was ready to take over, he'd make sure I had a position in upper management.

So first the daughter, then the cushy job with a view of the gorgeous terrain.

I made it to the elevator and mashed the button for the top floor, then closed my eyes and pictured the new dream I was chasing. Afternoons spent on the slopes, teaching the kids to ski. Finally being able to attend school events, holidays with my family, a community that didn't exist around a military life. I'd resigned myself to a long career of service, and Cheryl's decisions had ripped that right out of my grasp... but perhaps there was a better life waiting for me here.

The elevator slowed to a stop, and the doors opened.

Showtime.

Ellie

"Dad, I really have got to go. The preparation is going to take me all day," I made a show of tidying up my desk, hoping he'd take the hint.

"I know, Izzy. I just wanted to remind you about the golf tournament in a few weeks." He settled into my corner chair like he had no intention of leaving. I'd intentionally made it a cozy space with tall plants and a side table so I could curl up and feel like I'd escaped. I hadn't imagined my father would usurp it to hold me hostage when I was trying to leave.

The sigh poured from my lips like someone had punched me in the chest. "I really wish you'd listen when I ask you to call me Ellie. No one has called me Izzy for years."

"All the same, Zach said he hasn't heard from you in a while. Did you two have a falling out?"

My god, why was my dad discussing my love life with my ex?

"We broke up almost a year ago, Dad. You know that."

"Well, you two seemed pretty cozy at that fundraiser a few weeks ago."

"We're friends, Dad. We were friends long before we dated, and we're always going to be in the same circles. It doesn't pay for us to be enemies."

"Still, when I'm gone, you're going to need someone to help run this place. Zach knows all about how a place like this should be run."

My jaw clenched; sure, Zach knows all about it. Zach had huge plans for how he wanted to take over *my* family resort, which was the main reason we broke up. Not that I could tell my dad about it. He practically made Zach a member of the family ages ago, it would crush him to know what Zach's actual intentions were.

Instead, I just answered, "I have an MBA, Dad. I'm perfectly capable of running Lodging on my own."

"Still, I just don't want to worry about you struggling under all the pressure, Isabelle. It's a lot more than you think."

"I have a pretty good idea, seeing as how I've been here for the last few years as your 'Assistant CEO.'" I slammed my desk drawer a little harder than I meant to, but he was not getting the hint. At this rate he looked about ready to order a second breakfast and take a nap in my cushy chair.

"Well, it's a lot harder than it looks." His tone turned slightly defensive, as if I'd implied something about *his* ability to do the job instead of the other way around.

I closed my eyes and drew in a deep breath, letting it out before I settled my gaze directly on my father. His silverly hair and beard were perfectly neat, and the robin's egg-blue Aspen Ridge polo he wore matched his bright eyes. He was every bit the mountain executive: neat enough to be taken seriously, but casual enough to not to be too intimidating.

"I understand the responsibilities of the position, and I believe I am well-qualified to take over when you are ready to retire, Dad." I even managed a smile to go along with my patient-but-not-condescending tone.

Dad shifted in his seat. "Yes, about that, Izzy-"

I stood abruptly in frustration and snatched my purse. "Dad, I really have to go. I'll be at the reception hall all day. Call if you need me."

"Wait, honey, there's something I want to talk to you about-"

I was already on my way out the door. "I'm sure it can wait for tomorrow, Dad." I turned on my heel and crossed to the corner chair, bending to kiss his cheek before beelining again to the hallway.

With a final wave, I ducked through the doorway before he could call me back. "I'll see you tomorrow!"

Jake

I STRODE CONFIDENTLY UP to the reception desk, which was handsomely decorated with large polished letters spelling out 'Aspen Ridge Lodging & Hotels'. The young woman behind the desk eyed me curiously, but smiled in greeting all the same.

"Hello, how can I help you?"

I plastered on a smile. "Good morning. I'm supposed to ask for James Tremont, Junior. He's expecting me." I winced at my stern voice, and the girl's eyes narrowed slightly as if I were acting suspiciously.

"You mean JJ? Not a problem. I'll ring him."

"Thank you."

While she made the call, I glanced at my surroundings. Directly behind the desk was a beautiful panoramic photo of the ski resort at peak winter season on a sunny day, taking up an entire wall. Banks of cubicles ran the length of a room tucked away to the left, and to the right appeared to be a row of larger offices disappearing down a hallway.

Sweat gathered at my collar, despite the air conditioning. I resisted the urge to tug at the fabric as my eyes roved the room and made a disturbing discovery: no one else was wearing a suit. Most people wore polo shirts with the resort logo embroidered on the chest, and the few who wore dress shirts had them casually rolled to their sleeves.

Compared to the crowd, I was way over-dressed. Maybe it was a casual Friday. Don't people who work at billion-dollar companies wear suits?

"Jacob!" a deep, friendly voice called out from the direction of the offices, and I turned to see JJ approaching with a wide smile. He had on a polo and khakis like the front desk girl, and a full head of more salt than-pepper hair with a neat, matching beard. "So glad you finally made it. Quite a trip from Alabama! Did the kids enjoy the drive?"

"Jake, sir," I accepted his handshake. "They're troopers, they did alright. They're sort of used to moving. But it'll be nice to put down some roots."

"I can't imagine." JJ shook his head and patted my shoulder. "Thank you again for your service. We hope you like it here. Although it won't be quite as exciting as your former career, we get to have a bit of fun. Why don't we start with a tour? I'll show you your new office so you can leave your briefcase, and then I'll give you a rundown of our area of responsibility."

"Sounds good, sir." I followed him to a small, plain office. No expansive views of the ski hill, but it at least had a window. I could count on one hand the number of years I'd had one in my fifteen years of service.

"Okay, you've got to stop calling me sir, Jake. Never mind the white beard, you're making me feel old!" JJ chuckled at his own joke.

"Yes, si—I mean, sure thing, JJ. Sorry, habits." I clasped my hands behind my back to avoid fidgeting and squared my shoulders.

"Understandable. But you'll soon learn that things aren't that formal here. I'm sure you'll settle into it quickly."

"I'm sure I will." I set my briefcase on the chair and turned to him. "So, when are we starting?"

He gestured me down the hallway and we made our way back to the elevators. "I thought we'd start downstairs in the hotel, then I could take you to the condo registration, and if you like we could do a full lap of the resort, maybe grab lunch at the base of Peak 7. Our portion here only covers the lodging but the whole place is run by us and the Blackwells, so it's all sort of family business. Probably good for you to be familiar with the whole enchilada."

"Sounds great, sir, but I meant when we would start with your daughter?"

He chuckled. "So eager to get to work! No

worries, Isabelle isn't here today, so you get a one-day reprieve. She's setting up for the employee party." We boarded the elevator, and he selected the button.

"Employee party?" I questioned. "Like a GI Party? That's what we called a weekly cleanup crew."

JJ laughed again. "No, son, like a *party* party. We like to treat the staff well, and employee satisfaction has sort of become Izzy's baby. Most of them are college kids. We want them to have a good time working for us. We always have an end of the season party for summer and winter, our two biggest seasons. Besides the parties, we organize a lot of mixers and events throughout the year. We work hard, but we play hard, too. Izzy likes to plan them. She is pretty much friends with all the kids... which I suppose is part of the problem."

"Is that what you are hoping I can fix, for her to be less friendly with the staff?" I really wanted to get a better understanding of what I was here to do, as it had all been rather vague up until now.

"Yes, and no. We want them to feel cared for, but I think sometimes Isabelle forgets that she's not one of them anymore. She can't be going to keggers in the dorms with the kids at night and then giving their bosses performance reviews the next day, you know what I mean? She's got to start pulling back, acting more like a manager and less like their buddy, before I can consider handing the reins over. Aspen Ridge employs nearly a thousand people in lodging alone, so she needs to get a wider view."

I nodded seriously. "I know exactly what you mean. It's like when we promote a Senior Airman to Staff Sergeant. Suddenly they're a non-commissioned officer and they can't get away with acting like Airmen fresh from basic training anymore. For some of them, it's a hard transition."

"Sounds like I hired just the man for the job." JJ grinned as the elevator doors opened. "This is our main hotel lobby, but there are seven in total that span the base of the ski resort."

For the rest of the day, I followed along as JJ gave me a thorough tour of the main resort highlights. It was daunting to realize how many teams he had, which started with a network of VPs, plus a manager for each site, then each building, of the extensive resort. JJ filled me in on the other family he shared ownership of the resort with, which included the events center, stables, and ski hills. He and Robert Blackwell had equal shares in the business and, as they came of age, passed management onto their children with the plan of eventually handing over the reins entirely.

"So, how many kids do you plan to hand this off to? It sounds like you've expanded quite a bit on what your parents built with the Blackwells."

"Indeed." JJ leaned back in his seat and stretched. We'd stopped for a late lunch at a restaurant on the resort, and the remains of a savoury meal cooled on the plates in front of us. "My sister, Lily, didn't want much to do with the place. She's on the books, but really in name only. I don't hold out much hope for her son, Blaise, either. Bit of a flake, that kid. But my eldest, James the third, is already managing mountain operations, and Robert's eldest, Reece, works with the events center. Robert's daughter, Estelle, seems to prefer riding the powder to working, but Robert's certain she'll step up, eventually."

"And Isabelle is primed to take over all of lodging?" I asked. "Based on what you've shown me, that seems like more than one person's work. Especially for someone who likes to be so hands on."

"I think we manage pretty well with our team of VPs, but that's where I need you to help her, Jake." He leaned in and slapped me on the shoulder. "She needs to be less hands on, and try as I might, I can't seem to get that into her head. She's almost never in her office. If she wants to take over for me, she's got to be in meetings with the VPs, approving payroll, signing off renovation projects. Instead, I'm far more likely to find her out with the landscaping crew planting flowers."

"Right," I nodded. "She needs to transition to a macro view of the business, and right now she's fully in the micro."

"You've got it." JJ checked his watch, then wiped his mouth with a cloth napkin. "Well, I've got some meetings to attend tonight. Why don't you take the rest of the afternoon off? Or even better, go to the employee party tonight. I'll have Larissa at the desk send you the address. It'll give you a chance to see how we run things here, maybe make a few friends. It's sort of a send-off for seasonal workers, but most of our full-time staff should be there as well."

"Okay, what time would you like me in tomorrow?" I followed him outside to the golf cart we'd used for the tour, and we zipped off toward the offices the second I claimed my seat.

"Tomorrow?" He guffawed. "Son, tomorrow's Saturday. I'm going to be working on my golf swing. We'll see you first thing Monday."

"Don't I need to sign forms with HR, or fill out

a payslip?" I clung to the side of the cart to avoid spilling out. It didn't seem pertinent to mention that I assumed he wanted me to start on Friday because I'd be there through the weekend. Hence why I'd sent my kids to their grandparents.

"Nah, we already started your salary, and you can fill out paperwork on Monday. Go to the party and have a good time. Make some friends! We want everyone to feel like part of the family here."

"Yes, sir."

"I told you, stop making me feel old. JJ is fine."

"Yes, s—JJ."

"Better." He grinned and gave me a twinkly blue-eyed wink.

JJ dropped me directly at my truck, insisting there was no need for me to get my briefcase before I left.

I drove home in a daze, my mind churning on how I could make myself invaluable and earn a permanent place here. Aspen Ridge was a dream come true when it came to working environments. Everyone seemed genuinely happy, and JJ greeted everyone we passed, a lot of them by name. It was easy to see what he meant about it being a family business.

A text popped up on my phone just as I pulled into the drive, with a detailed message from

Larissa about how to get to the employee party. Obviously the suit would not be appropriate, but I honestly didn't know what to wear for an end of season employee party at a billion-dollar resort. I concluded neat jeans and a button-down shirt were appropriate for the brand new five-million dollar events center.

It's always better to be a little overdressed as opposed to under dressed.

Even if it was a little uncomfortable.

THE DOUBTS STARTED AS SOON as I parked in the lot. All the crowd heading toward the fancy events center was young—like fresh out of high school young—and the dress code appeared to be flip-flops and backwards baseball caps. The sun had long since disappeared behind the mountains, and twilight shadows were verging on darkness, stars already appearing in the sky.

Although I wasn't sure what I was expected to do here, JJ had asked me to attend and make friends. Honestly, I had nothing better to do on a Friday night, and the kids were happy at their grandparents' house. I decided it was an opportunity to see more about this 'treating staff as family' thing JJ was so proud of. I steeled myself for the culture shock and followed the others from the parking lot toward the building.

Once I got through the main doors, I glanced around at the stunning facility. They had built a marvel—it was modern and clean in the lobby, but it still had a decidedly cozy mountain feel. The employees streamed through a second set of double doors with loud rhythmic music pouring out.

To the right, a woman who was decidedly older than the crowd and clearly pregnant struggled with a heavy cart laden with boxes and platters of food. She had a giant crystal bowl of punch, covered with saran wrap, balanced on top of a cardboard box, and was trying to keep it from tipping over while she pushed the cart.

"Ma'am, let me help you." I crossed the lobby and picked up the bowl.

"Oh, thank you." She smiled. "But please don't call me ma'am. That makes me feel old."

"That's not the first time I've heard that today," I laughed. "My apologies, it's a habit. I just left the Air Force, and everyone is 'sir' or 'ma'am', no matter their age. I didn't mean anything by it."

"Well, that makes me feel a little better." She resumed pushing her cart, and I followed her to the double doors. "I'm Alyssa. I manage the events center."

"Jake, nice to meet you. Today was my first day, and the boss said to come to the party, so... here I am. Do you normally handle the food, as the manager?"

She laughed breathlessly. "No, not usually. But we wanted the staff to have the night off, so I figured if they made all the food, I could get it inside for them. We try to let everyone have a chance for fun. I just underestimated how many trips it would take, and how tired I'd be." She gestured to her belly. "They really take it out of you. You have kids?"

My throat seized up, and I swallowed to clear it. "I do, actually. Two."

"This is my first. I'm already planning to stay home once I have the little one. I just didn't realize the last few months would be so much harder. I really appreciate your help."

"Not a problem at all. I'm happy to assist." I followed her through the open doors and to an enormous banquet table, already half full. Despite the loud music and flashing colorful lights, most of the crowd was standing around the bar set at the far side of the room, opposite the dance floor.

There were small tables set up, but people were milling about, socializing.

Happy to have an excuse to avoid that exact scenario, I helped Alyssa unload the cart, and two more like it, until the buffet was filled. I escorted her back to the kitchen despite her assurances she was fine.

"Are you going to the party?" I asked, hopeful. She was closer to my age, and it was always nicer to know someone when you walked into a crowded room.

"Lord no," she laughed. "My ankles are two times their normal size and all I can think about is propping my feet up at home. But I can introduce you to some people before I leave, if you want?" She shifted her weight from one foot to the other, obviously uncomfortable.

"No, you're exhausted. You should get off your feet. I'll be fine. I'll just tell them I carried a watermelon or something."

She glanced around the kitchen in distress. "Oh shoot, did I forget something? My mind has been swiss cheese the last couple of months, I swear..."

My cheeks heated. "I'm sorry. It was an attempt at a joke."

Alyssa stared at me with a blank expression. "Why would a watermelon be funny?"

Cheryl always instructed me not to tell jokes because I sucked at it. I thought she just didn't have a sense of humor, but maybe I should have listened.

"You know, from the movie Dirty Dancing? Baby sees the guy juggling three watermelons, and she helps him bring them to the employee party, then when Johnny asks what she's doing there she says 'I carried a watermelon.' Because she didn't belong there, right?"

Alyssa's eyes narrowed, my only indication that she was trying to understand. "Yeah... I probably wouldn't open with that one. Or with the 'sir' or 'ma'am' thing. Just say 'Hi, I'm Jake.' It'll work about 100% better, promise." She gave me a wide smile. "It's nice to meet you, Jake. I'm sure I'll see you around. Thanks again!"

With that, she shooed me out of the kitchen and waddled to the exit door.

Squaring my shoulders, I lifted my chin and marched back into the party. I made a beeline for the bar, and ordered myself two shots of jack to soothe my nerves, and a long-neck beer to sip.

The party was sliding into full-swing mode now. People crowded the banquet tables, moving in groups through a set of doors leading outside that I had missed earlier. There was a large deck filled with tables and strung with Edison lights. I'd taken up residence at the furthest end of the bar, tucked into the corner, but most of the other drinkers were in a huddle closer to the dance floor.

A lot of them were dancing. Some in pairs, but most were in the awkward group circles that reminded me of high school prom. A fast-tempo song with a rhythmic beat pumped from the artfully concealed speakers, and the bass thrummed through the soles of my feet. My eyes traveled casually over the dancers while I sipped my beer, and instead of becoming more comfortable, I just grew more convinced this was a dead end. Everyone here had to be seasonal employees —they looked barely old enough to drive, let alone have a year-round job. A few slightly older people slipped out the doors with plates of food, and it occurred to me that people in management—or at least people closer to my age—might have hidden out there.

Just as I'd resolved to try my luck with the outdoor crowd, my eyes landed on a woman in a short red dress, and all thoughts of leaving immediately flew from my brain.

She was in a group of other people; although

she was still young and beautiful, she was clearly older than her peers. Her long blonde hair was damp with sweat, sticking to her bare back and neck, but as she spun around, her wide smile betrayed zero discomfort.

My heart thumped in my chest—this woman was like a glimpse of life and freedom that seemed so far removed from the world I lived in. My eyes were glued to her form. I couldn't stop watching her. There was something so... *free* about her, and envy made my throat too thick to swallow. She didn't have a care in the world; she was just living her best life in this one moment.

What I'd give to feel that way. I couldn't remember a time where my life wasn't filled with duty, obligation, and responsibility.

And then, as if hearing my silent plea, she turned and locked eyes with me.

Ready for more of Ellie and Jake's story?
Get The Wrong Girl in Amazon and Kindle
Unlimited

ABOUT THE AUTHOR

*S*asha Pierce is a long-time fan of romance and adventure. She's traveled the world, and currently resides in the shadow of the Great Smoky Mountains with her daughter Tessa.

ASPEN RIDGE IS BASED on one of Sasha's favorite places in the world, Breckenridge, Colorado, where Sasha tries to go snowboarding at least once a season.

COMING SOON

Aspen Ridge is a series of interconnected standalone that feature multiple relationships in the same breathtaking ski resort town. Expect at least three more novels set in Aspen Ridge with characters you already know and love. **The Wrong Girl** is out now, and **The Wrong Nanny** is coming February 2025.

Books 4 and 5 in the Aspen Ridge Series are projected to release in 2025 as well.

Join Sasha's newsletter at

sashapierceauthor.com/newsletter

to be the first to know more!